Jessica Vallance grew up in Bournemouth and studied law at Sussex University. Jessica's first novel for young adults, *Birdy*, has been optioned for film by Loop, and she has since written four more novels for young adults. In 2018, Jessica made her debut in adult fiction with her thriller, *Trust Her*. *Someone Else's House* is her second psychological thriller.

Also by Jessica Vallance

Trust Her

JESSICA
VALLANCE

SOMEONE ELSE'S HOUSE

sphere

SPHERE

First published in Great Britain in 2019 by Sphere

1 3 5 7 9 10 8 6 4 2

A CIP catalogue record for this book
is available from the British Library.

ISBN 978-0-7515-7265-0

Typeset in Caslon 540 by Palimpsest Book Production Ltd,
Falkirk, Stirlingshire
Printed and bound in Great Britain by
Clays Ltd, Elcograf S.p.A.

Papers used by Sphere are from well-managed forests
and other responsible sources.

Sphere
An imprint of
Little, Brown Book Group
Carmelite House
50 Victoria Embankment
London
EC4Y 0DZ

An Hachette UK Company
www.hachette.co.uk

www.littlebrown.co.uk

SOMEONE ELSE'S HOUSE

Part One

Chapter 1

I realised I had to break up with John when he came home with a carrier bag of cauliflower for the third day running.

'Felt like cauliflower cheese,' he said, setting it on the side.

'We had cauliflower last night,' I said.

He shrugged. 'It's on offer at Sainsbury's.'

'And I don't actually like cauliflower.'

He turned to look at me, his head slightly on one side. 'Yeah you do.'

I sighed. 'I don't.'

He continued unpacking the shopping. 'Well, first time you've bothered to mention it.'

'It's not. I said it last night in the shop and you put it in the basket anyway. And I've said it before. I've always said it. But you don't listen, because you like it, and you know how to cook it, and anything which doesn't fit in with your plans, you just ignore.' I put my mug down on the worktop. It landed more heavily than I'd planned, clanking against the granite.

He rolled his eyes. 'God, calm down.'

So – quite calmly – I picked up the cauliflower and dropped it into the bin.

I watched the colour rise up his face, from his collar to his forehead. He swiped his phone and wallet from the kitchen table and pushed past me, out of the kitchen into the study, slamming the door shut behind him.

'The study' was what he called it, but the room was actually the spare bedroom. My spare bedroom, in my flat. The flat that I'd found and viewed on my own, and the flat with a lease in my name, granted on the basis of my salary. However, shortly after moving in two years earlier – when things between us were still harmonious and the good days outnumbered the bad – John had commandeered the room as his own office. He'd filled the shelves with books by David Foster Wallace and Bret Easton Ellis, set his MacBook on the desk and began to shut himself inside for hours at a time, working on his writing. I'd never seen so much as a paragraph of this work myself. John was deeply private about it. If I knocked to ask him a question or to suggest he come out to eat, he would never call me inside. He would always get up to open the door himself and then stand there, defensively on the threshold. The only tangible output I ever saw was the rejection letters, headed with the names and addresses of agencies or literary journals, that I would find balled up in the waste paper bin. The letters were always addressed to 'Marshall T. John', I'd noticed, which was strange as his name was John Marshall, and he had no middle name at all.

'It's a pen name,' he told me witheringly when a letter I found on the doormat gave me the opportunity to query it. 'Most people have one. *John Marshall* doesn't exactly match my style, does it?'

I had no reply for that, having no idea what his style might be.

I worked full-time as a graphic designer for a dog re-homing charity, mostly putting together layouts for invitations to open days and choosing photos of puppies for the header of the monthly newsletter that looked scruffy enough to seem desperate for love but not mangy enough to be off-putting to potential adopters. 'Our mantra is, make people feel sad, not sick,' my boss, a formidable American called Caroline, had told me during my first week. John would sometimes refer to it as my 'artistic career', making it clear he thought it was nothing of the sort. I couldn't deny the work wasn't exactly what I'd had in mind when I'd studied illustration at university, but it paid the bills. And the fact that one of us had to was something John never seemed to acknowledge, much less appreciate.

A few minutes after the study door slammed, I heard the punching of the walls begin. I knew there'd be new holes when I went in there later. New grooves in the doorframe where he'd gouged away at it with a metal ruler. And probably new bruises on his hands too. I'd never witnessed John's outbursts first-hand – that's to say, I'd never seen one happen in front of me – but that didn't mean they were easy to ignore.

John moved through life inhabited by a constant low level of frustration that took not much at all to escalate to a level that needed to be released. The colour of his face was the first indicator that he was reaching his boiling point, closely followed by the way his eyes became fixed and unblinking. At this point he would excuse himself – to another room if possible, or if that wasn't an option, simply by walking around a corner out of sight – and I'd hear the tell-tale sounds: a boot making contact with a wall, shattering glass, a furious scream.

I'd tried to talk to him about it. It seemed absurd at first that I should pretend I didn't notice, that I couldn't hear, but I realised that's exactly what he expected me to do. When I suggested anger-management counselling, it was enough to provoke an episode on its own. When the outbursts were over, when the heat of the rage had cooled to a low-level sullenness, he would simply refuse to engage with any questions or comments that referred to what had just happened.

The one occasion I'd managed to get him to have a calm, rational conversation about his behaviour came after a night out at an Indian restaurant with some of my colleagues. Caroline's husband, another straight-talking American called Tony, had asked John, innocently enough, what he did for work. When John told him he was a writer, Tony said, 'Where can I read your stuff?' and John had been forced to admit that, as things currently stood, the only place anyone could read any of his writing was on his own computer. Tony had seemed genuinely taken aback by this.

'What, you mean, no blog? No web articles? Nothing published *any*where?'

I wasn't part of the conversation but nevertheless I felt myself tense as Tony strayed unwittingly onto this volatile ground.

'I don't believe in giving work away for free,' John told him coolly.

'Wow, okay,' Tony said, refilling his glass from his beer bottle. 'Sounds crazy to me, though. How can you call yourself a writer when there's no writing? You've got to get yourself out there, my man!'

With this, he gave John an encouraging slap on the back and turned to talk to the person on the other side of him.

Under the table, I put my hand on John's knee but he pushed me off.

'Fucking prick!' he shouted as soon as we'd returned to the flat. 'Fucking yank tosspot!'

He shut himself in the study and several minutes of the usual crashing and banging followed, before he emerged and stood at the kitchen sink to down pint after pint of water.

I wasn't sure if it was because I'd had a lot to drink, or if because, on this occasion, I could see John's point – Tony had been quite annoying – but I decided to steel myself and, for once, address the issue.

'He probably thought he was being positive. Supportive, even,' I said. 'You know – sort of inspiring you to be bolder.'

John grunted and moved to refill his glass, turning the tap on too high and spraying water down his front. 'Fuck's sake,' he muttered, roughly pulling his shirt off over his head.

'John you can't keep doing this,' I said. 'You can't let things get to you so much. You can't keep . . . losing it.'

I expected him to ignore me, to storm out and lock himself away again but, much to my surprise, he covered his face with both his hands and I realised he was crying.

'John?' I put my hand on his arm. 'Talk to me.'

'I'm sorry,' he said quietly. 'I wish I could stop. I do mean to. Every time, I think . . . what are you doing?' He paused and I didn't try to fill the silence. I wanted to give him room to speak, if that's what he was finally ready to do. 'But it's not like I hurt anyone, is it? It's not like I hit people. Hit *you*.'

'Well, no. But you damage stuff. You hurt yourself.'

He turned away from me and looked out the window. 'Maybe it's good to let off steam sometimes.'

I could tell his contrition was slipping away but I decided to persevere. 'There must be a better way, though. Sport, for example!' I could hear the desperation in my own voice. 'There are punchbags, aren't there? At the gym?'

He laughed once, the softness now gone. 'A gym! Fucking hell. I'd rather die.'

Then he walked past me into the bathroom. A few minutes later I heard the sound of the shower running and I knew the conversation was over. But although nothing had been resolved, it had given me a glimmer of optimism – there'd been tears, hadn't there, for a moment? A sliver of self-awareness. This optimism had bought our relationship several extra months as I continued to hope that John was on the cusp of a change. That one day soon he'd admit that he was suffering, that he needed my support to tackle his demons but that he would soon be a new man.

But suddenly, sitting there in the lounge that evening, the offending cauliflower resting in the top of the bin and the TV turned down low so that I might discern which parts of the flat would need to be replaced or repaired in the morning, I was struck by a sudden feeling of clear insight: This could be my whole life. This could be my future.

John could go on like this for years. Forever, perhaps. He would continue to search for recognition for his writing, for someone to tell him he was better than all the other people out there plugging away with the same ambition, but even if he got it, it would never be enough. He would always be angry. Because, deep down, he thought he was too special to live the kind of life that other people lived, and so even if he did make it as a writer, all the *un*special bits of life – the chores, the inconveniences, the small talk, the people with things to worry about other than him – were always going to confound him. For as long as I was with him, I would feel tense. I would be living with a volcano that could erupt at any time.

I didn't let myself think about it for too long. I stood up, walked past the study where I could hear the sound of ripping paper – I wasn't sure if it was his own work or that of one of his idols that was paying the price for the great cauliflower scandal – and went into the bedroom. I reached under the bed and pulled out the battered leather suitcase he'd had imported, for some reason, from Paris, then I took the entire contents of his clothing drawer out in one pile and laid it inside. I left the suitcase on the bed and returned to the lounge, turned the volume of the television up and waited for him to find what I'd done.

I had to sit on my hands to stop them shaking when, fifteen minutes later, I heard the study door open and John cross the hall to the bedroom.

'Lauren?' he shouted. 'Lauren!'

I stayed where I was. I put my hands in my lap and clasped them tightly together. I didn't go to him.

'What the fuck is this?' He was in the doorway of the lounge now, one hand pointing back behind him towards the bedroom. 'Seriously – what?'

There was plenty I could have said. I could have pointed out that I'd had enough of paying for everything because he thought getting a job with a salary was beneath him. I could have listed every episode of destruction, every item I'd had to replace, every occasion ruined by his temper. But in the end, I just said, 'I want you to go. It's my flat and I want you to go.'

He looked at me in disbelief for a moment and then he said. 'That's low. That's a low card to play. Kicking me out because I'm poor. What *is* that? Some kind of Marie Antoinette bullshit?'

I didn't reply. I realised I didn't want to win the argument. I didn't even want him to acknowledge his own behaviour. I was past it all. I had had enough. All I wanted was quiet.

'Where, exactly, am I supposed to go?' he said.

I could – should – have said 'That's not my concern' or something to that effect, but instead I said, 'Your mum's?'

John shook his head. 'Ha! My mum's. Right.'

Then he went into the bedroom and shut the door, and I heard the sound of objects being shifted around, things being dragged across the carpet. At first I thought he might be barricading himself in, staging a sit-in and refusing to leave, but after ten minutes or so he emerged, bundled up in his thick winter coat, his deerstalker hat on and the leather suitcase in his right hand.

He paused for a moment in the doorway of the lounge and I looked up. He looked sad and, in his layers of clothes, small, like a lost boy. I thought for a moment he might say something heartfelt, admit that he hadn't been perfect and ask me to get in touch if I changed my mind. But then his expression hardened.

'You'll regret this, you know. One day. You'll regret this.'

And then he was gone and I was alone in my flat. It was only some months later that I let myself wonder if his parting words had been right.

Chapter 2

The day after the break-up, it snowed – in March, for goodness sake – and I found myself slipping and sliding through London's icy back streets to find my oldest friend, Anya, for our bimonthly reunion in whichever intimidatingly fashionable bar she had chosen for us this time. She'd messaged me earlier that afternoon to let me know the place was called Smoke and I eventually found its doorway at the bottom of a steep flight of stone steps, marked by a sign that looked like it had been made from a bent coat hanger.

The lighting inside was dim and the room smelt, appropriately enough I suppose, of wood smoke. I squinted around the dark booths and spotted Anya at a table at the back. When the waiter came to greet me I pointed towards her and he nodded once, backing away.

I'd known Anya since our first day of secondary school when we'd been put in neighbouring seats in maths. She'd made me laugh by cutting a row of fake teeth out of the white cardboard at the back of her homework diary, slipping them into her mouth as the teacher came to speak to us. He'd recoiled and turned pink, clearly believing Anya was in need of some urgent orthodontic attention. A few teenage fallings-out excepted, we'd been best friends ever since. It was a source of quiet pride to me, that friendship. I might never have had a decent relationship, and my job might have been unimpressive and underwhelming, but at least, I told myself, I had clocked up seventeen years of a solid, real, closer-than-family bond. Not everyone had the staying power for that.

As Anya saw me approach, she let out an unselfconscious cheer. I was often nervous in the places we met, at least for the first few minutes. Not living in London, I felt like everyone around me knew I wasn't used to being here. Anya always seemed completely at home, engaging in easy banter with the staff and having no concerns at all about asking for customisations to the menu or sending back drinks that weren't quite what she'd had in mind. She'd lived in the city for nearly ten years, moving there to study at Kings straight from school, so I suppose it felt more like home to her now than Hoyle – the small coastal town where we'd grown up together.

'You're here!' she said, shuffling out of her booth seat and pulling me into a hug. As always, her hair was clean and perfectly styled, her shirt and work trousers were just the sexy side of corporate, and her perfume smelt sophisticated.

'Of course,' I said, smiling as I freed myself from my bulky blue anorak and the long woollen scarf I'd bought at a charity knit-sale. 'Would I be anywhere else?'

'Well, I just mean with this . . . blizzard!' Anya threw her hands towards the window dramatically, through which we could see snowflakes still swirling around the alley. 'I didn't know if the whole city might come to a standstill!'

I slid into the seat opposite her and she poured me a glass of red wine from the bottle that was already open. The waiter approached carrying a long rectangular plate. He laid it in the middle of the table. 'Smoked mackerel pâté with horseradish toast,' he said, giving us a grin and a quick wink.

'You ordered already, then?' I said, peering suspiciously at the pâté.

Anya shook her head and reached for a slice of the toast. 'Doesn't work like that. We don't order. They just bring stuff out every so often. The menu's different every day, curated by the chef. But it's all flame grilled or smoked. You know, hence the name – Smoke.'

'"Curated".' I repeated Anya's choice of word with a grin. 'I love how you say this stuff without even blinking now. You've been in London too long.'

As we worked through the plate of food and the bottle of wine, we covered off the topics that always featured when we got together – our jobs, books we'd read, television we'd watched, which people from home had got married or had babies since we last saw each other – but then conversation turned, as I knew it would, to my love life and it was time to admit the events of the last twenty-four hours.

'You threw him out?' Anya said, her wine glass halfway to her mouth. 'What did he do?'

'I didn't *throw* him out. I just put his things in a bag. It was just a hint. A serving suggestion.'

'But why? What triggered it?'

I shrugged. 'The cauliflower, I suppose, originally.'

I explained the story of the night's dinner and my growing impatience with John's self-centredness, his lack of consideration of my feelings and my general sense that life wouldn't go anywhere – anywhere good, anyway – with him in tow. I played down the destructive way in which he manifested his temper. Anya knew he was a generally angry man, but I'd never shared with her the full details, aware that, when said

13

out loud, it made him sound completely unstable – which perhaps he was – and that would likely raise the question of why I had stayed with him for as long as I had. A question I didn't really have an answer to.

'Oh my god,' Anya said, grinning as she topped up our glasses. 'You literally threw him out over a cauliflower. Wicked.'

I knew she knew it wasn't as simple as that, but it was Anya's style to make a joke of serious situations and, right at that moment, I was grateful for it. I had no desire to analyse how or when exactly the relationship had gone wrong, or what my future might look like now it was over.

'I'll tell you one thing I thought was weird about John,' she said, topping up her glass.

'Just one thing?'

Anya and John had only met a handful of times and it was clear the two of them were never going to get on. Anya had been – for her – diplomatic in her appraisal of him, but I knew her well enough to recognise that she thought him pretentious and uptight. Which, to be fair, he was. John had been less circumspect in his assessment of Anya, proclaiming that she was 'all right but kind of vacuous' which wasn't really fair given that she had a first-class degree in international relations and a senior job in the city's biggest law firm. But John essentially only liked people who were in awe of him in some way, and Anya definitely wasn't that.

Anya grinned. 'Why did he keep all those boxes of tissues in his study? Was he watching porn in there all day or what?'

'Oh. No. It's because he gets emotional when he writes. He says the only way he knows he's nailed a scene is if it makes him cry.'

Anya threw her head back and laughed loudly. 'Oh my god! That is too much! I'd literally prefer it if he was whacking himself off all day than weeping at his own beautiful prose!'

14

I couldn't help but join in with her laughter. 'So would I. So would I.'

When she stopped laughing, she put her hands on mine. 'Listen, mate. I know it will feel scary for a bit because it's a change and that's what change is like, and you'll doubt yourself and wonder if you should take him back, but this is the best thing. I am one hundred per cent sure of that. It's good to have a shake-up sometimes. You need to look at the rest of your life. Put some energy into other areas. What about that website you keep talking about putting together?'

'You talk about it more than me.'

'Exactly! Now is the ideal time to get on it. You need a project.'

After university, when I still had dreams of making art for a living – real art, not just nicely laid out adopt-a-dog adverts – I'd started keeping a sketchbook of drawings. I hadn't set out with a particular theme or style in mind, but I'd found that what I was best at was capturing series of little scenes from everyday life; a couple embroiled in a silent row in a restaurant, a group of strangers surrounding a car and waving their arms to guide its driver into a tight parking space. Across one page, and in just three or four frames, I began creating sort of visual short stories of what I saw – stylized, wordless narratives. Anya had a theory that they were distinctive enough to sell, in some format or other, and although I doubted many people had the money or the interest to buy original artworks by a graduate nobody, as Anya had put it: how would I know if I didn't try?

I sighed. 'Yeah. Maybe. I guess I'll have time to kill in the evenings now . . .' I looked around the room then back towards Anya. 'He was a dick, wasn't he? I haven't thrown away the best relationship I'm ever likely to get?'

Anya looked at me. 'I'm not going to list all the reasons

why I always thought he was a total waste of space because I've fallen into that trap before; I know that'll only make me the bad guy if you do ever take him back, but be assured I've got lots of reasons up here.' She tapped the side of her head. 'This is good. Good news and a fresh start.'

'Yeah.' I sighed. 'I'm sure you're right. It's just . . . you know, being single again. I'm not good at it like you are. I'm nearly thirty—'

'Not for a year and a half!'

'And it suits me, having someone to eat with. Having someone to go on holiday with.'

'When did you ever go on holiday with John?'

I thought about this. 'He took me to Brussels once.'

'That time when he wanted to set a short story there so made you traipse around the streets in the freezing rain while he made notes about the cobbles and the slate-grey sky?'

'That's the one. And I say he took me, but I paid, if I remember rightly.'

Anya shook her head. 'Christ. See? Waste of space. And – *and* – now that you mention it, I've had an idea. I've had it just now, this second.'

'What?'

'Let's go away. On a holiday. You and me. Like when we went to Croyde! Like that, but even better.'

When we were twenty, Anya went through a painful break-up with a boy called Stevie who left her for his mum's forty-year-old cleaning lady, and to cheer her up, I'd organised a trip to a windswept cottage in Devon. I'd booked it hastily, with little information on what to expect when we got there and no real plans for what to do with ourselves for the week we'd be together, but we'd ended up having a great time, getting lost on Dartmoor, drinking too-strong cider in tiny, dark pubs with crackling fires and making the most of the cottage's remote location by cranking the speakers right up to let Anya indulge her heartbreak by singing along to terrible power ballads.

'Yeah, could do,' I said. 'It would be nice to have something to look forward to.'

'Yes, let's do it!' Anya's eyes were shining now. She reached for her phone. 'Open your calendar, give me some dates. Let's decide now, make sure it really happens.'

Once we'd factored in work commitments, aunts' fiftieth birthday parties and shows we already had tickets to, the next time we could both clear a week was the first week in June.

'Is that . . . okay?' Her voice was serious now. 'To be away then?'

'It's fine,' I said breezily. 'Fine.'

She looked at me carefully, searching my face. 'You sure?'

I nodded. 'Yeah, honestly. It's okay. It's just a date. Just another day of the year.'

And I meant it. I remembered dates, but I didn't think there was much to be gained from getting unduly sentimental about them. The anniversary of my brother's death just marked another year since it had happened. It didn't change anything. It wasn't any sadder than any of the other days. He was still gone. He still wasn't coming back.

Anya nodded. 'Okay.' She typed quickly on her phone. 'That's it, then. That week is reserved. We're going away and we're going to have a bloody good time.' She smiled an excited smile and I returned it. It *would* be good. She was right. It was just what I needed.

Anya put her phone down on the table but as she did so, the screen flashed so she picked it up again to read the message. 'Oh. Okay. Cool.'

'What's that?'

17

'So I've got this new friend,' Anya put the phone back down and looked at me.

'Oh yeah?' I said with a smirk.

Anya often saved these divulgences until we were near the end of an evening. She'd mention a new 'friend' quite casually – that is, a man she was meeting for dinners and maybe more, but whom she didn't yet like enough to decline offers from other potential 'friends' – but refuse to be drawn on many details, claiming the person in question was unlikely to be around for long enough to make it worth our time discussing.

'Who's this one?' I asked. 'Big American banker? Flashy suit? Flashy teeth? You're due one of those after the plumber.'

'He was a joiner, not a plumber. And no. She's a musician, actually. She—'

'She?' I raised an eyebrow. 'Well, that's new.'

'Shut up!' Anya threw a balled-up napkin at me, but she was smiling. 'I mean honestly just a friend this time. She was my piano teacher, for a while—'

'Since when do you play the piano!'

'Since January. Until February. Thought I'd give it a go. I'd always fancied it and thought it might be . . . creatively fulfilling. Didn't want to shout about it, though, in case I didn't stick at it. Which I'm glad about now.'

'So it wasn't creatively fulfilling?' I asked.

Anya sighed. 'It was just *hard*. I suppose I thought I'd just turn up and learn a few scales and a few weeks later I'd be—'

'Performing Rachmaninov concertos at the Royal Albert Hall?'

'Exactly!' Anya said. 'But I couldn't even get *Twinkle Twinkle Little Star* right! So anyway, I thought, bugger this, who has the time? I'll just listen to other people playing the piano on Spotify instead. But Sophie – my teacher – was

18

lovely! And get this, it turns out she used to live in Hoyle, once upon a time. Not born and bred like us, just for a year or so. Anyway, I decided to pack in the lessons but didn't want to be like, "Thanks, bye, have a nice life" so I took her number, said we should go out for dim sum or something. She's not been in London long, so I knew she didn't know many people. And anyway, we did and it was fun so now we're—'

'Friends?' I grinned.

'Yeah! Anyway, that was her – that message. She's around the corner and wondered if I wanted a quick drink. I'll just see if she wants to come here, shall I? If that's all right?'

I shrugged. 'Sure. Let's meet this piano teacher friend.'

Fifteen minutes later, when the waiter had cleared away the latest plates, Anya said, 'Oh, here she is,' and half stood up in her chair to wave.

I turned to look towards the door and saw a woman with messy blonde hair smile and begin to make her way over. She was wearing denim dungarees and had a small backpack on both shoulders. This, together with the slight bounce she had in her step, made her seem childlike somehow.

'Hey!' Anya threw her arms around the woman's shoulders in a loose hug, then turned to me. 'This is Sophie! And this is Lauren,' she said to Sophie, 'My oldest friend!'

Anya beamed around at us like a parent whose children were all in the same place for the first time in years.

'Hello!' Sophie began cheerfully, but as she slipped her backpack off and turned to look at me properly, her expression changed. Her mouth froze in a half open position and her eyes widened, as if she'd seem something grotesque sitting on my shoulder. I probably wouldn't have noticed had I not been looking directly at her face – the whole expression passed in a matter of seconds – but it made me feel self-conscious.

Then she sat down in a chair at the end of the table, the waiter came to take her drink order and the moment was gone. But I couldn't help feeling unsettled.

Something about me had surprised Sophie – had troubled her – but I had no idea what it could have been.

Chapter 3

As the evening wore on, I told myself I must have imagined the strange look I'd seen on Sophie's face as she looked at me, because after that initial awkward moment, she was friendly, funny and charming. She asked interested questions about my job, told lively but not-too-long anecdotes from her own work as a music teacher and laughed at my and Anya's jokes so enthusiastically that there were several occasions where she was forced to wipe her eyes and gasp, 'Don't! Stop! You'll set me off again!'

It was different, of course, to how things were when Anya and I were alone, when we had our years of shared history and in-jokes running through the core of every conversation, but I was enjoying myself. It occurred to me how rarely I met new people these days, and how it was fun to have someone to get to know from scratch. Some fresh meat to interrogate.

Over the course of the evening I found out that, alongside her piano teaching, Sophie played in the orchestra of a musical theatre company and was one of four organists at her local church.

'I'm not religious, I just love the instrument. So . . . dramatic!' She mimed pressing the keys on the table in front of her, throwing her head back and forth in a way that made us laugh.

I also discovered that she was divorced – something I found surprising. I knew Sophie was little older than me and Anya, but only a by a few years, and really, I was still surprised when people our age got married, let alone had been through the whole thing already and come out the other side.

'What happened?' I asked, before immediately realising that was an intrusive question and she probably didn't want to go into it.

Sophie shrugged. If the subject caused her pain, she didn't show it. 'God. What *did* happen? Well, I suppose in many ways we were doomed from the start. When I met Caleb – that was his name – I was kind of nursing a broken heart, which isn't exactly the ideal time to begin something new. He was one of the first people I met when I'd just moved to a completely new town and I was so lonely I was willing to turn a blind eye to a whole load of glaring incompatibilities if it meant I didn't have to be on my own. He was a nice man – still is, I suppose, not that he'll talk to me any more – but I should never have forced myself into a relationship with him, much less married him. Eventually I had to tell him as much. It went down as well as you'd expect.'

'Christ,' I said. 'Sounds . . . emotional.'

Sophie smiled sadly. 'Indeed,' she said quietly.

'Lauren's fresh out of her own break-up actually,' Anya said.

'Oh, really?' Sophie gave me a sympathetic smile. 'How are you feeling?'

I nodded slowly, thinking about the honest answer to this. 'Okay, I think. Fine. It was my decision. These things run their course.'

Sophie nodded and sighed. 'Very true.'

When I checked my watch, I realised I needed to get going if I was going to make my train. Although I'd been sure I didn't want to return home to Hoyle after university, the thought – and the rental prices – of London itself had intimidated me, so instead I'd settled in Haywards Heath, forty minutes outside the city. I told myself it was the perfect compromise as this way I had ready access to both London and the seaside whenever I wanted, but I couldn't escape the knowledge that often several weeks would pass where I saw neither.

Before I could make my exit, Anya came around my side of the table, threw an arm around my neck and Sophie's shoulders, and held up her phone. 'I'm drunk enough for a selfie, I'm afraid.'

Sophie and I groaned but dutifully fixed smiles on our faces and tried not to blink at the flash.

'God, I bet that was hideous.' I wrestled myself free from Anya's grasp and pulled my coat off the back of my chair, ready to bundle myself up to face the snow again.

'It's all right actually!' Anya said squinting at the screen. 'In fact, we look hot. It's going on Instagram for sure.'

I groaned again but Anya was already tapping away on her phone. I told Sophie it had been a delight to meet her, hugged them both goodbye, and made my way into the cold night.

A few days after the dinner, Anya called me during my lunch break. 'I have a question: what did you think of Sophie the other day?'

'Yeah she was nice. Really nice. Too nice for you actually. Did you have to pay her?'

Anya laughed. 'Fuck off. I know what you mean, though, I don't normally go in for those sweeter-than-sugar types, but I think because she's funny too, she gets away with it. Anyway, good that you like her because I think she should come with us.'

'Where?'

'On our holiday! Which, by the way, we really need to get sorted.'

'Oh,' I said. 'Okay.'

I was a bit taken aback. I had liked Sophie and there was no reason why we couldn't grow to be friends in time, if Anya continued to invite her along to things, but I didn't think we were quite there yet.

'I know it sounds a bit random,' Anya said, obviously sensing my reservations, 'and it would be different to when it's just the two of us. But the other day I was telling her about what you'd said about being single and not having someone to go away with and she said something like, "Yeah, I wish I had someone to go on holiday with. That's one of the hardest bits, since the divorce." It must be harder for her than for you, because I don't think she really has any close friends. And you've got me.' She paused. 'This is where you say you're lucky to have me.'

I laughed. 'Yes. Of course. Blessed.'

'Exactly,' she said. 'And I don't think Sophie's got anyone like that. So anyway, I think she'd really appreciate being asked along.'

'Anya, you've already asked Sophie to come, haven't you?'

She was quiet for a moment. 'Well, not formally, but I did say . . . I can't remember what I said exactly. I think I just said it might be an idea.'

'And she was keen?'

'Yes. Very.'

I sighed. 'Well, it sounds like a done deal, then.'

24

Chapter 4

It was typical of Anya to move from having an idea to putting it into action without pausing to consider the details, but then, I thought, what did it matter? Sophie was nice. It was one week away. It would be fine. It would be fun.

The following Saturday afternoon, Sophie, Anya and I were assembled in Anya's flat, sitting cross-legged on the floor of her tiny lounge, the sash window rattling a little every time a car drove past four floors below.

Anya opened the notebook she had in her lap.

'I love that you're doing notes.' I took a segment of the chocolate orange that was sitting in its foil in the middle of our little circle. 'You mean business.'

'I do,' Anya said. 'I mean, it's April already! We've got to get on this!'

I laughed, but I knew she was right. June was only a couple of months away.

'First things first,' Anya said, pulling the lid off her pen. 'Where are we going? I say let's head for the sun. Biarritz. Marrakech. St Tropez?'

'Is that even a place?' I took the last segment of the orange.

'I thought it was fake tan. And anyway, aren't we getting a bit carried away? I thought we were thinking Devon or somewhere. You know – cute little cottage. Like before.'

'*Before* we were only twenty, Lauren!' Anya said. 'Now we are sophisticated women of the world we can set our sights a little higher. Don't you think?'

'I don't know. Can we? I hadn't really budgeted for anything major.'

'Barcelona,' Sophie said suddenly. We looked at her. 'Barcelona?' she said again, more tentatively. 'I was just doing a quick search for cheap short-haul flights and look.' She held up her phone. 'A flight to Barcelona is actually cheaper than a train fare to Devon. A train fare to lots of places, really.'

I squinted at the phone screen. 'That's probably true, actually.'

Anya nodded slowly. 'Barcelona . . . I like it.'

I liked it too. 'Yeah. Tapas. Sangria. The beach . . . sounds perfect'

'Does it have a beach?' Anya asked.

'Yeah,' Sophie said quickly. 'Have you been before? I've been out quite a few times, actually. It's one of my favourite places. Because it's a city with all the architecture and restaurants and city things, but then the beach too. Something for everyone.' Then she looked down, shy again. 'But obviously, it's totally up to you. I'm happy with whatever you decide.'

'It does sound like the best of both worlds,' Anya said. 'Best of *all* worlds. City and beach. Lively and relaxing.'

'Yeah, exactly.' Sophie was fiddling with a tissue in her lap. I felt sorry for her suddenly. I hadn't really given it much thought before, but now it occurred to me that coming on holiday with a pair of virtual strangers – especially ones who knew each other so well they'd finish each other's sentences

– was probably quite intimidating. Perhaps she wasn't actually looking forward to it as much as Anya claimed, but rather was making herself do it, forcing herself out of her comfort zone, aware that she had to make an effort if she was going to make a go of her new life in London.

'I think it's a great idea,' I said, giving Sophie my warmest smile. 'It must be pretty decent if it's one of your favourites.'

She smiled back, although she didn't quite meet my eye. 'And actually,' she said, 'I do have a friend there, who we could maybe stay with if we wanted to save money . . .'

Anya winced. 'I think I'd rather we got our own place.'

'Oh, okay sure,' Sophie said quickly.

'No offence to your mate,' Anya said. 'It's just, you know, being someone's guest, being on your best behaviour . . .'

'No. Yes. Of course,' Sophie said. She was smiling brightly but she still seemed on edge.

'Could we really afford it, though?' I asked. 'The flight's one thing, but what about hotels, meals out . . . It's all going to add up to a lot more than a cottage in the country.'

'We could stay in an apartment.' Sophie said. 'You know – when people let out their own places when they're away or whatever. It's cheaper than a hotel *and* it means you don't have to eat out every night because they've got all the saucepans, all the crockery and everything, so you can just stay in sometimes.'

'It's a good point,' I said.

I turned to Anya for her thoughts, but she groaned. 'I know people at work are always doing it, always going on about how great it is to "live like a local" or whatever, but honestly I've always found that whole idea a bit weird. Haven't you? You know, just moving into someone else's house when they're not there, with all their stuff – their books and teaspoons and their photos of great aunt Audrey on the wall. And then you might turn up and find it's not even there! Tell you what, my mum went to one in Italy and when she got to the flat there was just some old man in there making an omelette. He didn't speak a word of English. He had no idea who Mum was and had no intention of letting anyone stay in his flat. Turned out some scamster had just put a photo of the apartment online, taken the money and done a runner.'

Sophie looked at us earnestly. 'No, really, it's totally safe. I do it all the time. They have procedures for checking out people's credentials and everything.'

'Your mum can be a bit . . . slow . . . with internet stuff?' I said to Anya. 'Maybe she just didn't book it at all.'

Anya sighed and stretched across the carpet on her back. 'Quite possible, I suppose.'

There was a pause, then Sophie said, 'Why don't I find a few places and send them around? I don't mind doing a bit of research.' She was still fiddling with the tissue in her lap. Slowly tearing off shreds, rolling them into balls between her fingertips. 'Really. I'd like to. I do know that . . . that this is your event. Your old friends' trip away and I'm gatecrashing really. Sad old divorcee tagging along . . .'

'No! Not at all!' I said, at the same time Anya said, 'It'll be fun!'

'We're glad you're coming,' I said, putting my hand on Sophie's. 'Seriously. We are.'

Sophie smiled uncertainly. 'Well, thank you, but I would like to . . . earn my keep, if you know what I mean. I'm good at tasks like this. Methodical searching. Why don't I put together a shortlist of say, three flats, and then you can pick from there?'

'That's a great idea,' Anya said, making a note in her pad as I gave Sophie a supportive smile.

* * *

28

Two days later, Sophie messaged the group chat, which Anya had called 'No Spain No Gain'. I wasn't sure it made much sense, but it made me smile nevertheless.

Hello both! So as promised, I've been doing some research and have put together a shortlist of three for our Barcelona adventure. I have a favourite, but I won't try to influence you!

Below the message were three links, all to a site called www.rentmyhome.com. I opened the first one. Initial impressions were good – it wasn't so much a flat as a villa, with palm trees in the garden and a hot tub on the balcony. I'd thought we'd been going for a city break vibe, but I suppose there was nothing to say we couldn't kick back in a luxury house for a week. Nothing, that is, except the price.

We hadn't officially pinned down the budget, I realised now, but this place cost more per night that I was planning on spending for the whole week. I was worried that we hadn't made Sophie's brief clear enough, that we were going to have to tell her none of these were suitable. I had a feeling she might take that feedback badly, given that she already seemed to be feeling a bit apprehensive about the trip.

But when I opened the next link, I saw her second option swung to the other end of the spectrum. It was dirt cheap but it was tiny, with mismatched furniture crammed into a dingy lounge room. It claimed to accommodate three people but it was clear from the listing that one of those three would be sleeping on the sofa and I had a feeling that that person would end up being me. I closed the page again quickly.

I wondered if Sophie had just sent us the first three properties she'd found, or that, with it being a busy time of year, all the more suitable places were already taken. When I opened the third link, however, I relaxed. This was exactly the type of place I'd imagined. Bright, modern and airy, with white interiors and minimalist decoration. Simple furniture and clean-looking floors, and, best of all, a balcony with a stunning view over the whole city.

I opened the group chat.

Me: I like the third one!

Anya: What about that first one though! What a stunner.

Me: I know. Kind of pricey though, don't you think?

Sophie: Yes, sorry about that . . . I didn't notice the price till I'd seen all the photos and by then I was smitten

Anya: I say we go for it. I don't mind paying a bit extra if it's too much of a stretch for others.

Me: Don't be silly

I could see that Anya was typing but a few minutes passed and no reply came. Part of me was tempted to let Anya pay a bit more if she was so keen on the luxury option – the place did look nice – but a bigger part of me wanted to pay my own way. I suppose Anya realised that her offer could be construed as patronising because fifteen minutes later she replied:

Anya: The third one is fine by me.

Me: Yeah. Seems decent and the price is more what I had in mind.

Anya: OK. Cool. You all right to book no. 3 Sophie?

Sophie. I'm on it

A few minutes later Sophie confirmed that the apartment was ours for the week.

Chapter 5

Later that week, I caught the train from Haywards Heath via Brighton to make the familiar journey back to Hoyle to see my mum. It was something I did every eight weeks or so, not because I took any great pleasure from the visits or even because Mum requested my company, but because I felt a constant pressure that I should be there. The guilt that compelled me to visit was alleviated only for a day or so after I'd been, but then would steadily begin to grow like a pressure gauge creeping towards its limit, until around the two-month mark when I realised the only way to release it was by going down there and spending a few hours with her to reassure myself that she was okay. Or as okay as she ever was, anyway.

When I arrived at Chine Road, at the house that I'd grown up in, where Mum had lived since I was two and Reuben was four, when our father had left her for the mother of one of Reuben's nursery school playmates, it looked exactly the same as it always had. The same small, neat front lawn. The same statuette of a border terrier standing guard at the wall. As usual, Mum greeted me with a sort of weary resignation, like each time she saw me she was disappointed anew that I wasn't different, wasn't better. Wasn't Reuben.

She made us some tea – herbal; she wouldn't drink caffeine in the afternoon – and we sat at the kitchen table and Mum told me her news which, as usual, was a rundown of things her colleagues at the optician's had said; ailments they were worried about, educational milestones their children had reached. This was always the easiest part, where we hovered around trivial and impersonal ground. The atmosphere always grew more tense when I asked Mum what she'd been doing.

'Nothing.' She bristled. 'What would I have been doing? I go to work, come home. Do a few chores. What else is there?'

'What about Andrew?' I asked brightly, mentioning the man Mum had met at a colleague's leaving party, who I knew had asked Mum for a drink. 'Did you manage to meet up with him yet?'

'Oh, him. Not seen him. No.'

I wanted to ask why or what she thought of him or if she planned to see him at any point in the future, but I didn't have the energy to push through her prickliness. Instead I said, 'I broke up with John.'

Mum frowned. 'Dark-haired one? The poet?'

I nodded. 'Writer. Sort of. Yeah.'

Mum raised her eyebrows slightly, not so much in surprise as in an expression of 'suit yourself'.

'Oh right. Wasn't meant to be then, I suppose.'

'No.'

She didn't ask any other questions and I couldn't think of anything else to offer.

Mostly to give myself a break from the laborious conversation, I went upstairs to the toilet. On the way up, I glanced into my old bedroom, now stripped bare and painted magnolia, my single bed made up for guests, although I

32

couldn't remember the last time Mum had had any. Then I crossed the landing and looked into Reuben's room. The walls were still painted the same dark teal he had selected and applied himself when he was fifteen. On the walls were his posters – a still from *One Flew Over the Cuckoo's Nest*, a pencil sketch of a Stradivarius – and on his bed the same blue-and-white checked duvet cover he'd slept under the night before he died.

'What are you doing, sneaking around up there?' Mum's voice came from halfway up the stairs and made me jump.

I spun round. I could have said, 'Nothing,' and carried on to the bathroom – Mum would have been unlikely to mention my visit to Reuben's room on my return – but I decided to be brave.

'It might be better for you, to put some of his things away. Don't you think? You don't have to get rid of them if you don't want to, but it's probably making things more painful for you, leaving it like that. You might feel—'

'I don't need you to tell me how I feel, thank you.' She didn't snap, her voice was quite calm, but she turned and went back downstairs and I knew better than to raise the subject again when I returned to the kitchen a few minutes later.

Having had my attempt to tackle a difficult subject resolutely rejected, I made sure to keep conversation light for the rest of the afternoon, even prompting one or two chuckles from Mum as I recounted the mischievous antics of the dogs at work. In fact, we probably would have left our meeting on good terms, had it not been for my last-minute impromptu decision to casually mention my holiday to Barcelona.

'Oh yeah?' Mum said. 'Spain? When's that then?'

'First week in June.' As soon as the words were out I wanted to snatch them back.

Mum's face darkened. 'I see. Well, I hope you enjoy yourselves, laughing and drinking yourselves stupid. As if you didn't have a care in the world.' She paused. 'As if you never even had a brother.'

'I know, Mum, I'm sorry. But it was the only date we could do and—'

Mum stood up and began loading the dishwasher noisily, her back to me. 'It's fine.'

I was torn between wanting to smooth things over and feeling I had the right to defend myself. As I sensed my visit was nearing its end anyway, I plumped for the latter.

'It's just a date, Mum. It doesn't mean I won't be thinking of him. What do you want me to do? Spend every June the second sitting at home with the curtains closed?'

Mum turned back to face me, wiping her hands on a tea towel. 'Anyway.' Her voice was bright but brittle. 'I'm sure you need to be making a move for your train.'

16 October 2005

Lauren

I'd taken on an extra shift at work that afternoon, just to give me something to do. It was the day of the coroner's inquest into Reuben's death. I'd been surprised that one had been ordered – it was clear how he had died; 750 volts through the heart – but apparently it was about more than that. The 'wider circumstances' had to be established. It had become apparent that what that meant was deciding whether or not Reuben had intended to die.

I hadn't even thought of that myself. It wouldn't have occurred to me at all. Obviously it was an accident. Wasn't it? Reuben wasn't depressed. He wasn't suicidal. He was quiet but he was quiet because he had a creative mind, a busy internal world of thoughts and ideas and creations to keep him busy. He wasn't like the other boys in his year, the other seventeen-year-olds in Hoyle, moving around in big groups, spitting, shouting, riding rickety mopeds too fast down small streets, leaning against the doors of their first cars, windows open, R&B blaring out. Reuben would be in his bedroom, playing his violin, the special rubber plug in place on the bridge to mute the sound a little. Neither my mother nor I ever minded the sound of Reuben's playing. He was accomplished, grade eight before he was sixteen, not a beginner scratching his way through *London's Burning*, but the walls between our house and the one next door were thin, and Reuben was self-conscious. If he wasn't at home, he'd be in a practice room somewhere, or in the library, a book shop, the park. That was just who he was. He was self-contained, but he wasn't sad. I knew that. Our mother knew that.

But not long after his death, people who knew him only by sight, or from a brief conversation at school or in town, started speculating about his temperament and his state of mind. 'Troubled teen', one local newspaper called him. And later in the same article, 'brooding' and 'a loner'. I was indignant at first – they knew nothing about him, my kind, sensitive older brother. They saw his dark hair, flopping over his forehead, his long coat and the way he would walk, head down, his violin case bobbing on his back like a tortoise's shell, and they created the character for the story they wanted to tell. But the more the rumours circulated, the more I began to revisit my memories. To view them through a new lens.

After dinner each evening, it had been common for Reuben to shut himself in his bedroom. I'd never thought there was anything unusual about this; I did it myself often enough, but I now began to question what he had been doing. And then there were the two or three occasions when he had gone out in the middle of the evening and returned very late – when I'd assumed everyone in the house had been asleep. If I'd bumped into him on those nights, on the landing or in the kitchen when I'd got up to refresh my glass of water, he would seem distracted. If I asked where he'd been, he'd claim to have been out walking. Was walking the streets late at night normal, I wondered? Was it a sign of melancholy? Of depression?

After he died, I worried that it meant he'd started associating with a bad crowd. He worked two evenings a week on reception at one of the rehearsal spaces he used, but I knew the pay wasn't good and he'd been worried about ever having enough money to pursue a career in music. I wondered if he'd found some way to make faster cash. Drugs or something else criminal that would explain the late nights, the sneaking around. Had he got into something over his head?

But while I was allowing myself to wonder if what people were saying could be true, my mother remained furious at the suggestions that Reuben might have taken his own life. I felt this was because she saw the speculation as a judgement of her as a parent. What did it say about her as a mother if her boy saw no option but to fling himself on the third rail of the track?

I had put my own doubts aside and tried to reassure Mum. We *knew* Reuben, I would remind her. We were probably the only ones who really did. He was happy and he was looking forward to things. He was applying to the Royal Academy of Music, and everyone said he had a good chance of making it. And anyway, I had added, it just didn't make sense; you heard of people jumping in front of trains, but not just onto the track. That just wasn't how people did it.

But I knew that what really mattered to my mother was the public declaration. If the Coroner's verdict came back as suicide, then her grief would be complete. That would be the ultimate indictment of her life. I would lose her then, I knew. She wouldn't recover from that.

When I returned from my shift I was surprised to find the

lights on at home; I thought it would all go on for much longer yet. I opened the front door and Mum appeared at the top of the stairs. Her figure was silhouetted by the late afternoon sun from the bathroom window behind and I noticed how hunched she'd become over the last few months. How wild her hair was these days.

'So how—?'

'Open,' Mum said simply. 'Open verdict.'

I frowned. 'What does that me—?'

'They don't know,' Mum said. Then louder, her arms thrown up in the air. 'They don't even know!'

I looked up at her, squinting to see her face, to make out her expression. 'But . . . I suppose that's okay? Of course they don't know. Not one hundred per cent certain. How can a room of complete strangers know what he was thinking? But we know. We knew him.'

Mum came down the stairs quickly, brushing past me without stopping. 'That's not enough. Not enough for them,' she gestured out the window, to the town, to the world. 'Open means doubt, and doubt means they'll all think . . .'

She didn't finish that sentence.

Chapter 6

I was surprised at how much having our little holiday planned lifted my spirits. I found that with the apartment and the flights all booked, with the date circled in gold pen on my kitchen calendar, I was filled with a kind of optimistic energy.

In the days since John had left, I'd become slovenly. I told myself I was enjoying the freedom of having the flat to myself, of being able to cook what I wanted when I wanted, of being able to use my spare room to store my own things again, but I realised that eating microwave meals every night and never properly cleaning the kitchen were making me feel unhealthy and irritable. There were seven weeks until we went away, and I decided to use the time to get my new, post-John life in order. Then, when I returned, I would be in the best place to consider where I went from here. Perhaps I'd look for a new job, or put some proper thought into setting up that website for my sketches. I could move house even, maybe finally give London a go, and get a taste of the cosmopolitan lifestyle that Anya seemed to enjoy so much.

John still hadn't taken all his things but rather than have to engage him in conversation to arrange when and how he'd collect them, I tidied them into cardboard boxes and stacked them in a pile in the corner of the bedroom. Then I reinstated all the decorative touches to my flat that John had complained about so much that it had seemed easier to do away with; I laid scatter cushions across my bed, bought scented oil burners and lit them when I was watching TV in the evening. I took my teapot out of its dusty box in the back of the saucepan cupboard and put it in pride of place on the shelf above the kettle.

I also paid special attention to my diary, making sure I had a good smattering of social appointments planned in for each week. I rejoined the yoga class I'd let slide a few months earlier. I signed myself up to help out with the family fun day at work. I tagged along to any leaving or birthday drinks I got wind of. I also took on any overtime that was going, knowing that, aside from keeping me busy, the money would come in handy.

Two weeks into my new regime, I was pleased with how I was doing. Keep moving forward, I kept saying to myself. Chin up and carry on. I was surprised, though, at how many sad moments there were. On the day of the break-up, and the days immediately afterwards, I'd been so caught up in first my anger, then my relief at having John's oppressive presence out of my home, that I hadn't stopped to remember there were times when things had been good. When we'd actually quite liked each other.

Something I'd never given much thought to before it was gone, was how much of our shared life, although seeming automatic, had been specifically carved out by us, just for us, and weren't things that everyone had. There were things we did for each other and terms only we understood.

John knew I had an almost pathological fear of caterpillars and was quite used to clearing them away in those – quite

40

rare, to be fair – occasions when they'd cropped up. 'Bad men,' we would call them. I couldn't even remember when that had started.

'John!' I'd call from the bathroom when I'd found an unwelcome visitor on the pot plant.

'What?' He'd poke his head out of the kitchen. 'Need me to take care of a bad man?'

'Please,' I'd say. 'If you would.'

We had special words for so many things, I realised now. My winter coat was known as 'the grizzly' – a reference to a child who'd sat behind us on the bus one morning and loudly told his father, 'That lady looks like a massive bear.' John's frequent headaches, probably caused by too much coffee and too much screen time, were called, by both of us, 'a pan-face', due to him telling me once it was like being smacked in the face with a frying pan. If ever one of us ate something – leftovers, a packet of biscuits – we had been planning to share, we would tell the other there'd been a 'mouse situation', referencing a story a colleague had told me about his little girl helping herself to snacks in the kitchen but swearing blind a mouse must have broken in and stolen them.

It was an entire language that only we understood. Maybe one day I'd meet someone new and we'd develop our own but, for now, that one – that particular dialect – was defunct.

I heard nothing at all from John in the weeks after he left. In a way, this made it easier to feel I'd done the right thing, but I was still surprised by the silence. John didn't usually respond well to decisions that were out of his hands so in the days afterwards, every time I'd checked my phone, I'd turned on the screen nervously, expecting abuse and insults, whatever it would take to make him feel that he'd had the last word. But nothing came. Not at first anyway.

When he did finally get in touch it was three weeks after

he'd left and rather than the criticism I'd been expecting, I saw his message was warm.

Been thinking about you quite a bit.
Hope everything's going OK for you. X

I hadn't replied, partly because I couldn't think of the right thing to say, but also because I was nervous about how quickly I might crumble if he said anything affectionate or asked to see me. Instead, I switched my phone to silent, put it in a drawer and spent two solid hours scrubbing mildew from the bathroom walls.

When I checked my phone later, there were no more messages from John, but there was one from Sophie.

How are you?
  I just wanted to say, I know from experience the first couple of months after a break-up are the hardest. Stay strong. Stay busy!
  Let me know if you want a distraction.

I replied honestly, telling her that John's message earlier had shaken me more than I would have liked. Sophie got back to me straightaway.

I understand, of course. I'm in your area tomorrow afternoon with a new student. I'll have finished the lesson by mid-afternoon, if you fancy some company?

The following day was Sunday – the day I'd found hardest so far. The weekdays were okay, with work to be done, and after-work drinks or exercise classes to go to, and Saturdays were when I did my admin; went to the bank, called the heating engineer, changed the bed. But on Sundays it felt like everyone was with their family, their partners, the people closest to them. Everyone retreated inside. And those of us with no one inside to be with, retreated alone.

I let Sophie know that company sounded great and she said she'd be over in the afternoon with 'something delicious, something alcoholic, or both'.

The next day Sophie arrived wearing the denim dungarees she'd had on the night we first met in Smoke. This time, she'd teamed it with a striking rainbow jacket and a unicorn pin on the lapel.

'Cool coat!' I said as I let her in. 'Very . . . cheerful.'

Sophie groaned. 'Oh, I know. It's a bit much, isn't it? I try to wear bright clothes when I'm teaching younger children. I think perhaps it will make their lessons seem more fun, somehow.'

'Did it work?'

She shook head. 'Not today! Thea, she was called. Six years old. A horror. All she did for the entire hour was bash the keys with her palms and scream made-up songs about stealing cars. God knows where she'd got them from.'

'Wow,' I said. 'Sounds exhausting.'

Sophie sighed and gave me a weary smile. She took a box of shortbread out of her cloth bag.

'Sorry,' she said. 'It was the best I could do. I had to go to the shop before the lesson and I didn't want the parents to catch a glimpse of the hard stuff in my handbag. It's not a good look, when you're teaching children.'

I took the biscuits from her. 'Yes. Might cancel out the rainbow coat, I suppose.'

I led the way down the hall to the kitchen. When we were sitting at the table, our hands curled around mugs of tea, Sophie looked around the room and began a constant stream of fast chatter, making polite comments about the artwork on the walls, telling me which of my mugs was her favourite, asking me where I'd got my spice rack from and if I liked to cook a lot and if I'd ever thought of getting a built-in water filter because didn't I find the water was ever so hard down south? When we eventually moved on to the subject of John and how I was dealing with things, she seemed to calm down a little and become more contemplative in her conversation.

'I suppose what you've got to remember,' she said carefully, 'is that you know rationally that it's better he's not here, because that's why you made the decision you made. So, for the time being, for this interim period where you adjust, you just have to ignore your feelings. Don't stop them – I know that's not possible – just let them come in and think, Oh, there's a feeling, but don't act on it. And then eventually, the feelings will come less often.' She took a sip of her tea. 'Feelings can be squashed. Conquered!' She gave me a brief smile. Then she added more quietly, 'Eventually.'

'Did you miss your husband, when you first split up? Caleb, was it?'

Sophie thought for a moment. 'In a way. I suppose it took some getting used to – going from seeing him every day to barely any interaction at all but . . .' She hesitated for a moment and looked out of the window at the little patch of patio I'd dotted with plant pots of tangled weeds in a half-hearted attempt at creating a garden. 'I suppose I'd already had my big love before I met him. My heart had already been well and truly battered and bruised. And the scar tissue from that stopped the divorce having the impact it otherwise might have.'

'Scar tissue,' I repeated, considering the concept. 'Maybe that's what I need. How do I get some to form, I wonder?

Because right at this moment, I couldn't say for sure that if he turned up now and asked for me back, I would definitely say no.'

She looked at me for a moment, her eyes narrowed like she was trying to solve a puzzle. I thought she would offer me more advice or warn me not to entertain this unwise feeling, but in the end she just said, 'Okay. Well. Okay.'

I decided to change the subject. I didn't want to sit there all afternoon talking about John and my feelings and generally wallowing in my own misery. '*Singin' in the Rain*'s on Channel 4 this afternoon. Fancy it?'

Sophie agreed and we headed to the lounge. I was grateful for the cheery backdrop; the atmosphere felt more relaxed and it prevented the need for constant chatter. Near the end of the film, however, I caught a glimpse of Sophie's face and her expression seemed anxious, almost as if she was experiencing a wave of physical pain.

'You okay?' I said. 'You look . . . worried.'

She snapped her face into a smile. 'Oh! No. I'm fine. Was just thinking of all the stuff I have to do when I get home.'

I remembered then the expression I'd glimpsed on Sophie's face the first moment she'd seen me. For a moment, I toyed with asking her about it, but I decided not to. It would make me sound paranoid and I didn't want to make things uncomfortable between us now we were going away together. I wasn't even sure what I'd seen at all. Perhaps I'd imagined it. Or at least exaggerated it in my mind.

Chapter 7

When Sophie left that evening, the flat seemed quiet. I real-ised she was the first visitor I'd had since John had left. I'd been out to meet people, of course, but here, in this space, I was nearly always alone now. Remembering what Sophie said about conquering feelings, I didn't let myself dwell on that thought. Instead, I went into the kitchen, put the radio on and busied myself making a vat of vegetable soup that would serve as lunch for the coming week. As I was finishing decanting the soup into Tupperware boxes to store in the fridge, the doorbell rang.

I put the lid on the tub I was filling and went to answer it, and was surprised to find John standing on the doorstep, clean shaven and wearing a proper button-down shirt. Immediately I remembered what I'd said to Sophie in our conversation just a few hours earlier, about what I'd do if he appeared at my door. I had a strange sense that I'd conjured him up somehow.

'John,' I said, taking in his smart clothes. 'Hello.'

He smiled but it fell quickly. He seemed nervous.

'Hello. How are you?'

I nodded. 'Okay. You?'

He held on to the bottom of his jacket, pulling it down to straighten it. 'May I come in?'

I didn't think I'd heard John use the phrase 'May I' about anything before. I looked at him for a moment, then I nodded. 'Okay.'

I held the door open and he shuffled past me into the hall, pulling a bottle of red wine from inside his jacket as he did so. 'Maybe we could sit down?' He nodded towards the kitchen. 'Open this?'

I knew everything Sophie had said had been right. It had been everything I'd been telling myself. I needed to move forward, not back. To cut all ties. Not to let sentimentality or nostalgia get the better of me. I knew that seeing John, sharing a drink with him in the flat where we'd done just that so many times before, was definitely risky, but at the same time, I was curious. I wanted to know what he had to say.

I let him follow me through to the kitchen, and he made a show of pouring the wine courteously – showing me the label like a waiter in a restaurant might, making sure to fill my glass before his.

We sat down at the table and he asked me polite questions about work, and I was impressed when he managed to remember details of projects I was working on that I'd assumed he'd never paid attention to. He only swapped to share news of his own life quite late in the conversation, and when he did, it was to tell me that a story had been turned down by a Paris-based journal. He didn't whine or criticise the decision as he normally would have. Instead he showed uncharacteristic humility by saying, 'It just wasn't the standard they were looking for, unfortunately.'

After about half an hour of this strangely formal back-and-forth chit chat, he said, 'Anyway, there's something I want to

47

talk to you about.' He cleared his throat. 'I've received a message. From *Sean*.'

He said the name with heavy emphasis, watching me for a reaction.

I frowned. 'Who's Sean? Sean who?'

He closed his eyes very briefly then sighed as if my question had disappointed him in some way. 'Come on,' he said. 'You know.'

'Eh? I really don't.'

'Okay. I'll read it to you.' He took his phone from his jacket pocket, tapped the screen a few times and began to read. '"John, sorry to be the bearer of bad news mate, but I think it's right you should know that Lauren is seeing other people. I had a drink with her myself but it became clear pretty quickly that she was already spoken for and it's really not my style to tread on another man's toes. I told her I wasn't inter-ested once I realised the score but I wanted to do the right thing and let you know what she's up to. I've been messed around myself and I wish someone had told me what was going on sooner. Best of luck to you mate."'

John put the phone down on the table and looked at me. He was obviously waiting for me to offer some kind of explanation.

'What . . . ?' I reached out for the phone and John didn't try to stop me.

The message had been sent via Facebook by someone calling himself just 'Sean M'. The profile photo showed a man standing on a nondescript stretch of beach. It was taken from too far away to see anything about his appearance other than that he was wearing a black coat.

'John, I have no idea who this is. I don't know anyone called Sean. This message is . . .' I shook my head. 'A lie. Completely random.'

John frowned slightly and adjusted his position in his chair. 'I do realise that although we're not necessarily formally separated, we have been through a rough patch recently—'

'I would say we are formally separated.'

He continued as if I hadn't spoken. 'And I do get that while things have been up in the air you might have wanted to make yourself feel better by getting attention elsewhere. I do understand it. But I just wanted to see what you had to say about it. To see if there's anything to be worked out.'

'John, it's a *hoax*. Someone's winding you up.'

He continued frowning and took a deep breath as if to make it clear he was making a very big effort to be reasonable and I wasn't making it easy. 'Lauren, I just want to have an honest conversation. An amnesty, if you like. Everything out on the table, then we can clear the slate. If you just went out with this bloke to get my attention then—'

'There is no bloke!' I put my head in my hands and pulled at my hair in frustration. 'Who is he? What does his profile say? Did you reply?'

John shook his head. 'I'm not going to get into a conversation with a stranger. His profile's private. But why would someone make it up, Lauren? It makes no sense.'

'Well, I'm telling you. It didn't happen.' I knocked back the end of my glass of wine in one and slumped back in my chair, my arms crossed. The nostalgic feelings that had been creeping in around the edges over the last few days had evaporated. The man was impossible. John nodded once and stood up. 'In that case,' he said quietly, 'we're done.'

I couldn't help but smirk. 'We're done because I didn't go out with someone else?'

He picked up the cap from the table top and screwed it back onto the half empty wine bottle. 'No, because you can't ever be honest. We've reached a dead-end. There's nothing more for us to say to each other.'

He tucked the bottle inside his jacket and I was amused – but not surprised – to realise he'd decided to take it with him. He cleared his throat. 'If you change your mind in the next few weeks, maybe we can talk again. If perhaps over the summer—'

'I'm going away over the summer.'

I wasn't sure why I blurted it out. I think I just wanted him to know I definitely wouldn't be sitting around the flat lamenting his departure and hoping he might call by. I knew 'over the summer' was a clear exaggeration of the one-week holiday we had planned, but I liked the way it sounded. And, gratifyingly, it seemed to rattle him.

He frowned. 'Away where? Who with?'

'With some friends. You don't know them.' He didn't know Sophie, anyway.

'When will you be back?'

I turned away from him and began picking the dead leaves off the pot plant on the window sill. 'Not really any of your business, is it,' I said airily.

He looked at me with an expression halfway between confusion and disappointment, like a teacher whose pupils keep misbehaving, despite their best efforts to manage them. 'Why are you being like that, Lauren? I'm only showing concern. It's not safe to just go off with people you hardly know, to not tell anyone where you're going and when you'll be back. What if you *don't* come back? Who's going to come looking for you? Not likely your "work colleagues" are going to be bothered, is it?' He said 'work colleagues' like both the work and the colleagues were figments of my imagination. 'I'll be the first one to notice. You do realise that?'

'You know, I think I might just be okay.'

He looked at me, his expression dark. I thought this might be the point where he lost it, where the polite façade cracked and fell away, but in the end, he just muttered, 'Jesus Christ.' Then he marched out of the kitchen, down the hallway and out of the front door, letting it slam behind him.

Outside, I heard a frustrated shout – 'Bitch!' – echo around the empty street, followed by the sound of breaking glass.

When enough time had passed for me to be sure he'd gone, I looked out of my front window and saw he'd smashed the half-full wine bottle against my garden wall.

Chapter 8

I chose not to tell Anya or Sophie, or anyone else, about the bizarre and infuriating conversation with John. The more I thought about what he'd said, the more I wondered if he hadn't written the message from the mysterious 'Sean M' himself. I was seriously starting to wonder if he might have a genuine psychiatric disorder. Maybe he always had, but I'd been so scared of being on my own that I'd managed to convince myself they were just the understandable mood swings of a frustrated artist.

The whole of May passed quickly, and I was glad to be busy with work and low-pressure social gatherings. I didn't see Anya or Sophie at all, and didn't have much contact with either, until a week before our flight to Barcelona, when Anya sent me a message so late in the evening I was almost asleep when I saw my phone screen light up.

Anya: Do you think it was a good idea to invite Sophie?
Me: Hey, how are you? Yeah, why wouldn't it be? You invited her . . .?

Anya: I know, I know. I dunno. I was just feeling sad it wasn't going to be just us two, I suppose.

Me: Bit late now! It'll be good. Fun. More the merrier etc.

There was a long gap then and I assumed that was the end of the conversation. When the next message came through, I was nearly asleep again.

Anya: She said she went round yours, the other week? She told me, tonight.

I thought this was a strange thing to say. She made it sound like the quiet afternoon Sophie and I had spent drinking tea and watching an old film was some kind of illicit encounter.

Me: Yeah, I was feeling shit about John so she came to keep me company.

Anya: I would've come, if you'd asked.

Me: I know. It's not a big deal.

Anya didn't reply to this and it seemed the conversation was over. I lay on my back looking at the ceiling, feeling confused about the point Anya had been trying to make. At first I thought Anya was feeling guilty, that she felt bad that I'd had to ask for support from someone I'd only known a few weeks and that she was sorry she hadn't made herself more available. If that was the case, then she didn't have anything to worry about. Anya and I knew the other was there if needed; it wasn't our style to check in constantly or to send long affectionate messages of support unprompted.

The more I thought about it, though, the more I wondered if there was a hint of reproach in Anya's message, resentment that I had gone to a new friend – *her* friend, officially speaking – rather than her. That too was silly, and actually, quite unlike Anya. I toyed with the idea of following up the conversation with a message to clarify things, but I decided it was better to leave it. Whatever was on her mind would be long forgotten when we were drinking beers and watching the sunset from our Spanish balcony next week.

On the Saturday of our flight, the three of us met, as arranged, outside Gatwick departures hall. We greeted each other enthusiastically and quickly began exchanging questions about whether we'd packed the right things – 'How many plug adapters have you got? I've only got one. Should I buy another here do you think?', 'Forgotten my bloody hairbrush, haven't I. Can I just use yours?'

I was relieved to see that everyone seemed relaxed. Whatever issue Anya had had with Sophie when she sent that message wasn't evident now, and neither were there any obvious signs of the nerviness Sophie seemed to exhibit from time to time.

Our cheerful mood soon deflated when we realised our flight was delayed by nearly three hours. Anya, who never enjoyed having her progress frustrated, responded by melodramatically dropping her bag to the floor and saying, 'Fan-fucking-tastic, that's half our holiday gone already then.'

I met Sophie's eye across the row of metal chairs and saw a tiny twitch of amusement at the corner of her mouth.

'It'll go quickly,' I said. 'We can look at the shops, have a drink. You know they've got a Hugo Boss here now?'

Anya made a huffing noise, but she looked up and scanned the rows of shops on the balcony above us anyway.

I pulled my laptop out of my bag and logged on to the airport's free wifi.

'How come you brought that?' Sophie said. 'Bit heavy to lug about, isn't it?'

'Thought it was better to have it than to not,' I said. 'Just in case of work or something.'

The truth was that I'd taken the week as annual leave and nothing about my job was so important that anyone was likely to need to interrupt it. But I thought the holiday might be an opportunity to re-engage my artistic gears, if there was any downtime. When the others were reading or napping, I might want to open up a few of the old sketches I had tucked away on my hard drive, fiddle around with retouching them. Start to get my portfolio back together.

The three hours did pass by relatively quickly, and it was only near the end, as we were waiting at the boarding gate, that Anya's bad mood showed any sign of re-emerging. We were chatting idly about the flat, trying to remember the details we'd seen in the listing on the rental site. With the intention of reassuring Sophie, who I was worried might still be feeling the pressure of having made the choice, I said, 'It was such a good find, that one. Perfect.'

'I reckon Sophie had her sights set on that one all along. Only put those two others in to make us feel like we had options.' Anya said it without looking up from her magazine, in the flat weary voice she used when she was fed-up and bored. I knew her well enough to know there was no particular malice, or even forethought, behind the comment, but I immediately looked at Sophie to check her reaction.

Sophie's cheeks flushed. 'I didn't!' she said, looking at me anxiously. 'I thought they were all good options! I didn't mind which one we went for, I wanted you to choose.'

I shot Anya a brief look that said 'Back off, would you,' but she just calmly turned the page of her magazine. I reached forward and put my hand on Sophie's knee. 'We know. It's fine. Anya's just teasing because she's a moody cow.'

'Fuck off,' Anya muttered, still not looking up.

Sophie nodded and sat back in her chair, but her brow was still furrowed.

Chapter 9

The flight was uneventful but progress through Barcelona airport arrivals was sluggish and by the time the taxi delivered us to the edge of the city it was nearly 10 p.m. We stepped out of the air-conditioned car into the soupy night air.

'Jesus, it's hot,' Anya said, pulling her hair back from her face and tying it up in a messy ponytail. 'This place better have air-con.'

'Where are we going then, Sophie?' I asked. 'You got the address?'

'Yes. That way.' She pointed down a busy street with cars coming towards us in two lanes of traffic. Then she spun around suddenly and pointed in the opposite direction. 'No! That way! Yes. That's it.'

Anya raised an eyebrow. 'Sure about that are you?'

Sophie nodded firmly. 'Yes. One hundred per cent. I think.'

After nearly a full day of travelling, Sophie was the only one with any power left on her phone, so we had no choice but to follow her as she led us a meandering route through the narrow streets, every few moments checking the map and making a series of abrupt turns. I tried not to worry too much about how efficient a route we might be taking and instead focus on soaking up the atmosphere. This is it! I told myself, we're here! In one of the most vibrant cities in the world. Look around you! This is all part of it!

But my heart wasn't in it. I just wasn't feeling ready to soak up anything until I'd had the chance to change out of my crumpled clothes, have a shower and have a drink.

'Do you think she knows where we're going?' Anya muttered to me when we'd dropped behind Sophie enough to prevent her hearing. 'I think we've been down this street already.'

I shrugged and winced, adjusting my bag to shift it from where the strap was rubbing on my shoulder. 'I know . . . I was just trying not to undermine her.'

Anya sighed deeply and retied her ponytail. 'I think we're going to have to say something.'

I called ahead. 'Hey, Sophie? Why don't you take a break from the map reading for a bit? Let me have a go?'

She paused, obviously wounded by the implied criticism, but she nodded and passed the phone to me. Fifteen minutes later, I stopped and looked up at a grey tower block on a quiet road lined with plastic bins.

'This is it,' I said, letting go of my suitcase handle and rotating my shoulders to ease the ache. 'Torre Sonrisas,' I read from the sign above the door. 'Sunrise tower?'

'Tower of smiles,' Anya corrected. 'Apparently.' She surveyed the grey pebbledash sceptically.

'Okay,' Sophie said. 'Great. So . . .' She took her phone from me and squinted at the screen. 'The owner said we need to find the black metal box on the side of the building. It'll have a keypad on it, apparently. And when we type in the code we should find the key inside.'

We split up, walking up and down the street, scouring the walls for the box.

'Are you sure this is the right place?' Anya said, her hands on her hips as she looked up at the building. 'There *is* no box. There's nothing. I told you this was a bad idea. There really is nothing to stop just anyone setting up a profile, sticking a few pictures of a random flat on there and taking the cash. I tried to say this at the time.'

'Look,' I said, making a real effort to keep my voice bright, 'If we really can't find it, we just contact the website direct. They have guarantees for this sort of thing. That's the whole benefit of using these middleman sites.' I turned to Sophie. 'How did it work – you pay the money through some central system, don't you? You pay the site, they hold the cash and they only pass it on to the owner once we've confirmed everything's hunky dory?'

Sophie looked at me, her eyes wide. 'Well, that's the official way, yes. But the owner suggested we just do a direct bank transfer, because then he doesn't have to charge us the fifteen per cent admin fee.'

'Great,' Anya said. 'Some random bloke off the internet has run off with our cash. Fantastic.' She wandered away, running her hand along the edge of the concrete and shaking her head.

Sophie looked down. 'I was just trying to save us all money. I—'

'It's fine,' I said, putting my arm around her shoulders. 'It's going to be fine.'

'Oh, hey! Look!' Anya called from the corner of the building. 'I bet this is it! What's the code?'

We jogged over to join her and saw, just around the corner and hidden in the shadows, a black metal box with a keyboard, exactly as Sophie had described.

'Thank god for that! Okay, crisis averted. What's the code, Sophie?'

The key was released from its box and relieved – slightly

sheepish – smiles were exchanged as we let ourselves into the building.

There was no lift to the apartment but having been worried only moments ago that there was no flat at all, we dragged our suitcases up the two flights of stairs to the first floor with relatively little complaint.

'Surprised it's only on the first floor,' I said. 'The view from the balcony made me think it was much higher. Five floors at least. Maybe ten.'

At the top of the stairs, we dragged our cases down the narrow corridor, checking each door for a number. When we reached the door numbered 17, we stopped. 'This is it, then,' Anya said. 'The moment of truth.' She put the key in the lock.

It was hot in the corridor and we were all sweating from the exertion of the climb but somehow the air that drifted out through the open door to the flat was hotter. And more than that, it seemed stale somehow, as if no one had opened the door in a very long time.

Anya coughed and pulled a face. 'Christ, it's like opening the oven. What *is* that smell?'

'Is it definitely the right place?' I said, stepping back and looking at the number on the door again.

'Yeah,' Sophie said quietly, 'Number 17 is right.'

I could feel the awkwardness radiating off her. She was almost shrinking towards the ground, like she wanted to make herself smaller. It was obvious from the beginning she hadn't been totally comfortable, that she'd been acutely aware of her outsider status in our group, and now here we were, visibly, and vocally, disappointed by her contribution.

I flicked the light switch and we stood in the entrance of the flat. It was an open-plan space, the lounge to our right with two sofas facing each other running straight into a small kitchenette area. My first impression was how much smaller it was than the photos. It had looked light and airy in the pictures, but this room was cramped and cluttered, the furniture far too big for it. The heat was suffocating; there was no air conditioning to give any relief.

'Let's get a window open for a start,' Anya said, heading towards the main window and beginning to feel around behind the blind for a handle or catch to let in some air. But then she stopped suddenly, and held back the edge of the blind, looking out to the street below. 'Oh my . . . what! You've got to be kidding me, what the actual . . . ?'

Sophie and I went to join her and pulled back the blind to see what she was looking at.

I shook my head in disbelief. 'That is . . .'

'Oh my *god*,' Anya said. 'Oh my fucking god. Who does that?'

Behind the blind, through the window, we could see the balcony, all present and correct, and as per the photos on the website. We could also see the view beyond – the whites and browns of the rooftops and in the distance, the sea. But what was immediately striking about this view was that the sky was blue, the windows on the buildings glinting in the sunlight, even though it was past eleven, the sky inky black. The 'view' was, in fact, a photo. A huge city-scape printed on some kind of adhesive paper and plastered across a brick wall that sat a few feet in front of the balcony. In reality the apartment didn't have any view to speak of, but someone had come up with a very creative way to make it look like it did.

We all stood there for a moment, our faces poking through the gap at the side of the blind, staring at it in bemusement. It was almost funny.

'Can you do that?' I said, stepping away from the window

and looking around the room. 'It's false advertising, surely? Or something? Fraud?'

Sophie ran her hand through her hair. 'I was sure it was real! It looked real, in the photo. Didn't it?' She looked around at us for support. 'There was no way we could have known?'

'This is a joke!' Anya shouted suddenly. She kicked her suitcase over and it fell to the floor with a loud smack 'This is a scam. Okay so the place is *here*, but it's not *the* place. Not what we paid for.'

She spun around and looked at Sophie. 'Message the bloke now. Say this isn't good enough. We want our money back and we want him to find us a hotel.'

Sophie nodded, 'Okay.' She looked at me, tears in her eyes. 'So what should I say, then? I should tell him we want a hotel? Now? I don't know if—'

'Look,' I said firmly. 'Let's all just calm down.' Although I said 'all' I was looking directly at Anya. 'Let's get some perspective. We're tired. We're hot. Yes, it's disappointing and not quite how we imagined it, but we've all got beds for the night.'

'Have we, though?' Anya said coldly. 'Have we actually checked that? Might just be a cardboard box painted to look like a bed.'

I ignored her. 'Let's just get some sleep and reassess things in the morning.'

'Fine,' Anya said, heading towards the side-by-side doors that I assumed led to the two bedrooms listed in the flat's profile – one single and one twin. 'Anyone object if I take the single room? I take it you two will be okay to go in together.'

She wheeled her suitcase into the room nearest the kitchen and shut the door behind her. I was annoyed with her for being childish, for acting as though our day had been somehow worse for her than it had for us, but I also felt an underlying sense of unease. When things had gone wrong in the past, we had approached them as a united front. She was often grouchy and prone to melodrama, but this time it was as though she was angry with me. As though I'd done something wrong that I didn't know about.

Chapter 10

When I woke up the following morning, the bed next to me was empty and I could hear the sounds of shuffling about and low voices from the lounge. I grabbed a pair of shorts, pulled them on and went out to greet the day.

'Morning!' I said as brightly as I could. In bed the night before, I'd realised that I was going to need to take charge and set the tone of the following day. There was a strong chance Anya would continue to grumble and moan if she felt like it and Sophie would be too nervous and wary of getting things wrong to say much at all. It was going to be down to me to keep spirits buoyed.

Anya and Sophie were sitting on the sofas, Anya staring despondently at the mural of the city-scape through the window and Sophie staring into her coffee cup.

I sat down on the edge of Anya's sofa. 'How did everyone sleep?'

Anya just made a grunting noise but Sophie looked up and seemed to be making an effort to look cheerful. 'Fine, actually. Really it was okay, wasn't it? I thought it was fine?'

'Yeah. Wonderful,' Anya said flatly, without looking at us.

I rolled my eyes and smiled at Sophie to try to show her that she shouldn't worry too much about Anya's attitude. Then I made myself laugh to defuse the tension. 'Guys! Will you cheer up! We're on a holiday. We have an apartment. And really, it's fine!' I looked at Sophie now. 'Clearly we've all got something to learn about believing everything you see on the adverts, but it's not terrible. We've got beds, running water, somewhere to sit. And look!' I nodded towards the tiny strip of real blue sky that we could just see above the brick wall that faced our balcony. 'It's Spain! In June! The sun is shining, there's so much to see. Let's get dressed and get out there. We only have to come back to shower and sleep. We'll barely be here at all.'

Anya sighed and nodded, and for the first time since we'd arrived she seemed ready to make an effort to be more positive. 'Yeah. Okay.'

While Sophie took the first shower, Anya and I stayed in the lounge. Anya put her mug on the side table and wandered around the room, examining the space.

'What kind of person do you think lives here?' she said, picking up a glass ash tray from the desk and looking at the bottom.

'That's what I was thinking,' I said. 'This is someone's home, isn't it? It's not just some holiday apartment. And when you remember that, things like the big poster of the view . . . I mean, they put that up for themselves, didn't they? To make their home nicer. Not just to trick people. So, it's kind of . . . sweet, in a way.'

Anya raised one eyebrow, but she was smiling. She went over to the wall, which was covered with photos in frames. 'These are a bit weird.'

I went to join her. The photos were all of women, all on their own, from various periods in history, looking at the camera. Some of the women were expressionless, as if posing for a passport photo, but others were smiling in front of a beach view or standing beside a Christmas tree.

'Who do you think they are?' I said. 'Family? Ex-girlfriends?'

'He's got quite eclectic tastes if so.' She nodded towards one of the black and white photos that showed a woman of around seventy with a tiny tattoo of a cross on her right cheek and an eye patch.

I laughed. 'Good point. Also, he would have had to have been quite busy. There must be what, thirty women here?'

Anya shrugged. 'Who knows what this guy gets up to. I hope we never find out to be honest.'

Sophie emerged from the shower. 'All yours.'

'Great,' Anya said. 'Let's get dressed and get out of here.'

Chapter 11

As we emerged from the building, we were hit by the smell of drains.

'Wonderful,' muttered Anya darkly. 'I love holidaying in a sewer.'

No one responded, and neither did we say anything to her complaints about the noise of the cars, the heat or the price of beer listed outside a bar. It seemed that whatever resolve to be positive she'd had in the flat had left her.

'Anya,' I said eventually, stopping and turning to face her. 'Are you going to moan all day? About everything?'

I was prepared to have a fight on my hands, as I usually did any time I asked her to reflect on her own behaviour, but to my surprise she just nodded once and said, 'No. Yes. You're right. Sorry.'

I blinked, unsure for a moment how to react. 'Right. Okay.'

'I think I'm just going to go and have a drink.' She nodded across the road to a bar where a couple of old men with leathery brown skin sat drinking from tiny coffee cups and staring out in front of them. 'On my own. Just to . . . pull myself together. You two go on. I'll catch you up and meet you in an hour or so. Then I'll be all smiles, I promise.' She pulled her lips tight as if to demonstrate her good intentions.

I hesitated for a moment. 'Well, if that's what you want?'

She nodded again, already turning towards the bar. 'Yeah. I'll be fine. I'm just not used to being with people all the time. I live alone for a reason you know!' She flashed us a grin. 'I'll see you in a bit.' Then with a quick wave she disappeared inside the bar.

'Is she okay?' Sophie said, squinting into the sun after her.

I shrugged. 'I'd rather she had some time out than was a pain in the arse for the whole week.'

I wanted Sophie to think that Anya's sudden desertion was perfectly in keeping with her character and nothing to worry about, but really, it bothered me. Our holiday had only just started. It wasn't supposed to be like this. Anya and I were meant to be solid. Sure, inviting someone new would change the dynamic a little, but fundamentally Anya and I were supposed to be on the same side. Other people might come and go – boyfriends might leave, brothers might die – but through it all Anya would be there for me and I'd be there for her. She wasn't supposed to need time out from me.

As we ambled around the shops my phone kept buzzing in my bag. When I stopped to look at it, I was surprised to see I had three missed calls from John. I hadn't heard from him since the night he'd smashed the wine bottle outside my house. I considered what he could be calling to say. I weighed up a few options – perhaps something had happened to my flat, a fire, a break-in? – before deciding what was most likely was that he had thought up some new reason to criticise me and would act as though he was doing me a favour by giving me the opportunity to defend myself. As he tried a fourth time, I cancelled the call and held down the button to turn off the phone. Apart from anything else, receiving a call from overseas would cost me a fortune.

Sophie emerged from the souvenir shop where she'd been browsing corkscrews and fridge magnets. 'Who was that?' she said, nodding towards the phone in my hand.

'John.' I shoved it to the bottom of my bag. 'I don't know what he wants, though.'

'Are you still finding you're missing him?'

'No,' I said. 'Not really.' I thought about telling her about his visit to my flat, his strange accusations, but it seemed too long a story to go into, and one I couldn't properly explain. 'It is weird, though, living alone.'

Sophie nodded, trying on a pair of bright blue sunglasses from a rack outside a shop and checking her reflection in the mirror. 'Living alone has been the biggest shock for me. London is different, obviously, to where I used to live in the countryside, but I got used to the noise and smells and crowds quite quickly. What's been harder is getting used to knowing that when I get home of an evening, that's it. Just me.'

I nodded. 'Yeah. Exactly. Living with him wasn't always easy but . . .' I shrugged. 'I guess I'm just a natural cohabiter.'

She sighed. 'Yes. I feel that way too.' She turned to look at me. She was wearing a pair of Minnie Mouse sunglasses now and she grinned. 'Maybe you and me should move in together! Maybe that's the solution!'

'Yeah, maybe,' I said with a chuckle. 'We went from first meeting to holidaying together pretty fast. Why not go the whole hog and shack up together?'

Sophie laughed and it crossed my mind that I wouldn't have been so open with Anya about my feelings on living alone. Anya loved living on her own and couldn't understand how anyone could get lonely when they had a job and friends.

She thought having a space entirely of one's own wasn't just acceptable, but essential. Sophie, though, seemed to know exactly what I meant and I was suddenly grateful that she was there. The small moment of bonding gave me the confidence to bring up something that had been on my mind since we'd first met: that look she'd given me when Anya had introduced us.

'I thought you knew me already, you know!' I said. I added a short laugh to make it sound like a casual, throwaway comment, but it didn't quite work.

Sophie jerked her head to the side to look at me. She took the sunglasses off and put them back on the rack. 'What do you mean?'

'When we first met. When you arrived at the smoke place and Anya told you my name. I thought you gave me a weird look, like you'd known me in a past life! A life where you hated me!' I laughed again to try to show I was making fun of my own paranoia rather than suggesting she'd done anything wrong, but I wasn't sure that really was what I was doing. 'I thought maybe you'd seen me around? When you lived in Hoyle? Maybe we'd both gone for the last jar of Nutella in Tesco or something.'

She frowned for a moment, then she closed her eyes briefly and said, 'Oh. I see.'

Then she turned and continued to walk down the road, and I thought that was all she was going to say on the matter. But then she stopped abruptly and looked at me again. I stopped too.

'I did,' she said. 'Recognise you.'

I blinked. 'From Hoyle?

She nodded but she didn't smile. She continued to look at me, chewing on her lip. I really wasn't sure what was going on.

'I don't think I . . . I mean, did we have a mutual friend or something?' I asked.

She shook her head. 'Not really. I was a teacher. At Hoyle Boys?'

'Oh, okay. I thought you just did private pupils. I didn't realise you'd been an actual schoolteacher. I went to the girls' school. Hoyle High.'

She nodded. 'I know.'

In our small town, the main high school had been divided into two different but closely related schools – Hoyle High School, for girls, and Hoyle Boys – separated by a playing field. We shared some facilities and the boys came over for certain lessons, but it never worked the other way round; I'd never been inside Hoyle Boys. I was surprised that Sophie would recognise me simply by virtue of the fact that I'd gone to school next door. There had always been hundreds of kids swarming up and down that field every day – there was no reason why I would have stood out particularly. I certainly didn't remember her, at any rate. But I wasn't sure how to put all this to her without sounding unduly suspicious.

'So, I'm just wondering,' I began cautiously. 'How come you . . . I mean, where do you think . . .'

'I used to teach your brother, you see. For a little bit. That's the thing.' She stared at me intently, chewing on her lip again.

'Reuben?' As if there had been any other brothers.

She nodded. 'Reuben,' she said gently. 'I was an English teacher. I knew him in his AS Level year. The year he . . .'

I nodded and swallowed. I was glad she'd opted not to finish the sentence.

'I saw you together, a couple of times, outside the school, but it took me a moment to make the connection when I saw you. You two looked so similar. I'm sure you got that a lot.'

I nodded. We had.

'At first,' Sophie went on. 'I couldn't work out where I knew you from, but then when I did, I didn't want to say anything because . . . well, you know. I didn't want to bring up anything to upset you. Not when I didn't really know you.'

I nodded again. 'I see. Okay. That makes sense.' Then I added, 'Sorry,' although I didn't know why.

She gave me a sad smile and stepped forward to continue down the busy shopping street. I felt exposed suddenly, now I knew she knew more about me than I'd previously realised. Not only had she known Reuben, and what happened to him, but she would have been around to hear the rumours afterwards and probably read the local press coverage too. It made me feel uneasy that during the first few weeks of our friendship, during those conversations we'd had about my feelings about John, when she'd been to my flat, she'd known all the intimate details of my past but hadn't said anything. I could understand her reasons for not bringing it up sooner, but still, a part of me felt deceived.

Chapter 12

Anya came to join us again an hour later. Whatever pep talk she'd given herself during her solo bar expedition, whatever drink she'd had or – more likely – whatever male attention she'd received, seemed to have perked her up and the three of us spent a peaceful morning wandering around the streets, looking in shop windows, watching buskers and pointing out restaurants we could try.

At around one o'clock, conversation turned to lunch and we decided to buy some things from the supermarket to save eating out for the evenings. Laden with baguettes, precooked tortillas in plastic cases and bottles of fruit juice, we returned to our flat at Torre Sonrisas.

As we turned onto our corridor I noticed something was different; the whole hallway was brighter, and I quickly saw why. Whereas previously the only source of light had been a strip window about the width of a brick at the end of the corridor, sunlight was now flooding in from the entrance to one of the apartments, where the door stood wide open.

That door was number 17. Our door.

'What the fuck?' Anya said, standing in front of the doorway and looking inside. 'How's this happened? We shut it didn't we? Who shut it? You did, didn't you, Lauren?'

I nodded. 'Yeah. I definitely did. I checked it twice to make sure it was closed.' The door was bouncing gently on its hinges. I reached down to touch the lock, pushing down on the handle that controlled the in-and-out mechanism. 'The catch has been jammed open. You can't get it to do anything.' The metal block was stuck in a receded position, inside the door. In its current state, the latch wouldn't even hold the door shut in the frame, much less secure it. 'Who's *done* this?'

'Shit, what about our stuff?' Anya pushed past me into the flat and headed for her bedroom.

I stood in the middle of the main living area and surveyed the room. 'Everything looks the same?'

Anya came out of her room. 'All my cash seems to be there still, and my passport. But you should check yours.'

Sophie and I obediently went into our room. I unzipped the pouch inside my case where I'd stuffed my passport and the hundred euros of cash I'd brought with me. I realised now that this was a pointless hiding place – barely a hiding place at all, no better really than leaving it lying in the middle of the floor – so I was relieved when I saw my passport was exactly where I'd left it. A quick flick through the notes told me the money was all still present too.

'Everything's here,' Sophie said from her side of the room. 'I think it's all here.'

We reconvened by the front door and took it in turns to try to push down the handle, to coax the metal bar of the latch into action.

'Why bother to break in and then not even take anything? What's the point?' I said.

'Maybe they were looking for something that wasn't

74

here?' Anya suggested. 'Or maybe they've taken something belonging to the owner that we didn't notice? We didn't check everything.' She looked around the room again, but apart from the books and the pictures on the wall, it was hard to see what there was to take.

Anya groaned and threw herself down on the sofa dramatically. 'This is unbelievable!' she said. 'What are we supposed to do now? What are we supposed to do without a bloody lock, for god's sake?' We can't just go out, with the door hanging open like that.'

'Should we call the police?' I asked.

Anya sighed. 'Is there any point, when nothing's been taken? I don't see what they'll be able to do. All we really want is to have the door secured so we can go out again. Because until it's fixed, we'll just have to stay here. Imprisoned in this hovel. In the boiling heat!'

'We just need a locksmith,' Sophie said. 'Or a handyman or something. Someone to fix the lock, or fit a replacement.'

'We shouldn't have to be sorting this out, though,' Anya whined. 'This is the owner's job! The owner's problem. We've paid our money and he has a duty to provide us with proper accommodation. Including a working door.' She took her phone out of her pocket. 'What's his number?' she demanded. 'I'm going to call him, tell him to get here now.'

Sophie shook her head again. 'We don't have a number for him. Just email.'

Anya let out another groan of frustration and rested her head on the arm of the sofa.

'Okay,' I said, 'so we'll just have to get it fixed ourselves. What's Spanish for locksmith? I'll Google.'

'Why don't I try my friend?' Sophie said. 'The one I mentioned who lives out here? He's English but he's lived here a while so he speaks Spanish and everything. Maybe he can recommend someone to help. I don't know if he's definitely around but I could see?'

I shrugged. 'Worth a try.'

I assembled our supermarket purchases into a lunch and laid it out on the coffee table in the lounge while Sophie sat on the balcony typing quickly on her phone. When the food was ready, she came back inside. 'Right,' she said with a smile. 'He's coming over. He'll be here within the hour.'

'And you think he'll be able to help?' I said, passing her a plate.

'He said he'd try.'

Forty-five minutes later, there was a soft knock and a voice called out a cheery, 'Hello, anyone home?'

'Yes, we're in here,' Sophie said, going over to the door and pulling it open.

A man in cargo shorts and flip-flops with ginger hair and rosy cheeks stepped into the flat. As I looked at him and he looked at me, our surprised expressions mirrored each other's.

'Matt?' I said. 'Matt Fabian?'

'Woah.' He blinked. 'Lauren. Hi.'

Chapter 13

It had been a long time and he'd lost a lot of weight but his face was exactly as I remembered it.

He continued looking at me. He seemed bemused. Mesmerised, almost.

'No way,' he said, shaking his head. 'Lauren Henry.'

Sophie looked from Matt to me and back again. 'Do you know each other?'

'Yeah,' I said. 'Sort of.'

Matt Fabian was from Hoyle. He went to the boys' school, like Reuben. He'd been in his year. Reuben didn't tend to spend a lot of time with others, but I'd seen them together outside the school, on the field. He'd been to the house one or two times too, one of the boys who'd called by with odd-shaped music cases on their backs and left with a book or a bag of cables under their arm. I think we may even have given him a lift to a performance or an exam somewhere out of town; I had a vague memory of sitting next to him in the back of the car, the sleeves of his black hoody pulled down over his hands.

'Yeah.' He was looking at me with his head on one side. 'From way back.'

'Do you remember Anya, too?'

Matt looked her, his eyes narrowed, trying to remember. 'Yeah, maybe?'

Anya nodded. 'I think we saw each other around.'

'You knew my brother, didn't you? Reuben?' I said.

'Yeah,' Matt said quietly. 'Reuben.'

There was a moment of awkward silence where it was clear no one knew how to appropriately respond to the unscheduled mention of my dead brother.

I forced a bright smile. 'But . . . but so many questions! How do you two,' I pointed at Matt and Sophie with the index fingers on each hand, my hands crossing in front of me, 'know each other? And, Matt, what are you doing here, in Barcelona? Bit of a step up from Hoyle!'

Matt took a moment to adjust to the change of tone, but then he said 'Yeah!' He ran his hand through his hair leaving it sticking up. 'Well, Sophie and I actually met after Hoyle, I didn't know her there. We met here, in Barcelona! We only realised the Hoyle connection afterwards. Couldn't believe she'd taught at my school! I didn't remember her at all. But then I didn't take English after GCSEs.'

'We met at a music night,' Sophie said, but she didn't say any more.

I tried to visualise the shape of the black case Matt used to carry about the place. 'You used to play the . . . trumpet?'

'Trombone,' Matt said with a grin, miming the action of the instrument. 'Still do.'

'Oh, okay,' I said. I shook my head and laughed. 'Well, small world and everything, as they say!'

'Yeah,' Matt said smiling, shyly. 'Yeah. But anyway.' He gestured to the damaged door behind him. 'What's going on here? You poor buggers. Last thing you need on your holiday, I'll bet.' He crouched down in front of the door and looked at the lock closely, trying in vain to find a part that could be freed or adjusted. 'It's been completely done over, hasn't it? Stuck fast.'

'Yep,' Anya said with a weary sigh. 'Totally useless.'

Matt stood back up. 'Well, as soon as you messaged I called my friend Carlos. He's an electrician technically but he's pretty handy. We had a spare lock in the office from the refurb we had recently, so he's gone to collect it, then he'll be over to fit it.'

'Really?' Anya said, cheering up for the first time. 'He can just put a replacement in?'

Matt shrugged and smiled. 'He seemed to think so.' His cheeks flushed an even deeper pink. I expected Matt fancied Anya a bit. Or was at least struck by her looks. People usually were.

I got Matt a glass of orange juice and we sat on the sofas while we waited for Carlos to arrive. I asked him about how he'd come to be in Spain and what he did for work and he told us how he'd moved to Barcelona the summer after university, only ever intending to stay a few months to 'bum around for a bit' earning a bit of cash by gigging in bars with his friend who played double bass.

'We called ourselves Drunken Uncle. I've no idea why, it was lame. But we seemed to go down quite well. Just doing jazzy pop covers and stuff for tourists. I set up a simple website, mostly just to list our own gigs. But then I started putting similar ones on there too, just to drive traffic really, and over a few months, it really took off. We sort of became the main listings site for music in the city. Of course, then what happens is that advertisers start getting in touch and big names want to be on there . . . and anyway.' He shrugged. 'Eight years later and GigCity employs forty people and we've got an office in the Gothic Quarter.'

'Wow,' I said. 'Impressive. So you're the boss?'

Matt laughed, and ran his hands through his hair again, his cheeks flushing. 'I'm the majority shareholder and company director. I don't really do much bossing, though, if I can help it. I've got a good team and they mostly run the place themselves now.'

I grinned. 'Little Matt Fabian, company director. Who would've called it.'

Matt's phone rang and he pulled it out of his pocket to answer it. He spoke quickly in Spanish before hanging up. 'That's Carlos now. He's just coming up.'

A few minutes later a short, stocky man with bushy black eyebrows and dark stubble appeared in the open doorway.

Matt stepped forward to shake his hand and Carlos said a low 'Hola' to the room without meeting any of our eyes. He went over to inspect the damaged lock. After a few moments, he turned to Matt and said something in Spanish. Matt raised his eyebrows in surprise.

'I think maybe the lock is broken from the inside,' Carlos said, swapping into English for us. 'You can see from how it's stuck.'

I looked at the others. 'So whoever did this, let themselves in first, *then* broke the lock?'

Carlos shrugged. 'I'm not certain. Is just a maybe.'

'But how would they have got in in the first place?' I asked.

Matt rubbed his hand over his chin, scratching his stubble. 'With a key, I suppose? That's the thing with these home-from-home rentals. You're never the only one with a key.'

Chapter 14

'What?' Anya said. 'Someone has a key and is just letting themselves in to this flat whenever they feel like it? Jesus!'

She was looking at Carlos, aiming her outrage directly at him as if he was the one who'd caused the problem rather the person there to fix it.

He held up his palms in protest. 'I don't know. I say maybe. But maybe not. Is like you say – why? It makes no sense.' Carlos shook his head, then he slid his toolbox across the floor to the door, knelt down in front of it and got to work.

'Okay well, we're getting out of here then, either way. Aren't we?' Anya turned to me. 'We're not going to stay here.'

'Oh,' Sophie said. 'I mean, do you think we . . . ?'

Sophie trailed off. Both she and Anya were looking at me – Anya's expression was outraged, Sophie's nervous, but both seemed to expect me to make the call on what happened next.

'Let's just try to think about this calmly for a minute,' I said. 'I suppose the reality is that getting burgled could happen to anyone, anywhere. Anya, your flat in London's been broken into before, hasn't it? When your work phone

81

and your camera were nicked. You didn't decide to move out then, did you?'

'Well, yeah. But this is different. It was done from the *inside*. Someone just let themselves in. That's the issue. That's what I'm not happy about.'

We turned to look at Carlos who had finished unscrewing the old lock and was carefully lifting it out away from the wood of the door. I didn't really want to speculate about the validity of his theory in front of him when he was only trying to help us.

'Sorry,' I looked at Matt and Carlos. 'Could you just excuse us for a moment?' Matt nodded and I gestured for Anya and Sophie to join me in the kitchen where I spoke to them in a low voice. 'Look, this Carlos guy didn't seem to know one way or the other what happened to the lock. I don't really see how he could tell anyway, just by looking. I don't think we should do anything dramatic based on that.'

'But let's be honest,' Anya whispered. 'This place is a shithole. It just gives me a bad feeling. I say let's move on anyway. Find somewhere better.'

'Where, though?' I said. 'Without anything booked? I'm not sure that's a realistic plan.'

Anya stuck her head out of the kitchen and called across the apartment. 'Matt?'

Matt had been busily examining the books on the shelves, clearly not quite sure what to do with himself while Carlos was busy with his toolbox and the rest of us were occupied by our furtive discussion. On hearing his name, he spun round. 'Yep? Yes?' He crossed the lounge towards us. 'You okay?'

'We were just discussing our options,' Anya said. 'Specifically, if we've got any.'

Matt frowned. 'Options?'

'If we want to ditch this place,' she explained. 'Accommodation options.'

Matt's face cleared as he understood. 'Oh, yes of course. Well, of course, that's fine. I mean, my place isn't huge but if you'd rather not stay here then I totally—'

'Oh, no,' I jumped in to save him. I could tell by the deep flush of his cheeks that he'd felt he had no choice but to offer. 'That wasn't what we were angling for, sorry.' I knew the last thing Matt would have expected when he'd agreed to take fifteen minutes out of his day to help an old friend would be to wind up with three uninvited houseguests for a week. And really, sharing a cramped lounge floor in a virtual stranger's flat wasn't exactly the vision I'd had for our holiday either.

'No, sorry,' Anya said. 'I just meant, have you got any ideas? Tips on where to stay? Knowing the city so well and everything.'

Matt pushed his hands into his pockets. 'Yeah, I get you . . . well . . .' He thought for a moment. 'I mean, you're going to struggle at this short notice. In the winter you'd be all right, but we're in peak season now. There are a couple of people at work who I think rent out rooms to exchange students and that sort of thing. There may be one of those free. Not sure there'll be one person who could fit all three of you, so you might have to split up and head to different places, but if you'd prefer to—'

'Oh, it's okay,' I said quickly. 'Thanks, Matt, but really, don't worry.' I turned back to Anya. 'Come on, this is mad. We can't go and stay in separate houses! The lock's getting fixed. We have a place to stay. We're only here for a week. It's just a bit of bad luck. Let's not overreact.'

When Carlos finished fitting the lock, he held up a bunch of three keys. 'New keys.'

I took them from him. 'Thank you,' I said. '*Muchas gracias.*'

'At least now you've got a brand new lock you know you're secure,' Matt said.

'Exactly.' I turned to Anya. 'Even if the weirdo owner did want to let himself in and have a look at us while we're asleep—'

'Oh gross, do you think he . . . ?'

'No,' I said firmly. 'I was joking. I really don't. But anyway, we've got new keys now, haven't we? The only copies in the world.'

'I guess.' Anya picked moodily at her nails.

'What do we owe Carlos?' I said, reaching for my bag. 'For his time?'

Matt shook his head. 'It's okay. He works for me, so he'll charge it to the company.'

'What do we owe you, then?' I said.

Matt smiled. 'Oh, don't worry about it. It's not a big deal. Just happy to be able to help. Must be a nightmare on the first day of your holiday.'

'Well, listen,' Anya said, looking at her watch. 'We're going to head back out in a bit. Get some beers, some food later. Why don't you come? Let us buy you some drinks, at least?'

Sophie laughed nervously. 'Anya! It's not even four yet. We're not going out already, are we?'

It was the first time on the holiday that Sophie had expressed an opinion about any of the decisions that had been made. Up to now, when any ideas had been floated – what to do, what to buy, which road to turn down – she'd just shrugged or smiled slightly absently, said 'okay' or 'sounds fine.'

Anya waved her hand, dismissing Sophie's concerns. 'Sure, why not? We're on holiday!'

We looked at Matt expectantly. He seemed uncertain for a

moment but then he smiled and shrugged. 'Okay, cool. That would be fun. Thanks.'

While Anya and Sophie were in their rooms getting ready, Matt and I were left to wait alone in the living room. As he was busying himself browsing the bookshelves, I suddenly remembered he'd sent me a Facebook message, maybe a year or so after Reuben's death, saying he was there if I needed him and giving me his number in case I wanted to talk. It had been sweet, in a way. Although perhaps a little over-familiar. I sensed that he hadn't been sure how to deal with us, Reuben's family, in the aftermath of his death. Like most seventeen-year-old boys, it probably wasn't something he had much experience of. I suspected that it had taken him almost the full year to decide that the message was the best way to go.

'It's weird, isn't it?' Matt said, from his position at the bookcase. 'I've done a few of these myself, and it's always odd being in someone else's home. Looking at their stuff, trying to work out what kind of person they are, what kind of life they have.'

I nodded. 'Yeah. Anya and I were saying that. Sort of a weird level of intimacy to get to with someone you've never even met. There's not much to give anything away here, though. Doesn't feel like he's here very much. Whoever he is.'

Matt nodded and wandered over to the wall of photos we'd all looked at the previous evening. The strange assortment of women.

'I wonder what made him go for this lot?' He shook his head. '*Very* weird choice of photos.'

I joined him at the wall. 'Oh yeah, we were wondering about that. I mean, they're are a funny collection, aren't they? Why is it all women? And why are they all on their own in the photos? Is it his family or . . . ?

Matt laughed. 'Unlucky family if it is!'

I looked at him blankly.

'I mean, I don't recognise all of them. But that lady – ' he pointed at a black-and-white of a woman with a heavy blonde fringe and dark eyes looking directly at the camera, 'was the first victim of the Yorkshire Ripper. And these three – ' He nodded towards images of dark-haired women, all in their fifties or sixties ' – were murdered by a serial killer who roamed around the Spanish east coast a few years back. And you must recognise this one? From the news?'

I peered at the photo he was looking at now. It showed a young woman in her early twenties wearing a graduation cap and gown.

'Yeah.' I nodded slowly. 'You're right, I do. It's that poor girl who went missing on her way home from work, isn't it? Family kept doing emotional television appeals and then it turned out the brother had strangled her and . . . what was it? Hidden her body in the forest.'

Matt nodded grimly. 'Yep. That's the one. I don't pretend to recognise every woman but I think there's a pretty clear theme here. A pretty sick theme.'

'Murder victims,' I stared at the sea of faces, seeing them in a new light. Women who had met untimely, violent ends. 'Why would anyone want these on their wall? Do you think he's a policeman? A criminologist?'

'Who knows.' Matt shook his head and sighed. 'Maybe, or maybe not. People get their kicks in mysterious ways.'

Chapter 15

When we headed back out into the hot mid-afternoon sun, Matt offered to take us to a good place he knew. 'You don't spend most of your twenties investigating the best place to get wankered in a city without coming away with a bit of useful knowledge,' he told us with a grin.

Happy to have someone to lead the way, we followed him across a busy square, the bright sun reflecting off the smooth paving slabs and making us squint. When Sophie and Matt had moved ahead enough for us to be able to talk without them hearing us, Anya said, 'I do actually remember him now, I think. He was quite a lot chubbier then, wasn't he? Always wore a black hoody that seemed way too big for him.'

I nodded. 'Yeah. That's right. His hair was a bit longer. Ginger curtains, sort of thing.'

Anya smirked but not unkindly. None of us had been at our sartorial best in our teens. 'Well, I suppose it's been ten years since we laid eyes on him. People change.'

I remembered then that it hadn't been ten years. Not quite, not for me.

'Oh, you know, I did actually see him once. In Hoyle when

I was back home from uni for Christmas. Must've been seven, eight years ago. Bumped into him on the high street. I think he asked me for a drink?'

Anya looked at me, amused. 'Oh really?'

I laughed. 'Not like that. We literally bumped into each other. We said "hi" and "how are you" and I think he wasn't sure what to say next, it was just the first thing that came into his head! He looked quite relieved when I said I had to get back for Mum.'

'How funny,' Anya said. 'I wonder if he remembers.'

When we reached the edge of the square, Matt took a sharp left and led us down a narrow shady alley where a small bar with a faded pink awning was set back slightly from the road. We dragged two extra metal chairs across the pavement and the four of us crowded round the small square table.

We ordered drinks – beers for Matt and Anya, a big jug of sangria for Sophie and me – and we were finally able to relax, out of the stuffy apartment, out of the heat and away from the bustle of the main road.

I was worried that the afternoon might feel awkward, given that Anya and I barely knew Matt now and that the one person who connected all of us, Sophie, had hardly said a word all day, but in the end, conversation flowed easily. We exchanged anecdotes about university and work and Anya made him laugh with the stories of the outrageous things she'd said to senior colleagues that could very well have got her sacked but usually resulted in a pay rise.

We kept things light for the first few hours. It did occur to me that it was perhaps strange that we weren't mentioning Reuben, when he was the reason Matt and I had recognised each other in the first place, but I was hopeful that we would make it through the whole evening without having to dredge up the memory of the circumstances of his death.

'You still drawing a lot, Lauren?' Matt asked. 'I remember that was always your thing, wasn't it? Didn't you do graphics at uni?'

'Illustration,' I said. 'Useful as a waterproof teabag.'

'She does still do it,' Anya said. 'She's been taking a creative hiatus for a while, but she's just coming out of it now. Aren't you?'

I rolled my eyes. 'Yeah, yeah. Absolutely.'

When the sun started to go down, we moved to a different bar. I didn't remember ordering, but the table was covered with baskets of bread and small terracotta bowls of vegetables in tomato sauce. Sophie seemed to be in the process of giving Anya an impromptu piano lesson, tapping out the notes on the edge of the table in front of her and Anya copying alongside.

Matt lowered his voice and leant closer to me. 'I was wondering, how's your mum doing now, Lauren? Elaine? Is she okay?'

'Oh. Yeah,' I said brightly. 'She's okay.' I nodded, slightly too earnestly. 'She's good.' There was a pause and I felt I should add more, that I should address more directly the subject he was trying to bring up. 'Still working at Optemma. I see her when I can, but it's not always easy. She can be a bit . . . closed off. Hard to talk to.'

Matt nodded slowly. He dipped his bread into one of the bowls of sauce. 'I remember she was very angry. Not before Reuben died, but after. I don't remember much about her at all before really. She was just Reuben's mum. But after-wards, I think she blamed everyone? Not for what happened,' he added hurriedly. 'I know it wasn't that. She was just angry about . . .'

He didn't finish the sentence and I felt a brief shot of panic about what he could be alluding to. Matt didn't know, did he? How could he? But then I realised he just meant Reuben's death in general, and the ensuing reaction from our town. He was right. Mum was angry – angry with people for not reacting in the right way. She felt that if it had been Connor Huw or Joe McMillan who'd died on the tracks, one of the cheery, noisy, sports-mad boys known for their cheek and their charm all over town, people would have been more horrified, more shocked. They would have demanded answers. As it was, Hoyle reacted to Reuben's death with a kind of collective sigh. A sad nod and a 'Well, we can't say we're totally surprised.' That's what she'd been so angry about. And although I had been too, I suppose the difference between us was that I could understand why people felt that way. Why they had seen Reuben as they did.

'I remember Reuben was very protective of you,' Matt said. 'Back at school.'

I nodded. I remembered that too. At the time it had annoyed me – it was just sexist, I had thought, the way he thought I might not be able to look after myself, just because I was a girl. Mum, of course, thought it was admirable, that his sense of responsibility towards his family was kind and chivalrous. There was a short time, just after his death, when I'd thought she was right, and that I'd been mean-spirited and ungrateful not to have appreciated his care and attention when he'd been alive.

But then the police officer with the blonde hair had visited and told me what they'd found on Reuben's body and I no longer had any idea what to think about him at all.

'I sometimes think I should've protected *him* better,' I said, eventually. 'If I'd gone to the beach that night with everyone else. If we'd walked home together.'

Matt nodded sadly, and I realised that Sophie and Anya had stopped their mimed piano playing and were listening in, their faces solemn, respectful. No one said anything for a moment, then Sophie put her hand on mine. 'He probably wouldn't have let you anyway. Others tried, but he was stubborn.'

I moved my hand away. She was a bit drunk, I could tell. But it riled me, that she was offering me platitudes when she had no idea what Reuben wanted that night or what he was really like. She was his teacher, saw him only once or twice a week to listen to him read aloud from *Death of a Salesman* or to discuss William Blake's portrayal of class. It wasn't really appropriate for her to console me like she was part of the family. I was still uncomfortable about the fact that she hadn't let me know about her connection to Reuben sooner, however minor it was. It made me realise that, although she was pleasant, and although we had certain life circumstances in common, I didn't know very much about her at all. And, it seemed, she had no problem keeping things to herself when it suited her.

'How would you know?' I said. My tone was probably uncalled for but I'd been stewing all day.

Sophie looked stung for a moment but she quickly set her face back to neutral. 'Sorry,' she said. 'You're right. Of course, I have no idea. I'm just going on what Anya's told me.'

Anya opened her mouth in surprise, her cheeks flushed.

I turned my attention away from Sophie and Matt and looked at Anya. 'What did you tell her?' There was no aggression in my voice, no accusation. It was a genuine question; I wanted to know.

Anya closed her eyes, just for a second. Then she said, 'I was there – at the beach that night. Not for long, and I hardly saw Reuben at all. But I know he left on his own and I know he wasn't in the mood for company.'

I thought back to the night of the beach party. The night the last of the sixth formers finished their exams. Word had got round both schools of a big piss-up on the beach, to the west of the pier. Anya and I had talked about tagging along. We were still in the middle of our exams but thought we could take a break from revision for a couple of hours to blow off some steam. In the end, though, she'd pulled out. Said her mum wasn't happy about her going and decided it wasn't worth that argument. So I'd stayed at home. I'd sat in the garden shelling peas, then I'd cooked them into a risotto and gone to bed early.

'You said you weren't going to the beach. You said you'd changed your mind?'

'Like I say, just for a really short time.' Anya kept looking down at the plates of food, not able to fully meet my eye. 'Fifteen minutes. Literally.'

'But why? Why didn't you tell me you were going? And why didn't you tell me after that you'd been. Especially after—?'

'Because I was going to make a move on Reuben, okay?' She did look at me now. 'Because I thought at the time, for some mad reason, that that would be a good idea. And one that would be less awkward without his little sister hanging around.'

For a moment, I didn't know what to say. I looked at her. 'You were . . . ? With *Reuben*? You weren't into Reuben. You thought he was strange.'

Anya squirmed uncomfortably in her seat. She folded her arms across her chest. 'I did a bit, yeah. He *was*, really. But he interested me. He wasn't like other people.'

I just looked at her. I knew it was ridiculous to be put out that she'd gone to a party without me thirteen years ago. I knew it was ridiculous to be annoyed that she had – what, flirted with? Propositioned? – my brother without getting my permission first. But it wasn't really about either of those things. That night my whole life changed. Anya having lied to me about it felt significant.

'So did you and Reuben . . . ?'

Anya sighed. 'It was a stupid idea. Obviously.'

We were all quiet for a minute. Matt used a paper napkin to wipe away a splash of beer from the edge of the table and I sensed that he felt uncomfortable. Sophie too was looking up and down the alley, like she was hoping to catch sight of some oddity – a brightly coloured bird, a unicyclist – that she could point out to get conversation back on lighter ground.

'Why didn't you tell me, afterwards, that you'd been with him that night? Didn't you think that was important?'

Anya shrugged. 'I don't know. I told the police, obviously. I wasn't about to lie to them. They spoke to everyone at the party. But like I say, I wasn't really with him. I barely spoke to him so I didn't tell them anything that made a difference to anything. I thought they might tell you, tell your mum, that I'd been there, but I guess they had no reason to. And then there just didn't seem a time or a place or a *need* to bring it up with you, to tell you that I'd decided to go to the party and why. Time went on and it seemed less and less like something I could, or should, just come out with. It felt like telling you would make it seem like it meant something it didn't.'

2 June 2005

Anya

Anya walked from the bus stop through the woods that led to the beach. She was nervous. She'd downed two glasses of her mum's scrumpy cider standing up in the kitchen to relax her but the bus had taken longer than she'd thought it would and the effects were wearing off. Now she just felt sleepy and slightly nauseous.

She was very aware that she was likely to be the only non-sixth former on the beach that night. People in her year had got wind of the party, but their year had their end of year maths exam the following morning so the general consensus was that this event wasn't for them.

Anya felt bad lying to Lauren but, she reasoned, if it all went to plan, then she'd explain the whole story to her afterwards. Lauren was her best friend and Reuben was Lauren's brother, so if she and Reuben got together, Lauren would be the first to know. Of course she would. And she felt

94

sure Lauren would understand why she'd had to tell a few white lies to orchestrate a bit of privacy for the sensitive early stages. It wasn't so much on her account, but she was sure it would put Reuben off his stride if Lauren was anywhere around. He was unlikely to succumb to seduction with his little sister looking on from the sidelines.

The beach was already busy. Some of the older ones had been there since mid-afternoon and she could tell from the reclined positions and the occasional whooping that erupted from the middle of a group that many were already drunk. There were a couple of girls in the sea, just up to their thighs. They were tossing a beach ball between them. They looked cold, though, and they kept missing the ball and having to do an ungainly wade, the edges of their shorts hitched up, to collect it.

Anya saw Reuben sitting apart from the others looking at the sea, his legs loosely crossed and a can of lager in his hand.

She was hit by how beautiful he was – and beautiful was really the only word. Not handsome. Not fit. His hair, like Lauren's, was so dark it was almost black and his long eyelashes and the slight flush of pink on his flawless cheeks made him look delicate, like he had been put together with great care in a craftsman's workshop.

She was surprised by how quickly the crush had gathered pace. She'd known him for years, without ever really knowing him. For a long time, he'd been nothing more than a shadowy presence, a brooding older brother, skulking up and down the stairs with his hood up, playing music from behind his closed bedroom door.

But in the last six months he'd changed. Maybe it was just his age – there was a big difference between a sixteen-year-old and seventeen-year-old – but he'd seemed to open out somehow. His posture had become less hunched. He smiled more. He chatted to Anya when she came to the house, asking her about her schoolwork. The type of boy she was used to talking to were idiots – football players, pot-heads. Neanderthals. Reuben was an entirely different species.

Anya made her way over to Reuben. He must have heard her footsteps on the shingle as she approached but he didn't turn to look at her. He still didn't turn when she sat down next to him, her knees tucked to the side, her skirt just covering them. He just took a swig of his beer and continued looking at the sea.

'Hey!' she said brightly, hoping that the sound would snap him out of his trance and he'd turn and smile and say, 'Oh hey, was miles away there!' or something normal that she could work with.

But instead, there was a pause, then he said, 'All right,' in a flat sort of a voice.

'You okay?' she said.

'Uh huh.'

Anya wasn't sure where to go from here. Reuben was self-contained, she knew that, but she also knew him to be passionate. He'd come into Lauren's room sometimes to show them something – a rare edition of a book he'd found in a charity shop, an obituary of an artist he admired in a magazine – and he'd talk to them about it, presenting it almost, in short, enthusiastic sentences, reading out snippets or holding up the photos. Then he'd leave again, without waiting for their response, not caring if they'd listened or not. It was as if the excitement had just bubbled out of him and he'd had no choice but to share it.

Because of these incidents, she'd hoped that this conversation would be easy. That by providing a dedicated ear, by simply being there and letting him know she was interested in what he had to say, he might use her as a receptacle for whatever idea or fact or art had excited him that day. Still, she thought, perhaps here was an opportunity. Perhaps she could use his bad mood to her advantage. She could be the shoulder to cry on that he obviously needed.

'What's the matter?' she said, her voice gentle. 'Has something happened?'

He sighed and looked down. 'Not really. Just some bad news, I suppose.'

Her spirits lifted slightly. It was a proper answer at least. He was talking to her.

'What kind of bad news?'

He didn't reply. He didn't say anything at all. He just continued staring.

Then, all of a sudden, she thought perhaps he was crying. He rubbed his hand over his face and held it there.

'Reuben?' she said. 'What's going on? Tell me.' She reached for his hand and tried to hold it but he shook her off.

'Don't,' he said.

'I care about you,' she said, realising only afterwards that it was true, in a way.

But again, he pushed her away. 'I'm not interested, okay? I've already got someone, you know. For that. For whatever it is you want.'

She sat there for a moment. She was surprised to find that she was blinking back tears. It had been so abrupt. She wasn't the type of girl to just say things like 'I care about you' without taking it seriously and she didn't like that, now that she had, it had been thrown back at her in such a dismissive way. It made her feel cheap and unattractive. She was embarrassed and quickly, the embarrassment turned to anger.

'All right,' she snapped. 'Jesus.' She pulled her hand away.

Reuben got to his feet then and, without saying goodbye

or where he was going, turned and walked away from her. She watched him go, marching across the sand, his stupid tight black jeans hanging way too low and sliding down his arse. Why didn't he pull them up? And why did he always have to wear black? It was so pretentious.

He was talking to that fat ginger kid now, the one she'd seen playing the trumpet or the tuba or something outside Sainsbury's last year. Matt, she thought his name was. She was glad to see that Matt too was on the receiving end of whatever it was that had put Reuben in the dark mood. Matt put his hand on Reuben's arm, as if to hold him back, as if to get him to stay, explain his problem. But Reuben shook him off, just as he'd done to her. She saw – but didn't hear – Reuben shout something and pull his arm away from Matt so roughly that Matt had to take a step backwards. Then Reuben left the beach, disappearing into the woods.

After he'd gone, Anya made her way over to Matt. She didn't know him to speak to, but she didn't think that mattered. It was a party. People were there to be spoken to.

'What was up with Reuben?' she said. 'He was moody with me too.'

Matt shook his head. 'No idea,' he said. 'Wouldn't say.' Then he gave her a helpless shrug and ambled off to join a group of boys who were playing a makeshift game of boules with large pebbles.

Anya realised what a stupid error of judgment she had made, ever thinking she and Reuben could have been a thing. She didn't even like him. She didn't know him. She didn't *want* to know him. She didn't even want to talk to him, never mind anything else. She decided that Reuben was rude and sullen and performatively angsty. Just another pathetic teenage boy who was all image and no personality. She hadn't even given that much thought to the mention he'd made of having someone 'for that'. She'd assumed that had been a lie, just something he'd said to add clout to his brush-off.

It wasn't until weeks later, when Lauren told her about the visit from the police, about what they'd found in the pockets of Reuben's jacket, that she revisited what he'd said. And that she realised how disturbing it really was.

Chapter 16

The conversation about Reuben had dampened the mood of the evening and although I still had more questions to ask Anya about that night, I suddenly felt drunk and tired, too exhausted to be around people any longer.

'I think I'm going to head back,' I said, the metal chair scraping nosily on the ground as I stood up. 'I need to go to bed.'

I could see from the surprise on their faces that they took my departure as a sign that I was upset or angry, but I actually wasn't sure how I was feeling. Just that I wanted some time to myself.

Sophie made a half-hearted attempt to come with me but I brushed her off and headed off alone into the night, hoping I would be able to retrace the route back to Torre Sonrisas on my own.

When I eventually found our block having taken several wrong turns down narrow side-alleys and having to double back on myself, I was surprised by how dark it was in the corridor. I felt around the walls for the light switch but when I eventually found it and flicked it on, the long strip light I knew was on the ceiling didn't respond. As I fumbled with the new key Carlos had given us, I couldn't help but think how quiet the block was. Surely there should be sounds coming from the other flats? Televisions or radios playing? Footsteps, people walking around? The silence felt unnatural.

Inside the flat, I went around the room turning on every lamp I could find. Just to reassure myself, I ducked my head into first the bedrooms and then the bathroom to make sure everything was as we'd left it. Thinking rationally, I knew we were more secure now we had the new lock than we had been before, when who knew how many people may have had access to the key, but I just couldn't make myself feel it.

With us all bundling out the door for drinks so soon after the business with the broken lock, I hadn't had a chance to really think about the wall of photos and what Matt had told me about them. I'd meant to talk to Anya about it but we'd got caught up in the coincidence of seeing Matt again and I hadn't had a chance to bring it up.

I stood in front of them. Now I knew what had happened to these women, the expressions on their faces seemed to have shifted. Although I knew they'd had no idea about the fates that awaited them, as I looked down the rows of pictures, I felt I could see something afraid, haunted even, in their eyes. What possible reason could anyone have for exhibiting the images like this? The owner being some kind of true crime enthusiast – perhaps even an armchair detective – seemed the only explanation I could imagine, but really, that was no excuse to have this macabre display set out so openly.

There was a shout outside and I jumped, thinking it was a child's scream before realising it was just a woman laughing. I shivered despite the heat. I wished we'd brought a radio with us, or that there was a television in the flat. Even a

Spanish chat show I didn't understand would be welcome if it helped fill this unnerving silence. I picked up my phone but without a wifi connection I couldn't stream and the only song I had stored on the device itself was 'The Chapel of Love' – something I'd downloaded to use as the soundtrack for a congratulatory video we'd made for a colleague before his wedding day. I put the song on now, turning it up loud and setting it to repeat. By the third rendition, though, even that was putting me on edge, the a cappella introduction reverberating mournfully around the flat.

I stopped the music, undressed and climbed into my bed, pulling the sheet right around my neck. Sophie and Anya would be home soon, I was sure.

Chapter 17

After a disturbed night's sleep, broken by nightmares of intruders and Sophie and Anya's eventual noisy return, I emerged into the living room, where Sophie was already busying about making coffee and chattering brightly.

'I was thinking, how about we have a beach day today?' she said, as I joined her on the sofas. 'Some proper relaxing?'

'Yeah,' I said. 'Okay.'

When Anya got up, Sophie talked to her, and I talked to Sophie, but I felt Anya and I were avoiding any direct conversation. I still wasn't sure how I felt about the revelation of the night before. I thought maybe it didn't matter, but I didn't want to rush into saying so in case I decided, on reflection, that it did, and then it would be too late to raise my grievances. In the end it was Anya who brought up the subject when she came out to find me on the balcony.

She sat down on the white plastic chair next to me. 'I think we should talk about last night.'

'What about last night?' I said automatically.

'You know.'

'Yeah.' I nodded slowly but I didn't say anything else.

If she wanted to talk, she was going to have to do the talking.

'I am sorry,' she began, 'that I went to the beach. When I told you I wasn't going to.'

I rolled my eyes. 'Anya, we're not fifteen now. I don't care that you went to a party without me.'

'I know. I *know*. But you know what I mean. After everything.'

'Why didn't you tell me then? As soon as we found out about the accident you should have told me that you'd been with him. Didn't you think it was relevant? Didn't you think we'd want to know what he'd been doing the evening before?'

'Of course. Of course I did. Which is why I told the police. And I know we're not fifteen now but back then I *was*, wasn't I. I was still fifteen. And when you're fifteen, things like going out without your best mate to hit on her brother seem like a big deal. The kind of big deal you don't really want her to find out about. Obviously as we got older I realised what did and didn't matter – that the fact I'd gone to the party without you wasn't the point – but . . . I don't know. It just got too late to say anything.' She shrugged. 'I just thought, you know, least said soonest mended.'

I nodded and looked out over the edge of the balcony. I wished there was a proper view that I could pretend to be lost in, rather than having to stare at a wall to avoid meeting her eye.

'Okay,' I said eventually.

'Okay?'

I nodded. 'Okay.'

'It's the second today,' Anya said quietly. 'Second of June.'

'I know.'

'Thirteen years ago exactly.'

'I *know*.'

Anya hesitated and I thought she might be going to say something else, but after a few moments of silence she just slid the glass doors open and went back inside the apartment.

Chapter 18

We took a taxi to the beach. Anya and I were together in the back seat, but I kept my head turned towards the window and let the chatter – mostly Sophie asking the taxi driver polite questions in slow English and his dutiful replies – wash over me.

'Torre Agbar,' he said, pointing out of the window at a cylindrical glass tower. 'Is very famous.'

Anya looked out the window and raised an eyebrow. 'Looks like a big knob,' she said without enthusiasm.

'Anya!' I scolded. I doubted the taxi driver understood but I thought we probably shouldn't be rude about his city. Normally when I told Anya off she would smile or wink or at least roll her eyes, but this time she just mumbled 'sorry' and looked down at her hands. She'd been quiet since our conversation on the balcony.

The beach was busier than I'd imagined, and the tall glass buildings of the city loomed around the edge, giving me the feeling of being hemmed in, despite the expanse of water in front of us. Only after walking up and down the sand for ten minutes, weaving our way around the tanned bodies stretched out around us, did we find a space big enough for the three of us to lay out our towels.

As we got settled, I put my headphones in and the others took books and magazines out of their bags. It was approaching midday and the sun was intense. Most of the people on the beach with pale sun-starved bodies like ours had had the sense to bring with them parasols or even small pop-up tents to protect themselves, but we hadn't thought of that. I closed my eyes and tried to relax.

After a few minutes, the podcast I was listening to was interrupted by the chime of a notification: John had updated his Facebook status. I didn't know why it did that – singled out specific people to keep me informed on – but curiosity got the better of me.

I opened the page and immediately saw his update spanned several lines:

As I sit here down to the last five-pound note in my wallet I realise I don't know how I'm even going to eat tomorrow. People have told me my writing has moved them, has made them feel less alone and has made them consider ideas they never had before. It's comments like these that have made me so determined to stick at it, to dedicate my life to my work, whatever the personal cost. But now the woman I thought I loved has realised the road is rockier than she thought – and that it's not going to be a route to fast riches – and I find myself kicked out of the home I helped create, with very little to truly call my own. So, if you value artists in your society, if you're having a luckier year than me and want to throw ten, twenty, fifty quid in my direction, here are my PayPal details.

'Jesus *Christ*, John.' I threw my phone down on my towel in frustration.

Sophie looked up. 'What's happened?'

I picked the phone back up and held it out to her. She took it from me, shielding her eyes from the sun with her hand as she squinted at the screen to read.

Her eyes widened. 'Right. Okay.' She looked at me as if to work out what I had to say about it before delivering her own assessment.

'How dare he say that about me! Publicly! Like I was only with him because I was hoping to live a life of luxury once he hit the big time. I paid for *everything* for years.'

Sophie nodded and frowned. 'Yes. It does seem a bit . . . odd to say that.'

'And,' I went on, jabbing the phone screen with my finger, 'what's all this about not knowing where his next meal's coming from? He's living with his mum, in their five-bed detached house in Cuckfield. She cooks him three meals a day and brings up a tray of biscuits at 4 p.m.!'

Sophie's nose twitched. She was trying not to laugh. So I did laugh and Sophie, seeming relieved by this, joined in. Anya, who had had her earphones in, noticed our conversation for the first time and looked up.

'What?' she said. 'What's funny? What's happened?'

'Oh, it's just John,' I said, waving my hand to show it wasn't a big deal. 'It doesn't matter.'

It wasn't that I'd intended to block Anya from the conversation, just that it felt like it was coming to an end. I was shocked and outraged at his brazenness, but we'd laughed about it and now the conversation was over and I just wanted to forget about it. I could see immediately though that, by refusing to let her in on the joke, I'd offended her.

'Oh,' she said quietly. 'Okay.' She rested her head back down on her arms. I looked at her for a moment, wondering if I should say something to reassure her but I couldn't think how to put it.

'Do you fancy a swim?' Sophie said, sitting up and putting her magazine down on her towel.

'Sure.' I shoved my phone into my bag and stood up. 'I'm boiling.'

'Anya?' Sophie said.

Anya lifted her head and twisted her neck to look at the sea. 'Maybe.'

'Oh, I suppose someone should stay with the stuff, though,' I said, looking around at our bags.

I'd only meant that I would be happy to stay behind if Anya and Sophie both wanted to go swimming, but that clearly wasn't how Anya interpreted it.

'It's okay,' she said. She lay down again quickly, her face buried in her arms. 'You two go.'

When we got back to our towels after our swim, Anya was lying on her back but her sunglasses had opaque lenses so I couldn't tell whether she was awake or not. I checked my phone and saw I now had a missed call from John. As I was looking at the screen wondering what else he could possibly have to say, it started ringing in my hand, John's name on the screen. I hit the 'cancel' button quickly, hoping the speed at which he'd been sent to my voicemail would let him know that the rejection was deliberate.

'He's calling me now,' I said, holding my phone up to Sophie as she settled back down on her towel. '*Calling*, for god's sake.'

'You're not going to answer?'

I shook my head firmly. 'God, no.' I pushed the phone to the bottom of my bag.

As I lay back on my towel, the sun quickly drying my wet skin, I could feel myself getting worked up, going over and over the words of his bizarre post in my head: how he was going to be starving by tomorrow, how I had got bored of him because he was poor, how I had thrown him out of the home he'd helped – what was it exactly that he'd said? Helped *build*? I reached for my phone and opened his Facebook page, wanting to check the detail of the obnoxious message again. But the update was gone from his profile. I scrolled for a while, in case some algorithm meant it had slipped down to another part of the page, but it was definitely missing. It had been deleted.

As I moved to replace the phone in my bag, John's name appeared on the screen once more. A message this time:

I'm sorry about the Facebook thing. I know you saw it. I shouldn't have said that about you. I'm a bit of a mess here, to be honest. I've been doing a lot of thinking over the last few weeks. I just want the chance to talk to you. Can I come and see you?

I replied:

I'm in Barcelona, John

A few moments later, he wrote back. Just two short words:

I know

Sophie lifted her sunglasses from her eyes and gave me a questioning look, so I showed the phone to her and waited while she read the message exchange.

'Strange,' she said.

I nodded. 'He is certainly that.'

I wasn't sure what John wanted me to say to his last message, so I switched my phone to flight mode, put my earphones back in and resumed listening to my podcast.

By three o'clock we'd had our fill of the unforgiving sun. Despite having done very little most of the day, we were lethargic from the heat and none of us spoke much in the taxi back into town. As we made our way up the stairs to the flat, though, Sophie seemed to have a sudden burst of energy. She started walking quickly, taking the stairs two at a time and pushing past Anya. 'Woah, all right,' Anya called after her. 'What's the rush?'

Sophie was already at the top of the stairs, fumbling with the key in the new lock. 'Just need the loo,' she called back.

But when Anya and I joined her inside the apartment, she wasn't in the bathroom. She was standing in the middle of the lounge, looking around her anxiously, chewing on the nail of her index finger.

'Thought you needed the toilet,' Anya said, kicking off her flip-flops and collapsing down on the sofa.

Sophie looked up. She blinked then said, 'Oh. Yes. Just going.'

'Weirdo,' Anya muttered. I smiled, but Anya didn't. She was just staring at the ceiling blankly.

'It's crazy hot in here again,' I said. 'I'll get the windows open.'

I headed over to the corner of the desk where there was a handle that, when fully rotated, let us pull the window open wide. I stood there for a moment, grappling with the lever, trying to work out if I had to turn it clockwise or anti-clockwise to release the catch. I heard the soft click that indicated the mechanism was engaged but before I could ease the glass away from the frame, there was a loud crack, a dark black shape in front of my eyes and a wrenching sensation as my head was jerked sideways. A few seconds later, the pain arrived at the side of my head.

Chapter 19

I was sitting on the floor, my legs straight out in front of me like a doll. I didn't think I'd fallen, but then I didn't remember making a conscious decision to sit down either. My right hand was stinging so I lifted it up slowly to inspect it and saw blood on the palm. I realised I must have pressed it down on the shards of glass that surrounded me.

Sophie knelt down at my side. She kept reaching out towards me and then retracting her hand at the last moment, like she was afraid to touch me. 'Lauren,' she kept saying, in a quiet voice, almost a whimper, 'Lauren Lauren Lauren.' There were tears on her cheeks.

'What?' As I turned my head to look at her, more pain shot up the back of my neck and forced me to stop moving. 'What's going on? What happened?'

Anya was standing in the middle of the room blinking in confusion, stunned. Next to her, the square pane of glass of the nearest window had an almost perfect round hole in the centre, a web of cracks spiralling out from it to the frames, like a piece of modern art. She bent down and picked up the spherical red and white object that had hit me.

She held it in her palms, like a fortune teller gazing into a crystal ball.

'It just came through the window,' I said, lifting my hand weakly to indicate the broken glass. 'What . . . is it?'

'It looks like a . . . skull?' Anya said. She turned it around in her hands, and held it out so I could see it properly. 'It's a kind of painted skull ornament.'

I looked at it. It was about the size of a grapefruit and had been painted with an intricate floral design. The intertwining vines and petal shapes were in the style of Mexican Day of the Dead festival decorations. I knew that's what the design was because I'd seen the skull before. On the window ledge, in between the flowering cactus and the Lego Luke Skywalker – in my kitchen at home.

'It's mine,' I said quietly.

Sophie stared at me, her mouth hanging partially open.

Anya looked down at the skull. 'That one you've had for years? The one that used to hold your text books on the shelf above your bed? The one you got—'

I nodded. 'From Hastings. From the shop with the crystals.'

Anya looked at me. 'The one Reuben bought for you.'

28 July 2004

Lauren

Anya and I sat in the back of my mother's Ford Focus. Reuben was in the front seat, every ten minutes or so moving his hand towards the stereo to turn it up. Mum slapped his hand away affectionately.

'Leave it, you monkey. I need to be able to hear myself think when I'm on the big roads.'

Mum was sitting forward in her seat, her nose inches from the steering wheel. She wasn't a confident driver so I'd been surprised when she'd agreed to drive us all down to Hastings for the day, and even more so that she hadn't backed out of her promise when we woke up to sheets of rain bouncing off the pavements as the heatwave of the last few weeks came to an end in spectacular fashion. But then, it had been Reuben's idea, and our mother never liked to deny him.

I didn't really understand why Anya had agreed to accompany us on our little day trip either. I couldn't see what

Hastings had to show for itself at all apart from a beach and we had one of those in Hoyle, but as Anya said, at least it was something different to look at for a few hours. I'd thought we might postpone the outing when we saw the weather, but Reuben insisted towns were at their best in the rain, so at ten o'clock that morning, off we had set.

We spent the day making our way slowly through Hastings' vintage shops and junk yards, Reuben meticulously examining each object – enormous ornate harps, rails of military uniforms from centuries ago, hip flasks engraved with the initials of people long since dead. It was in some new-age shop that I found the skull, a cluttered space that smelt of patchouli, selling tarot cards and wind chimes, and wall hangings with yin and yang symbols on them. The skull was white, made of some kind of opaque solid glass, and decorated with petals and vines standing proud of its smooth surface and painted red with gold highlights. I stood for several minutes turning the object over in my hands, tracing the lines of the pattern with my index finger.

'Gruesome,' Mum said, coming to stand behind me.

'I think it's pretty,' I replied.

'Twenty pounds!' Mum nodded towards the sticker on the skull's base. 'For a useless lump of glass!' She shook her head in disbelief. 'Honestly, the things they think people will spend money on.'

I sighed and replaced the skull on the shelf. Twenty pounds was four weeks' pocket money and Mum was right; I could hardly say I *needed* a decorated skull ornament in my life.

That evening, when we were all at home, me curled up in an armchair sketching while Mum worked on her crocheting in front of *EastEnders*, I'd gone to my bedroom to find a pencil sharpener and had found a small parcel wrapped in green tissue on my bed. I peeled back the paper and carried it down to my mother in the lounge.

'I thought you thought it was gruesome?' I said, holding it carefully in the palms of both hands. 'But you bought it for me anyway?'

Mum looked up. She shook her head. 'Nothing to do with me. Unsightly, it is. If you ask me.'

I left the lounge and went to Reuben's room. I knocked softly and found him lying on his bed, writing out careful notations in his music manuscript pad. 'Roo? Did you buy this? For me?'

He looked up and grinned. 'Maybe I did.'

'But it was so expensive!'

Reuben just shrugged and turned the page of his pad. 'You liked it.'

I frowned. 'I know but . . . it just seems a lot. To spend on an object that just sits there looking nice.'

'Maybe that's enough.'

I looked down at the skull. I ran my fingers over the raised petals as I'd done in the shop.

Reuben pushed himself up and sat in the middle of his bed with his legs crossed. 'Listen, Lauren. Let me give you some advice. Two bits of advice, actually. Big brother to little sister. Wise man to apprentice.' I rolled my eyes and Reuben grinned, but he carried on. 'Number one, when you feel enthusiastic about something, even if you're not sure why, just go with it, okay? See where it takes you. Even if what you feel enthusiastic about is a little glass skull. Even if what you're enthusiastic about is . . . growing turnips. Because before I really knew what playing the violin would even feel like, I just had this feeling, in my gut, that it was for me. And now look at me.' He grinned again. 'Virtuoso. The best the world has ever seen.'

116

I raised my eyebrows, but I was smiling. 'Uh huh. If you say so. What's the second piece of advice?'

He stood up and began putting away the folded, freshly laundered T-shirts our mother had delivered earlier that evening. 'Advice number two is: stay away from boys. Boys are all arseholes.'

Chapter 20

Anya turned it over in her hands, running her finger over the narrow ridges created by the paint. She still seemed dazed. 'It looks similar, I know, but I don't think it can be the actual exact one from your kitchen. I mean, think about it, they would have made hundreds at the factory, so there must be loads out there.'

I'd always liked to believe it was a one-of-a-kind, hand-painted by an elderly Mexican man in a workshop on a hillside somewhere outside Mérida, but I realised Anya was probably right.

'We need to get her up! We need to get help!' Sophie spoke so suddenly and so loudly that I jumped. She was looking at Anya and gesturing to me as if Anya might not have noticed me sitting there surrounded by shards of glass, my palm bloodied and my hair dishevelled.

Anya looked momentarily surprised but then she nodded once and approached me, and together the two of them carefully lifted me from my position on the floor and eased me down on the sofa. Anya took a tea towel from the kitchen and used it to brush my clothes down, removing the crumbs of glass. Then she crouched down in front of me and examined my face closely, looking from one eye to the other. 'Are you okay? Do you feel dizzy? Do you feel sick? What hurts, exactly?'

I rolled my shoulder experimentally. 'I'm okay, I think. My ear hurts a bit and my hand stings. But I think it was mostly just a shock.'

Sophie was standing a few feet away from the sofa, near the strange wall of murder victims. I looked up at her and noticed there were tears silently running down her cheeks. 'Sophie!' I tried a gentle laugh. 'It's okay. I'm okay.'

She nodded slowly and wiped her eyes, an index finger under each one. She sniffed. 'Sorry. I know. It's just . . . you could've been . . . I don't know. I don't know.' She sat down on the other sofa and took three or four deliberate deep breaths.

Anya began to move around me efficiently, bringing her tweezers from her bedroom and a bottle of vodka from the kitchen, sitting down beside me with my hand resting in her lap and beginning to extract the shards of glass from my palm. When each small area was clear, she wiped it down with a ball of vodka-soaked cotton wool. 'Best antiseptic we've got,' she said.

'Seems a waste,' I said.

Anya grinned, apparently relieved that I was able to make a joke, then she got up and collected an ice pack from the freezer, wrapped it in the hand towel from the bathroom and held it against my head.

'I just don't understand,' I began, looking at the red and white skull that Anya had left sitting on the corner of the desk. 'Why would someone do that? Why would someone throw that through the window?'

Anya shrugged. She'd found a dustpan, but no brush, in

the kitchen, and she was trying to sweep the glass on the floor into the plastic tray using a cushion from the sofa. 'Just vandalism, I suppose. I don't know. I mean, why does anyone ever do vandalism? Boredom? To show off?'

Suddenly there was a voice behind us. A woman saying something in Spanish. We all turned to look in its direction and I realised we hadn't shut the door behind us when we'd come in. The woman was standing in the doorway looking into the apartment. She was in her fifties, I guessed, and holding a rolled-up cigarette that wasn't yet lit.

'Sorry,' Anya shook her head. '*No entiendo*. We don't speak Spanish. *Inglés*.'

The woman nodded in a weary way that suggested she was used to hearing this kind of thing. 'The window is broken,' she said, pointing towards it with her unlit cigarette.

'Yes.' Anya gestured to me, as if to say 'we are quite aware of that, thank you.'

The woman sighed. 'The man who live here,' she went on, her accent thick, 'he . . . leave the flat with other people always. He work away, all around the places. So always, different people coming up and down the stairs. Up and down. Different noises. Sometimes too much!' She laughed suddenly, catching us off guard. 'Too much noise.'

She turned then, but before she headed down the corridor she said 'work,' again, this time making quotation marks in the air. 'I say his work is . . .' She did a mime, someone dealing a deck of cards. 'Drugs, you know? Party drugs. Ibiza.'

'Oh,' I said. 'Okay.'

Before we could ask her anything else about the man who owned the flat – like, for instance, how we could get hold of him and ask him exactly what kind of place he'd brought us into, she turned and left.

'That explains a few things,' Anya said, tipping the

contents of the dustpan into the kitchen bin. 'He's a drug dealer. This is a drug den.' She sighed, and shook her head. 'Of course.'

'We don't know that,' Sophie said, sitting down on the sofa now. '*She* didn't know that. She was just speculating on the basis of not much evidence, as far as I could see. Of course, he's away a lot and of *course* there are different people coming into the apartment. That's just what happens when you rent a place out for holidays. I think she was just gossiping.'

Anya didn't look convinced but she didn't argue. She looked down at me, slumped against the back of the sofa, still holding the ice pack to my head. 'Do you want to go to hospital?'

'No,' I shook my head. 'No, no. No need for that. We'd have to wait for ages and what can they do? It's just a bruised head and a cut hand. It'll heal up fine on its own.'

Anya took one of my hands and turned it over to examine the cuts. 'But maybe we should get someone to check you over, just to make sure.'

'It'll cost a fortune,' I pointed out. 'They'll charge us hundreds just for having a look. It's not like at home, with the NHS.'

Anya looked uncertain. 'Isn't it?'

We were all quiet for a moment.

'Let's just get a hotel,' Anya said eventually. 'Just leave here, close the door behind us and check into a nice, modern, *safe* hotel. There must be one with space. There are hundreds in this city. I just cannot believe that every room would be booked up.'

'But how much is that going to cost?' I said.

'I'm sure we can get somewhere perfectly decent for probably no more than one-fifty a night. We must be able to.'

'A hundred and fifty a night! Anya! I can't afford that. Especially seeing as our chances of getting our money back

121

from this place seem like less than zero. He isn't even replying to our emails.'

'I can pa—' Anya stopped. I thought she'd been about to offer to cover our share but had cut herself off, obviously doing some fast maths and realising it was a more generous offer than she'd had in mind.

'I say we do nothing,' Sophie interjected suddenly. 'As you said, Anya, the most likely explanation is that this is just random vandalism. Some children, teenagers probably, just found the skull on the floor and decided to toss it at a window for japes. And even if that isn't the case, even if – and let's just say for argument's sake – it *is* a personalised attack on the man who lives here, because of whatever drugs shenanigans he may be tied up with, their issue is with him, not us. So I suggest we leave well alone, and he can sort out the mess when he's back.'

I was surprised how quickly Sophie had rallied. Just minutes ago she'd seem shaken by what had happened – more shaken than me, in fact – crying and sniffing in the corner. But now, here she was, taking charge of things and arguing that it was nothing to worry about. I knew her logic made sense, but I was still unsettled by this brisk closing off of the topic. The skull itself was still playing on my mind. That design was so specific. It was *so* similar to mine. But with the others apparently unconcerned – or unconvinced – by my claims, I had no choice but to let the subject drop.

We headed out for a low-key dinner, keen to escape the oppressive atmosphere of the flat and whatever dangers lurked beneath its windows. I was anxious about what we might find when we returned, but thankfully there was nothing amiss. As Sophie and I lay in our beds, I stared up at the ceiling and decided to bring up the issue of the skull again.

'Do you think it's weird, about the skull? That it's the same as one I own myself, I mean?'

Sophie didn't reply immediately, and I thought she might already be asleep but then she said, 'Is it the same, though? I thought Anya said it was just similar?'

'It is the same,' I said. 'I'm sure of it. I looked at it properly. Exactly the same. The way the lines sort of fan out from the crown, the petal shapes around the eyes . . . all of it.'

Sophie sighed, and I got the sense then that she was tired of the topic. 'If I'm being totally honest, I don't think it's that strange, no. Decorated skull ornaments like those are quite common, really. There must be hundreds of them like yours. Thousands, even.' Then, in the kind of voice you would use if you were settling an agitated toddler, she added, 'If I were you, I'd stop thinking about it at all. Put it behind you and try to get some sleep. Tomorrow's a new day.'

I nodded silently in the darkness and turned onto my side.

Chapter 21

Over the next few hours, I tried the whole gamut of techniques to summon sleep, but when the glowing hands on my watch told me it was 5.30 a.m., I was still awake.

My ear was throbbing, despite the two paracetamol I'd taken just after 3 a.m. I lay on my back and watched the shadows move across the ceiling, feeling hot, uncomfortable and uneasy. With Sophie breathing peacefully next to me, I was suddenly filled with a feeling of frustration: why was nobody taking what had happened seriously? Someone had thrown a missile at my head! A missile identical to something I owned myself! I didn't care whether there were two or two thousand of those skulls in existence. The point was, I had one and one had smashed through the window of our apartment and hit me. That couldn't just be coincidence. Or maybe it could, but it didn't mean it definitely *was*.

I sat upright in bed, hoping that forcing my body to consider the possibility that it was time to get up for the day might cause it to protest, realise it was, in fact, exhausted and let me get some sleep. I still didn't feel tired, though. I felt overheated and claustrophobic. Not specifically on account of the size of the space, but because I knew I was trapped – I was stuck there, in that flat, without my own room, my own space. I couldn't even put the light on without worrying about waking someone else. I had an impulse to get out, to stand on the balcony, to get some air.

I disentangled my legs from the sheet and got out of bed. I stood for a moment in the middle of the bedroom looking down at the floor, trying to make sense of the dark shapes and plot a path to the doorway that I could take without tripping over a suitcase or slipping on a discarded bikini top and waking Sophie.

As I peered at the shadows, I noticed a movement. The strip of light coming under and around the side of the door was moving like a door or a window had been opened some-where, changing the angles of the shadows. I could hear my pulse in my ears. I stood completely still, trying to keep my breathing quiet and steady as I listened out for sounds.

There were footsteps, I was sure of it. Shoes being placed carefully and deliberately on the tiles. They weren't coming from the corridor outside our flat; they were definitely in the lounge, by the back wall, by the gallery of murder victims. I crossed the bedroom silently, picking my way through the bags and clothes on the floor, and stood just to the left of the door, so I could see through the gap where we'd left it ajar.

There was a figure, exactly where I thought I heard it, over the far side of the apartment, standing still with its back to me, arms hanging down by its sides.

Chapter 22

My body jerked into action before I could consider the best response to the sight. I slammed the bedroom door shut and spun around, leaning my back against it heavily and breathing hard.

Sophie woke with a jolt. 'What?' She sat up and fumbled for the lamp on her bedside table. She looked at me squinting in the light, her hair in a lopsided topknot. 'Lauren? What are you doing?'

I stayed in position, my back still resting against the door. 'There's someone in the flat,' I whispered.

Sophie's eyes widened. She froze, her hands hovering just above the bed sheet. 'Where? Who? Are you sure?'

I nodded slowly. 'Yeah. I think so? I saw a person in the lounge. I'm sure I did. I did.'

'Was it . . . Anya?' Sophie peered at me closely, obviously trying to work out if I'd had a bad dream, or even perhaps if I was still having one now, standing there and talking to her in my sleep.

Sophie pulled back her sheet and got out of bed. As she approached me, I moved aside to let her tentatively open the bedroom door and look out. I stood at her left shoulder looking past. There was nothing obviously amiss in the room outside. The lounge seemed empty.

There was a loud click as the other bedroom door opened and we both jumped. Anya appeared in the hallway.

'What's going on?' Her face was screwed up with sleep and confusion. She was pulling her arms into a cardigan. 'Are you two okay? Why are you stood there like that?'

'Have you been out of bed?' I was aware I was holding myself in an unnaturally rigid position, my hands hovering at waist height.

'What? When?'

'Just now.'

'Lauren thought she saw someone.' Sophie looked past Anya, out into the lounge.

Anya looked behind her. 'Someone where?'

'Out there,' I said, nodding to the empty space.

'What did they look like?' she asked. 'What did you see?'

I could tell from her voice she wasn't totally convinced there'd been anyone at all.

'I don't know exactly,' I said. 'I couldn't make out the details. It was more . . . a presence.'

There was a pause.

'A presence?' Anya repeated. She frowned, confused.

I realised how it sounded. I closed my eyes, trying to bring the image of what I'd seen back to me, but the shapes kept shifting, undefined patches of dark and light. Perhaps Anya was right to be sceptical. Perhaps my mind had pieced things together to create an image of something that wasn't really there.

I sighed. 'I'm sorry. I guess I'm just on edge with everything that happened . . . that thing being chucked at my head, John being weird.'

'John?' Anya looked at me. 'What did he do? When?'

'Earlier. Just a couple of messages that didn't make sense.'

'What did he say?'

'He said he wanted to come and see me and then when I said I was here, in Spain, he just said "I know".'

'Well, what does *that* mean?' Anya looked alarmed. 'Why didn't you say anything?'

I shrugged. 'It wasn't a big thing.'

She looked hurt. 'I don't understand why you have to keep everything a secret. I'm meant to be your best friend. I know you've had a hard time of stuff but it's not good to keep things bottled up. You—'

'I told Sophie,' I blurted out.

Anya looked briefly taken aback but then she nodded once and looked away. 'Right. Of course,' she said quietly.

Immediately I regretted implying that Sophie had replaced her as my trusted confidante. The incident with the skull seemed to have pushed aside the tension between us that had begun with Anya's bad temper before we even arrived in Barcelona and had been exacerbated by the conversation about the night of the beach party. Now, though, she was distant again.

'I don't think that's got anything to do with it anyway,' I said. 'It's not like the figure *was* John. It was the wrong shape, for one thing.'

'How can you be sure?' Anya said. 'If you're not really sure what shape it was at all?'

'Well, it wasn't John-shaped. I'm sure it wasn't.'

Anya nodded but she still looked concerned. 'Okay.' She flicked on the lounge light and sat down on the sofa. 'I'm wide awake now anyway. What time is it? It must be gone six. Shall we just stay up? I guess none of us feel much like sleeping now.'

'No,' I said sitting down next to her. 'I couldn't if I wanted to.'

'Does your head still hurt?' she asked.

I shrugged. 'A bit. But it's more just . . .' I gestured loosely at the room in general – the broken window, the skull still grinning at us from the desk.

'Yeah,' Anya said quietly. 'I know.'

Sophie moved to sit down on the other sofa but as she crossed the room, she stopped suddenly and looked over towards the back wall. 'What's that?' She nodded her head at the floor, frowning for a moment, then she bent down and picked something up. She held it out to us in the palm of her hand. It was a cigarette, only half smoked, flattened.

'He must have dropped it.' I looked around at them all. 'We don't smoke. How else would it have got here? Someone must have brought it in. I *told* you there was someone.'

Anya picked it up from Sophie's palm and held it between her thumb and forefinger, examining it carefully. 'Maybe,' she said doubtfully. 'Although we could just as easily have carried it in on one of our shoes.'

I sat back in my chair. I knew that was a possibility.

'Although . . .' Anya got up and went over to the area from where Sophie had retrieved the cigarette. 'What's this? Look.' She crouched down, her hands resting on her knees, looking closely at the ground. 'Come and look.'

I went over and bent down beside her.

'A footprint.' I reached out to touch it, but she knocked my hand away.

'Don't touch it,' she said. 'Just in case . . . I don't know. Just don't.'

'Is it one of ours?' I asked.

Anya shook her head. 'I don't think so.' She held a vertical palm at either end of the shape and brought them upwards, keeping the distance between them steady to show us the size of the print in the air. 'It's too big,' she said. 'And the shape too. The tread. That's not a flip-flop, is it. It's a boot. A big man's boot.'

'Maybe Matt or Carlos left it when the lock was being fixed?'

'I've swept since then. It would've gone.'

I paused. 'So what you're saying is . . . you think someone else has definitely been in here?'

Chapter 23

There was a loud sound suddenly, like the horn of a car, and Anya screamed.

I frowned. 'That's the sound the door buzzer makes, I think? I've heard it in the other flats.'

I stood up and went over to the door. Tentatively, and with Anya and Sophie standing behind me for back up, I reached forward for the handle and pulled it open.

'Morning!' It was Matt, smiling broadly and holding a cardboard coffee cup. He looked at the three of us crowded around the doorway. 'Everyone's up! Oh good, I was worried I'd have to haul you out of bed. I'm so sorry it's so early.'

I was suddenly aware how a story about an early-hours intruder, evidenced only by a cigarette butt and a dusty footprint, had the potential to sound silly and hysterical and I didn't want to be the one to tell it. With the sun coming up and filling the apartment with a gentle orange light and Matt standing there with his rosy cheeks and Bermuda shorts, it suddenly seemed less likely anything had actually happened at all.

'You guys all right then?' he said, looking at us with his

head slightly on one side. I realised the way we had gathered to open the door en masse must have seemed strange. I forced a laugh. 'Yeah! Yeah fine. We thought we'd have an early start, make the most of the day.'

'Oh wow, okay!' He nodded encouragingly. 'Keen. I like it. Well, I won't keep you. I just called in on my way to work, number one to check you were all right with the lock and everything and number two, to see if I left my travel card here the other day, in the kitchen.'

I wondered if he'd notice the black bag we'd taped over the hole in the window pane. If he did, and he commented on it, I felt sure we would have little choice but to give him a full account of the events of the last fifteen hours. In a way, I wanted him to notice so we could report everything to him, but I was wary of burdening him with our problems unprompted, in case he felt obliged to offer his assistance in some way. He'd helped us out once, but that didn't mean he wanted a full rundown of every mishap we encountered.

'Oh yeah,' Anya said, holding the door open for him. 'I thought I saw that in there. I'll get it for you.'

'It's okay,' he said, stepping inside and heading for the kitchen. 'I'll get it. Someone had smeared something . . . delightful on the banister so I could do with washing my hands.'

'Ugh, this *place*,' Anya muttered, picking at the paintwork.

She started to say something else – which I could tell by her expression was going to be another complaint – but she was cut off by a loud blast of music that made us all jump. It was classical, a full orchestra playing something booming and frantic. I thought I recognised it as one of the more intense passages of Vivaldi's *Four Seasons*.

I saw Anya mouth, 'What . . .?' but the music was too loud to hear her. The sound was coming from the kitchen. We all turned in its direction, but before we could move to investigate its origin, there was another sound: a loud pop, like a firecracker.

I was the first to respond. 'Matt?'

I stopped in the doorway. Matt was on the floor of the kitchen, his knees bent and his head resting against the wall.

Chapter 24

'Holy mother of fuck,' Anya said.

'Matt!' I went over to him. 'What happened?' I held out my hand to help him to his feet but he waved me away and clambered to an upright position on his own.

He stood for a moment in the space between the window and the worktop, looking dazed.

'My god,' he said, shaking his head. '*God.*'

He stepped forward and looked down at the radio on the counter. It was a small, digital model, black and square with a metal volume knob protruding from the top. He seemed to be examining it but at the same time being careful not to actually touch it. His hands were down by his sides, his palms facing backwards. He turned his head to look at me. 'Have you got anything wooden? A wooden spoon or something?'

'Uh . . . yeah,' I rummaged in a drawer and held a spatula out to him.

Matt took it from me and prodded the radio experimentally. 'Wow,' he said quietly. 'Okay.'

'What?' Anya asked from the door. 'What *happened* in here?'

'It's been rigged,' he said, nodding towards the radio.

'Connected to the live wiring of the flat somehow. Or something like that. It started up just as I came in here. Scared the life out of me it was so loud. So I reached for the volume dial and . . .' He shook his head. 'Boom.'

We all stared at the radio.

'Where's the fuse box?' Matt asked. 'Have you seen it?'

All three of us shrugged blankly and Matt spent a few moments opening cupboards before locating the grey plastic shell above the bathroom door. 'I'm just going to shut the power off for a minute. Just to be on the safe side.' He dragged a chair over from the table, climbed onto it and flicked the row of switches above the door into a downward position. The corner of the lounge that had been illuminated by a floor lamp went dark.

'But why?' I asked. 'Why would someone do that to it?'

Matt pushed his hands into his pockets and shook his head again. 'Honestly no idea. No reason that I can see. Except to give anyone who touched it a sizeable electric shock.'

'And that's what just happened to you?'

Matt looked down at his hands, turning his palms upwards to examine them 'Well, yeah. I mean, it was a hell of a jolt. But these shoes have got a decent rubber sole, so I was lucky. But if you touched that dial when you were just in your bare feet, for example. Or with wet hands . . .' He shook his head again and breathed out slowly.

'Well, maybe it's just broken?' Anya said. 'Maybe it's just a crappy knock-off thing, off the back of a truck or something. You know, badly made, dodgy wiring?'

Matt winced and shook his head. 'I really don't think so. I think the way—'

'Hang on,' I said suddenly, cutting Matt off. 'Where did the radio even come from? It wasn't here before.'

Matt frowned. 'Before when?'

'Before now!' I said. 'I wanted to put some music on the other day and I was annoyed when I couldn't find anything. No radios, no stereos, nothing. It wasn't here.'

'Maybe it was hidden away, tucked behind something?' Anya said.

I shook my head. 'I looked everywhere. I would've seen it.'

'Also,' Anya said. 'I don't understand why it would just start playing on its own? And why it was set so loud.'

Matt shrugged. 'I'd guess it was on a timer. Like a radio alarm clock. Probably turned up loud specifically to get someone to reach for the volume dial.'

There was a pause while we took this in.

'So it's like someone's set a trap?' I asked. 'To hurt us?'

Matt shrugged. 'I don't know who it was meant for. But to hurt someone, I would say. Yeah. But I don't know how it would've got here, if you're sure it wasn't here before. Have you had any trouble with that lock Carlos put in?'

'It was while we were asleep,' I said suddenly. I turned around to look at Sophie and Anya. 'This is what he was doing. This must have been why he came in here!'

'Who?' Matt asked. 'When?'

'Lauren thought she saw someone in the flat in the night,' Anya explained. 'A man in the flat.'

'I *did* see someone,' I insisted. 'I'm sure of it. And when else would this radio have appeared? It wasn't here yesterday. It arrived in the night, no two ways about it.'

Matt looked at each of our faces in turn. He looked anxious. Wary. Almost as if he was waiting for one of us to laugh and admit we were just teasing him. 'So you're saying someone crept into your flat last night and, while you were all sleeping in your rooms, set a trap to electrocute you? Who? Why?'

Anya shrugged helplessly. 'We don't know, do we? Maybe the same person who chucked that through the window.' She

136

nodded towards the decorated skull, still sitting where we'd left in on the desk.

Matt looked towards the skull and then from there he noticed the black plastic bag covering the broken window. 'What . . . ?'

In the end Anya was the one to explain how the hole had appeared. She left out, I noticed, the detail about the skull itself being the same as my own.

'Woah,' Matt looked at me, his grey eyes fixed on mine. 'Are you . . . okay?' He reached out and touched the top of my arm gently.

I replied with something halfway between a nod and a shrug.

'Do you know what? I've had enough,' Anya said suddenly. She left the kitchen and stood in the middle of the lounge. She looked at the sofa but seemed to have second thoughts about sitting down and remained standing, her arms hugged around her. 'It's fucked *up*, man. It's fucked up. What *is* this place?'

Chapter 25

I nodded slowly. I too was hit with the sudden, overwhelming feeling that enough was enough.

'It's obviously mixed up in something.' Anya said. 'This flat, the owner. Maybe drugs, like that woman said. There's something weird going on here. The photos are creepy enough, then the break-in. But now . . .' She looked around the room. 'Whatever's going on here, I think we should go now. Just leave, go wherever we can. We don't know what's going to happen next. I just don't think it's safe.'

Matt nodded. 'If it was me, I'd definitely be out of here. Get your money back off the guy and just get a hotel or whatever.'

'Maybe we should just go home,' Sophie said, speaking for the first time in a while. 'Maybe we should just head to the airport and jump on the first—'

Matt laughed suddenly, cutting Sophie off. 'Good luck getting a short notice flight at this time of year. You can expect to be sleeping on the floor of the airport for at least a week.'

Sophie looked down, chastened. Perhaps Matt noticed

because when he spoke again, his voice was gentler. 'Look,' he said, 'why don't you all stay with me?'

We looked at him.

'Seriously,' he said, his smile shy, almost hopeful. 'It's a bit of a boy's place, I'm afraid. Bachelor pad, type thing. You know. But I've got the room and I know you'll all be out and about doing your own thing anyway. Just use it as a base. I'll be glad of the company, to be honest. And it would be better than here. You'd be safe, at least. Secure.'

'Oh! Well . . .' I began. My instinct was to thank him for the kind invitation but to decline, embarrassed that our loud deliberation of our unappealing options had left Matt feeling obliged to offer again. But this time, I didn't dismiss the idea out of hand. This was partly because it felt slightly less uncomfortable now that we'd actually spent a bit of time in each other's company, but mostly because I had a feeling we were all thinking the same thing: it didn't look like we had much choice.

'Are you sure?' I said eventually. 'We'll try to be out the whole time. And we can pay you rent and board and—'

Matt laughed. 'It's fine! It's fine. It's a few days. It will be nice to have visitors. It gets boring living on your own. Honestly, the most exciting thing I had planned this week was watching the football with my neighbour.'

'Well, if you're really, really sure—'

'I am.'

'—then that would be amazing. Thank you.'

With the decision made, we packed up our things and left the keys on the desk in the flat. Anya wanted to leave a strongly worded note to the owner but, as we pointed out, we didn't even know when he would next be there in person. We knew that any contact we were able to make with him would probably have to be online and could take a long time.

I already sensed the chances of us seeing any of our money again were slim, but at this point, I just wanted to cut our losses and be grateful things hadn't been even worse.

Matt helped us carry our bags on the fifteen-minute walk through the streets to his flat near the Arc de Triomf. From the outside, his apartment block seemed unremarkable and even inside the lobby, the only real difference between this and the one we'd just left was the presence of a fully functioning lift. However, when we arrived at the top floor and found just one door in the hallway, Anya said, as a joke, I was sure, 'You got the only flat on this floor then, Matt?' and he'd replied simply, 'Yeah.'

When he opened the door to his apartment and we saw the space inside, we realised why. His flat extended the entire footprint of the building. The front door led into a vast kitchen space – gleaming white tiles, dark marble workshops, sparkling chrome metalwork.

'Bloody hell, it's enormous,' I said, gazing around in wonder.

Anya, who had cheered up considerably since we'd made the decision to vacate Torre Sonrisas, gave Matt a nudge and a wink and said, 'Bet it's not the first time he's heard that!'

Matt blushed. I wasn't sure if it was at the crude joke or just because he knew – he must have known, surely – that his place made quite an impression. I shot Anya a disapproving look and she pulled a face to signal that I was being uptight.

Beyond the kitchen area was a hallway lined with a succession of closed doors. 'Bedrooms and bathrooms and that,' Matt said, nodding his head towards them as he led us through. 'But mostly I hang out here.'

The hallway opened into a huge square room with white sofas lining the edges and big black beanbags dotted around the floor. Mounted on the wall was a TV screen and, on a shelf below it, a number of boxes with flashing lights and digital displays.

'Probably a bit too much seating for one, I know,' Matt said, going over to the window and fiddling with a dial. 'But sometimes the guys from the office come round for PlayStation so it works well then.'

'Yeah,' I said. 'I bet.' The others nodded mutely, gazing around them.

I'd thought Matt had been playing with the buttons by the window as a way to avoid looking at us directly – it was almost as if he was worried that giving us this tour was bragging in some way – but I realised that he'd been adjusting the setting for the blind on the window and it was now slowly retracting upwards and disappearing into a narrow vault in the ceiling. We all turned and looked as, inch by inch, the window behind was revealed, and through it we could see a huge terrace with a free-form swimming pool in the middle, and a stunning view of the city's rooftops beyond.

'Woah,' I said, staring mesmerised. 'Is that yours? All yours?'

Matt came to stand alongside us, his hands pushed into his pockets, his head angled down shyly. 'Yeah,' he said. 'I do love it out there, I can't lie.'

'This is insane!' Anya stood in the middle of the room, spinning, her arms outstretched like the woman from *The Sound of Music.* 'Seriously how much is this place worth? Like millions, surely?'

Matt said, 'I don't honestly know now. But I got a good deal on it. And I did a lot of the work myself. And . . .' He shrugged. 'Basically, I got lucky. I worked hard at the business, but I also had a lot of lucky breaks. Deals that went my way when it counted.'

Suddenly I noticed that Sophie had her eyes closed. She was standing in the corner and seemed to be making an effort to keep her breathing steady. 'Sophie?' I went over to her. 'You okay?'

Her eyes snapped open and she fixed a smile on her face. 'Oh! Yes. Sorry. Just felt a bit queasy for a minute. Too hot, probably.'

Matt looked at her for a moment, almost curiously, then he said, 'I'll get you some water.'

After Matt had handed Sophie the glass, he took us back down the hallway and pointed out the two spare rooms. 'They've both got double beds, so someone can have their own, but two of you will have to share, I'm afraid. Lauren, I thought maybe you could do with the space to yourself after your bump and every—'

'Oh, I think I should come in with you,' Sophie said quickly. 'Keep an eye on you. You have to be so careful, with head injuries. Symptoms can appear hours or even days later.'

'I'll be fine, I'm sure,' I said, smiling at Sophie warmly. I was grateful for her consideration but really, I would have quite liked the room to myself. But Sophie was adamant and I didn't want to risk offending her so I let it go.

As we moved into our new rooms and Sophie chattered away about nothing very much while we put our things away, I was hit with a sudden urge to be on my own for a little while. Sophie was lovely but I wanted half an hour or so where I could just be with my own thoughts, and not have to keep up a cheerful stream of conversation or to watch people carefully to see how they were reacting, how they were feeling.

'I'm going to go out and get some food.' I picked my bag up from the floor. 'Where's good to go?' I called to Matt from our bedroom door.

'Oh, I'll come and give you a hand,' Matt said, appearing from the lounge. 'Help you carry things.'

'I'll be fine, honestly.'

'I can go with her,' Sophie said, and within seconds she was by my side, empty shopping bag on her shoulder. 'You must be late for work, Matt! You were on your way ages ago!'

She smiled at Matt brightly. He paused in the hallway and looked at us, and for a moment I thought he was going to say something, but in the end he nodded and said, 'Yeah, true,' and picked his keys up from the worktop. 'There's a little supermarket at the end of the road,' he said. 'Turn right out the main door. You can't miss it.'

Sophie and I walked down the street in silence for a few minutes, but before long I was compelled to say something to fill it.

'Matt's place is lovely, isn't it? I've never seen anything like it. So nice of him to let us all barge in.'

'Yeah,' Sophie said, but her voice was flat and she didn't offer any observations of her own.

'What's up?' I said. 'You seem a bit preoccupied?'

'Oh,' she said. 'Oh no. Not really. I was just thinking that Matt's quite good at playing the hero. I think he likes the role. I think it makes him feel good.'

This was such an unexpected thing for sweet, gentle, give-everyone-the-benefit-of-the-doubt Sophie to come out with, I wasn't quite sure how to respond.

Eventually I said, 'Does he? Really? It seems to me that it's not so much playing the hero as *being* the hero, isn't it? In this instance?'

Sophie was quiet again and I thought she wasn't going to reply at all, but a few moments later she just said, 'Maybe,' in a way that indicated she didn't want to discuss it any further.

Chapter 26

Over the next couple of days, we settled into a pattern. We'd emerge from our rooms once we'd heard Matt leave for work, breakfast leisurely on the terrace, have a gentle – and often half-hearted – attempt at sightseeing, before returning to the flat for a swim and more lounging mid-afternoon.

'It feels like this is the holiday we should have had,' Anya commented.

'Yeah,' I said, dipping my hand into the pool to test the temperature. 'It's almost like the freaky couple of days in that weird place were just a trial we had to go through to appreciate true comfort when we found it.'

'Ha,' Anya said, tipping her face towards the sun. 'Maybe. I don't think I'd need any trial to appreciate this, though.'

I had hoped that now we were out of the stressful environment of Torre Sonrisas, and that Anya was being accommodated in the style she was used to, she might start to relax a little, to be more like the Anya I knew – more like the Anya I'd hoped I'd be coming on holiday with – but, although things were improved, I still felt there was a distance between us. She still seemed distracted. It was hard to pinpoint concerns

145

substantial enough to warrant raising, but there were a series of small incidents that told me the problem wasn't entirely in my head.

One afternoon we were making drinks in the flat and Anya had taken a tray of ice cubes out of the freezer and put them on the side. She forgot to close the freezer door and it was only as we were leaving the kitchen that I noticed the door was still wide open, leaving Matt's frozen goods at the mercy of the Spanish summer heat.

'Oh, the freezer,' I said, nodding towards it, my hands full of drinks. 'The door.'

'Oh. Yeah,' Anya said, returning to it and closing it with her foot.

'That, my girl, is a very fast road to where?' I said in my best comedy Irish accent.

When we'd been at school, Anya and I had had a food technology teacher called Mrs O'Shea. She was a stout, Irish woman of sixty who was very particular about how we did things. If she caught us preparing our recipes in a way she didn't approve of – perhaps melting chocolate in a microwave rather than over a bowl of boiling water – she'd shake her head and say, 'That, my girl, is a very fast road to where? To disaster, that's where.' It had been a turn of phrase that had stuck with us well into our twenties and when either of us was contemplating doing something unwise – texting a boy we shouldn't, telling a boss what we thought of them – we would adopt Mrs O'Shea's accent and tell the other, 'That, my girl, is a very fast road to where?' And the other would reply, 'To disaster, that's where.'

But my attempt to orchestrate a nostalgic bonding moment between us fell flat. Anya just smiled without replying, and to deliver the line myself seemed pathetic somehow, so the joke, the reminiscence, went unfinished.

Sophie looked at me, bemused. 'What do you mean? What road?'

'Oh, it's nothing,' I said, feeling sadder than seemed reasonable. 'Don't worry.'

I told myself that, although back home Anya and I would speak or message often, we didn't spend extended periods of time together any more. And as Anya had lived alone for the last five years, she wasn't used to spending extended periods of time with *anyone*. All I could do was try not to take any irritability personally and try to give her the space she seemed to want, leaving her to it when she dragged her lounger over to the far corner of the roof terrace, not asking her why she had chosen to read her magazine on her bed in her room rather than join us on the sofas.

I wasn't lonely though by any means; Sophie was as friendly as Anya was aloof. She would gravitate towards me wherever I was, I noticed. If I went inside to get out of the sun for a while, she would follow me in a few minutes later, ostensibly to read me a funny paragraph from her book but then she'd sit down beside me, saying something about how it was nice to cool down for a moment. Then if I said I was going to lie down on the bed, she'd yawn and say, 'Yes, good idea. Tiring, somehow, isn't it, doing nothing?' and follow me through.

I had an idle theory that it was something to do with the fact that she'd got married so young, she had never really learnt to be in her own company. I thought that perhaps if Anya had been more forthcoming, less distant, Sophie might have shared her attention more equally, but as it was, she obviously felt I was a safer target.

More confusing to me was the nature of her relationship with Matt. Sophie had offered up his apartment when we were first planning the holiday so I had assumed they were close, but now we were here there seemed to be a formality between them. I had imagined there'd be conversations about times they'd shared, people they both knew, but there hadn't been much of this at all. The questions they asked each other were about restaurants they'd tried, bands they'd heard – the types of thing you might discuss with a fellow tourist on a bus when you'd only just met. Polite and friendly enough, but not intimate.

I mentioned this observation to Anya but she just shrugged and said, 'I guess it's a bit rude to talk about people we don't know when we're there.'

I began to realise that of the three people I was sharing the week with, it was actually Matt with whom I felt most relaxed.

Matt seemed to move through his life with a calm, unshowy competence. He was an excellent cook, returning home from work most days with paper bags full of fresh ingredients he'd picked up from markets – chorizo, squid, onions the size of a head – and preparing simple but perfectly flavoured meals. He also knew his way around an engine, once ducking out of the flat late one evening to help a neighbour whose car wouldn't start and coming back with blackened oily hands and a grin to let us know he was back on the road. Although I knew it was to be expected from someone who had lived abroad for several years, I couldn't help but be impressed by the way he would swap into fluent Spanish whenever he needed to. We later found out, when we bumped into a colleague of his in town, that he could do the same with German. But he never talked about these things. He wasn't modest in the sense of needy self-deprecation, he just genu- inely seemed to think his skills were unremarkable. When I complimented him – on his cooking, his language skills – he'd just shrug and say nothing at all. I realised that in this way, he was the complete opposite of John, who would talk at length about why he was superior to others but offer little in the way of evidence.

There had been no word from John since his strange message about wanting to come to see me. I realised he'd probably been drunk when he sent it and even if he hadn't been, his moods were always so ephemeral that my lack of reply would no doubt have vanquished any sentimentality he'd been feeling and he would now be furious with me again. The thought made me tired, but also uneasy, and any time my phone buzzed I felt a small spike of adrenalin that only abated when I saw it wasn't him.

When, one morning, I heard my phone ringing and I saw a Haywards Heath area code on the screen, I did worry it might be him, but deciding there would be no reason for him to call me from a landline and that it was more likely to be work, I answered it.

'Hello, Lauren? This is Valerie Marshall.'

It took me a few moments to place the name. In the few times I'd met John's mum, I'd been unsure whether 'Val' or 'Mrs Marshall' was more appropriate, so I'd decided the best option was to avoid addressing her altogether.

'Oh.' I was surprised. 'Hello there.'

I never said 'hello there'. It was just part of the bizarre formalness I found myself slipping into around other people's parents.

'Sorry to bother you,' she said. Her voice sounded careful and measured, like she was making an effort to use her most polite telephone voice. 'I just wondered if you'd heard from John at all? In the last day or so?'

'He sent me a message a few days ago. Monday, I think. But not since then. Is everything okay?'

'I'm just not sure where he is, just at the moment. You knew he was staying with me, did you?'

'Yeah. Yes. I knew.'

'Well, he went out early yesterday morning, but I haven't seen or heard from him since.'

'Right, well. Okay.' I didn't want to be rude or to upset Valerie Marshall by telling her that her son's whereabouts were no longer any of my business. Instead, I searched my brain for something helpful to offer. 'Have you tried . . .' I paused. Where could she try? I couldn't name a single friend or even acquaintance he might be with. ' . . . the pub?'

'No.' She sounded doubtful. 'Not yet. I'll ring the Bull and see if anyone has seen him.'

'Yes, good idea,' I said, having no idea where the Bull was or if it was the type of place John would frequent.

I ended the call with a renewed irritation with John. It was so typical of him to take himself off for a destructive drinking binge, to go AWOL while he indulged his self-pity, without giving any thought to how worried his mum might be. Without giving any thought to anyone but himself.

After the call, I found Anya and Sophie out on the terrace, their loungers in opposite corners facing outwards towards the city. Although Sophie probably would have been a more sympathetic audience for my report of the call from John's mum, it was Anya with whom I wanted to share the news. She was the one who'd known John, who I'd told when I'd first met his mum.

I approached Anya's lounger and sat down on the end of it, forcing her to shift her legs aside. 'Guess who I've just had a call from.'

'Who?' She looked up at me, holding her magazine over her face to shield her eyes from the sun.

'John's mum.'

She seemed disappointed by this answer. She opened her magazine and resumed reading. 'Oh. Okay. What did she want?'

'She said she hasn't seen him for a few days. She sounded worried.' I paused but Anya didn't say anything. 'I wonder where he could have gone.'

Anya usually jumped on any suggestion of scandal or intrigue and would once have joined in the speculation as to where he could be with gusto. I'd expected her to have delighted in coming up with some far-fetched explanation for his absence – 'I bet he's been arrested for trying to pass himself off as someone famous.' 'Maybe he's joined a cult!' – but all she said was, 'Yeah. Strange,' before turning back to her reading.

I wasn't ready to give up just yet, though, so I tried one more time to prod her into conversation. 'He did this to me once. He just upped and went out, didn't come back for twenty-four hours. I can't even remember where he said he'd been but I remember I was worried.'

I expected her to say, 'Really? When was that?' Or even, 'You never said,' but instead she just sighed and said, 'Well, you've always attracted weirdos, haven't you.'

And it stung. Because although maybe it had been a throwaway comment, maybe she was being dismissive and not vindictive as it felt, I still felt hurt that she hadn't considered how it might sound. Because it sounded very much to me like she'd been making reference to a thing that we both knew, but that we never *ever*, no matter how bad a fight was, said out loud.

6 June 2005

Police Sergeant Maggie Larsen, Hampshire Constabulary

Everything Maggie had had to do with the family of the railway death boy, Reuben Henry – the sister, the mother – had reaffirmed everything she'd ever thought about having children. Specifically, why she could never be up to the job.

It was one thing, wasn't it, to look after them when they were little, when you could wrap them up, tuck them up, keep them with you at all times and put them to bed in the evening, but teenagers were a whole different business. She didn't think people thought carefully enough about teenagers, when they were deciding to become parents. Maybe they just didn't know any to realise how they could be – how headstrong, how reckless, how vulnerable, how confusing. The Henry kids were certainly a good illustration.

For the past few days, she'd been immersed in the world of Reuben Henry, and by all accounts, he seemed to have been a strange boy. Nice looking, if the photos were anything to go by, but he'd messed around with himself. That hair was too long, and she could never understand why anyone went in for facial piercings. She'd heard a lot – from the mother, mainly – about his musical talents. There did indeed seem to be the certificates to back that up, but he was clearly one of those tortured artistic types. 'Loner' is the word that had come up several times in the door-to-doors and, once or twice, 'odd' or 'quirky'. It wasn't all bad; lots of people said he was nice too, that he kept himself to himself and didn't give anyone any trouble. But that was what people always said when they didn't really have anything of substance to contribute but wanted to have their say anyway.

Today, though, things had taken an uncomfortable turn, and any warm feeling she'd felt towards the boy had faded, especially when she learnt she was to be the one to let the sister know what he'd been up to.

The girl was sitting opposite her now at the kitchen table. She had the same face as her brother – that elfin, sharp-eyed look. It suited her better, though. Looked better on a girl. The mother was there too, standing over by the counter, cradling her mug and frowning anxiously. Maggie felt for her, she really did. In fact, when she saw her, she saw she was thinking exactly what she herself would have, if she'd been in this situation: How did my chubby little babies get themselves into this? How did it all turn out like this? It was never meant to be this way.

Officially, the purpose of the conversation was to ask the girl if she knew about the photos. It was clear to Maggie, however, that the answer was no. Of course she didn't. How would she know? Which meant Maggie's real job today was to break the news. And to break the mother's heart even further, if that were possible. And to leave the poor girl feeling she could never trust anyone again, no doubt.

Maggie laid the pictures out on the table in front of her. She'd warned Lauren they might be hard to see, but she didn't want to introduce them any more than that. She couldn't influence her impression of them. She wanted to see what she had to say about them herself.

Lauren's initial reaction was exactly as Maggie had anticipated – the shock creeping across her face slowly as she recognised herself in the images, turning quickly to disgust and then embarrassment as, pink-cheeked, she tried to cover them.

She looked up at Maggie. 'Who took these?'

'Well, we're not totally sure at the moment, love,' Maggie said.

In fact, they were already quite sure that there had been no one behind the camera at all at the moment the image was captured. A clear webcam job. Why people were so enamoured with the internet, Maggie had no idea. For every benefit it offered it seemed to present ten problems. You could tell from the field of vision that the camera had been installed up high in Lauren's bedroom, hidden by books on a shelf perhaps. A team had already searched her room – although without letting Lauren know exactly what they were looking for – and identified several spots where the little pervert could have feasibly concealed his kit, knowing which times of day he'd be most likely to catch the footage he could best use to get his thrills. Or to get his money from whichever mates he was flogging the stills to.

Her mother appeared at her shoulder, took one look at the photos and covered her mouth in horror. Then, in one swipe across the table top, she knocked them all to the floor. 'What is that? Where did those come from?'

But it was Lauren she was looking at as she spoke. It was from her daughter, not Maggie, that the mother was demanding the answers. Maggie realised then that it was as if the mother was suggesting Lauren had been complicit in their creation. That she had wanted them, even. Maggie was surprised she could think that. But then, as she'd suspected, this is what it must be like, parenting teenagers. You had no idea what they were going to do next.

'I don't know when they were taken!' Lauren said again, her voice high-pitched. 'Or how! I haven't even had anyone in my room.'

Maggie put her hand on Lauren's, pulled out the calming, gentle voice that was so useful in her line of work. 'We know, love.' And then to the mother, 'The camera was hidden. We believe on a shelf somewhere in Lauren's room. A high-tech business. A webcam, you know. Accessed remotely. These images are stills from the footage.'

The mother looked at Maggie, her face twisted in horror. 'Why? Why . . . ?'

Maggie picked the photos up from the floor and placed them in a little pile in front of her, being sure to keep them face down. 'We don't know. That's what we're looking into.'

'Reuben had these? He . . .' Lauren's voice was barely audible.

Maggie nodded. 'They were found in the inside pocket of his jacket.'

Lauren swallowed and looked blankly at the wall in front of her.

'Now obviously it's an . . . unusual thing, for him to have on him.' Maggie felt herself blush, which wasn't something that happened often. 'And we don't want to jump to conclusions about why he had them. One possibility is he intended to distribute them, to sell them. We know he was keen to study music and the fees were a concern so—'

155

'No,' the mother said. 'No. No.' She shook her head firmly, over and over again.

Maggie wasn't sure if she meant 'This can't be happening' or 'He wouldn't have done that.' Probably both, she supposed.

'I don't understand,' Lauren said. But her voice was flat, her face was blank.

Maggie put her hand on Lauren's. 'Boys can be confusing things, love.' She plastered on her softest, mostly kindly, benevolent-grandma smile, but Lauren shook her head and pulled her hand away.

'Boys are all arseholes,' she said.

Chapter 27

When Friday night arrived, we began to make our preparations to leave Barcelona and return to our lives at home. We were subdued as we shuffled around the apartment, gathering up towels and magazines and throwing away nearly empty sunscreen bottles that it wasn't worth carrying on the journey home. I found I had a melancholy Sunday-evening feeling; I was surprised by how sad I felt to be leaving.

On paper, I knew the holiday couldn't be considered to have been a total success, but it was the very fact of its drama that made me feel that we'd been in Barcelona much longer than a week. In the time leading up to the holiday, I'd viewed it as a marker of sorts. A formal end to the messy, infuriating, miserable business with John. I'd planned that I would go back to my flat fully rested and rejuvenated, with a new enthusiasm for work, for my social life, for my fitness. For my future. For all the areas of my life that it would be easier to concentrate on now I only had myself to worry about. I was disappointed then, to find that the only feeling I could muster about my return was a heavy weariness.

It suddenly hit me that the reality was that it was all going to be the same as before. One week in the sun wasn't going to transform my fortunes, or my personality. I would slip back into my meaningless life of Photoshopping dogs' coats for the adoption mail-outs and sitting at home on my own all evening, eating microwave meals straight from their black plastic trays. John might continue to send me messages with fluctuating tones but eventually he'd lose interest and I'd be alone, with only a fortnightly drink with Anya or the odd night out with colleagues I barely knew to look forward to.

I had this whole sorry insight as I was standing in the kitchen, my hand on a pile of magazines that I'd intended to collect and distribute to the others for the plane trip. The misery of the vision had briefly engulfed me and I realised I'd been standing completely motionless for a few moments, staring blankly at the table.

Matt, who was standing at the hob poking at a stir-fry with a wooden spoon, noticed I hadn't moved for a few moments. He looked up. 'You okay?'

'Oh, yeah.' I laughed and shook my hair. 'Yeah. I'm okay. Just thinking that I wasn't really looking forward to going home, that's all.'

'No?' he said, turning back to his cooking. 'Thought you'd be glad to get back. I know this holiday didn't exactly turn out how you planned.'

'Well, the beginning, yeah. But this bit. This half. This place . . .' I gestured to the bright room, the evening sun streaming through the glass doors and lighting up the row of wine bottles lined up along the counter. 'I could stay here quite happily forever, really. To be perfectly honest.'

Matt reached for a bottle of sauce from a shelf above the hob. 'You can,' he said casually. 'If you want.'

I laughed, but he turned to look at me. He turned down the heat and put the wooden spoon on the side. He came over to where I was standing, his hands in his pockets. 'Okay, not forever. I don't like you that much.' He grinned and I laughed again. 'But you're welcome to stay on for a bit. More than welcome. You say you work from home a lot anyway, so what difference would it make if you did it from here for a while instead?'

'I couldn't just . . . not go home. That's mad.'

He looked at me. 'Is it?'

'What about my flight? It's all booked. I can't just not turn up. How would I—?'

Matt shrugged. 'You'll lose a bit of money, sure. But, I'm telling you, Barcelona in the summer. It's a pretty special thing.'

I looked around me. I imagined myself working here, at this table, in the day while Matt was out. Then, come five thirty, I could take a cold beer from the fridge, step out onto the terrace, look out at the city below me. It could be good for me, couldn't it? To watch all those different lives being lived right in front of me, in this exciting city, all the different choices people had made, all the different routes they had decided to explore. And to think about the path I could take. To think about what options were open to me now I didn't have to consider what would and wouldn't please John.

'But I know there's nothing like sleeping in your own bed.' Matt turned back to the stove and picked up his spoon from the side. 'I get that you probably just want to get back to normality.'

I sensed Matt was already retracting the offer and the idea of staying on evaporated as quickly as it had arrived. Of course I had to go home. That's just what you did at the end of a holiday. I consoled myself with the knowledge that it was at least a sign of a good time, that I should have thought so seriously about extending it.

I was taking a break from my packing and watching the sunset over the city from the terrace when I saw that Mum was calling me. She knew I was abroad; had something happened? But when I answered I realised she'd simply got her dates confused and thought I was already home.

'I was just going to say, there's a letter from Student Loans here, if you want to collect it.'

'Can you not forward it on?'

Mum sighed heavily, like I'd asked her to package the letter in a gold-plated case and carry it to my house on her back. 'I suppose so.'

There was more huffing and puffing while Mum wrote down the address of the flat where I'd been living for the last three years, and where she'd already sent me a number of other forwarded letters, but had apparently never before felt the need to store the details.

'Still sunning yourself, then? Not got work to get back for?'

So here was the reason for her barely concealed dissatisfaction with me: she was annoyed that I was still away. And I was annoyed that she was annoyed. I wasn't on a no-expense-spared, six-month luxury cruise on borrowed funds I had no prospect of repaying. It was one week in Spain that I had saved for and I hadn't had a proper holiday for four years. Sometimes it really was like she'd prefer it if I was miserable.

'Yeah,' I said, hearing the defiance in my voice. 'Still here. Actually, I was thinking of staying on for a bit. I'm having a good time.'

'What do you mean, "staying on"?' Mum snapped. 'For how long?'

I shrugged, even though she wasn't there to witness my deliberate display of nonchalance. 'Don't know really. As long as I like, I suppose.'

Mum laughed then. 'Right you are.' She sighed. 'Give me strength.'

When I'd ended the call, I went to find Matt in the kitchen. 'You know what we were just talking about? About me not going home quite yet? About me staying here?'

He spun round to look at me. 'Yeah? You should. Seriously. You should.'

'I mean, are you totally sure?' I said. 'You wouldn't mind if I stayed for a bit? I really thought you'd be desperate to get rid of us by now.'

Matt looked at me again, but he didn't smile. He seemed confused for a moment. Hurt, even. 'No,' he said frowning. 'Not at all.'

And then he turned back to his cooking and it occurred to me for the first time that maybe Matt was lonely. I realised he'd hinted at it a few times – his not having many plans, his friends being mostly colleagues from work and, as he was the boss, he was never completely sure how people felt about him – and I realised that perhaps I'd been shallow to assume that because Matt had a nice flat and his own business he was completely happy.

'Okay,' I said. 'If you're really sure, then that would be amazing. I'd love to stay.'

He turned to look at me again. He blinked almost in disbelief for a second, then he smiled widely. 'Seriously? Great! That is so great.'

I fiddled with a loose thread on my top suddenly nervous. 'Is it? It is, isn't it?'

He nodded and swallowed, and his expression shifted slightly. He was still smiling but his eyes were sad. Wistful, almost. 'Yeah. Honestly, it will be so nice to have you around the place.'

* * *

'Stay?' Sophie had been bent over her bag trying to wedge her book into the pocket at the top and she jerked her head up to look at me. 'What do you mean?'

Anya was sitting on the floor by the mirrored wardrobe, straightening her hair. She too turned to look at me. 'Yeah – what? Why?'

I shrugged. 'I just want to. I can work from here, I've got my computer and that's all I need. And Matt says it's fine. So, I just thought, why not, really?'

'So you just won't come to the airport? You just won't show up for the flight?' Sophie was staring at me. I could see she was gripping her bag quite tightly; her fingers were white at the ends.

I shrugged. 'Yeah. I can ring them and let them know, but they must get no-shows all the time. I doubt it matters much.'

'All right for some,' Anya muttered grumpily. This wasn't really fair of her. As she was fond of telling me, she didn't believe in envy. As she saw it, if you looked at someone else's life and wanted what they had, you had to get off your arse and go and get it for yourself. She'd chosen her important corporate job in the city, hadn't she? She enjoyed the big pay cheque they gave her every month. It wasn't my fault that her job placed greater demands on her than mine did on me.

Later, I was in our bedroom, taking my things back out of my bag and placing them once again in the drawer next to my bed, when Sophie came in. She hovered by the cupboard for a moment, like she was looking for something.

'Lauren,' she began in a low voice. 'Are you sure Matt won't mind? I know he's very quick to make these generous offers but I've known him a while and I do think he has a tendency to say things without thinking them through.'

'I've known him a while too.'

162

She frowned. 'You know what I mean. You haven't seen him for years. You don't know adult Matt. Not really. Not like I do.'

I looked at her carefully. 'Sophie,' I stopped. It was hard to think of a way to say what I wanted without it seeming cruel. What I wanted to say was that I could understand why she might be jealous. I knew it was hard starting again in a new town at the end of a relationship. I knew she didn't have many friends – she wouldn't be on holiday with us, virtual strangers, if she did – but that didn't mean she needed to be possessive about her old friends. I was no threat to that. I wasn't going to steal Matt away from her. I just wanted a place to stay.

In the end, though, it seemed too difficult a subject to tackle so I just said, 'It'll be fine. And if it's not, if I get the feeling Matt's had enough and wants his own space, I'll just come home.'

'Lauren!' Sophie put her hands on her hips, seemingly suddenly exasperated. 'That'll be so expensive! Last minute flights aren't that easy to come by!'

I was tempted to point out that she hadn't been so worried about that when she wanted to head home immediately when things had started to go wrong at Torre Sonrisas, but I didn't. Her fussing was beginning to grate. She hadn't been there when Matt had made the suggestion. I wasn't so obtuse that I couldn't spot when someone was issuing an invitation they didn't really mean. I was sure Matt hadn't felt pressured into making the offer. In fact, I was sure he was happy I'd taken it up.

'It'll be fine, Sophie. Really.' Then I turned my back on her to show the conversation was over.

Part Two

Chapter 28

The day Sophie and Anya left for the airport and Matt went into work for a few hours, I realised how much I'd missed being alone. It had only been a week but sharing a room with Sophie meant I'd only ever managed to snatch short pockets of time to myself – in the shower, reading in the lounge before one of the others came to join me. At home, I often got lonely, but there, in that apartment, with that view, it felt luxurious to be alone with my own thoughts, where I could do exactly what I wanted without having to run the idea past anyone else. I drifted through the rooms in my bare feet, running my hand along the smooth marble worksurfaces, standing at the window and watching the life going on in the streets below, lying fully stretched out on the white sofa and looking at the clouds through the skylight.

Over the next few days, I established exactly the routine I'd had in mind when I decided to stay.

I emailed Caroline at work to let her know I was going to be working remotely for a while. At the last minute, I added, 'I'm actually abroad at the moment, but available on email all the usual hours.' I told myself that I'd included that detail in case they asked me to pop into the office for a meeting, but really I think I just liked the way it sounded. Spontaneous and intrepid. Caroline seemed neither impressed nor concerned by my location, though, simply saying that it suited them for me to be out of the office for a while as they had a new intern starting soon and it would be useful to give him my desk. This, together with the tense call with Mum, left me with the definite feeling that no one in England would miss me much, or in fact notice my absence at all.

Every day, I waited until I'd heard Matt leave for work, then I got up, showered, ate breakfast on the terrace and was at the kitchen table in front of my computer by eight. I'd spend the morning replying to emails, tweaking layouts, searching image libraries and tidying whiskers in Photoshop. If I worked steadily, I could be finished by one, so I'd make some lunch out of the bread, cheese and fruit that I made sure the flat was stocked with – it seemed the least I could do in exchange for free accommodation – and head out to explore.

When Sophie and Anya had been there and we'd gone out on our little afternoon jaunts to see the city, our day trips had been lacklustre. We'd ambled about dutifully commenting on the architecture and ticking the main sights off our list, but I think we all were looking forward to the moment when we decided we'd done enough to earn a sandwich and a drink in a pavement café. Now, though, on my own, I roamed the city in a different way. I wasn't looking for anything in particular or aiming for specific monuments highlighted in the battered copy of *Barcelona: Your Pocket Guide* I'd picked up in a charity shop the week before we'd left. I would always choose the narrowest side street, the quietest option at any junction. The path least trodden. I'd come across things I knew must be famous, that I should probably know the history of – an enormous statue of a cat, cathedrals, wide squares – but I didn't stop to look them up. I knew that probably made me a philistine, but what I was interested in was the details. The small children in matching uniforms holding hands as they made their way to school. The smart women in high heels shouting crossly into their phones. The young shirtless men veering around on noisy mopeds shouting out greetings – or insults, I had no way to tell – to people they knew on the pavements. I wanted to see the real life. I wanted to be part of it. Or at least to pretend I was. I took my sketch book out with me and made quick drawings of scenes that caught my interest and supported these with photos so I could continue work on the pieces later. I had in my mind that I wanted to make a study of the hidden corners of Barcelona life, the interactions and events that characterised life there. Then perhaps, I could travel to other places, other cities, and do something similar there, building up a series of works giving a glimpse into how people lived around the world. I was surprised by the idea. Embarrassed really, and I would never have told anyone else about it. Honestly, I thought to myself, who do I think I am? A week in the sun and I think I'm Michael bloody Palin.

In the evening, Matt and I would eat together. I insisted on cooking at least some of the time. He said over and over that he didn't expect me to, that he didn't want me to feel like 'some kind of housemaid, or whatever' and we both knew he was more skilled in the kitchen than me, but it seemed only fair that I should do something, given that he wasn't charging me any rent and he already had Luisa, his cleaning lady, who washed the floors and changed the bed sheets every week. He would ask me what I'd been doing in the day and I would tell him about my drawings, although always batted away his suggestions that I show him my works in progress. One step at a time.

One evening, as we shared a Moroccan chicken dish that I'd made that hadn't quite worked but Matt insisted was 'perfect', he said, 'I was meaning to check: how are you feeling now, about everything that happened in those first couple of days? At that dive you found yourselves in? Are you still . . . I don't know . . . shaken up?'

I thought about this for a moment. I thought I *had* been shaken up, at the time. Certainly, that night I'd seen an unknown figure hovering in the lounge in the middle of the night I'd been quite terrified. But now it was over, I didn't think I was experiencing any lasting trauma. My overriding impression of that place, now we were out of it, was of discomfort. The heat. The smell. The claustrophobia.

I shrugged. 'I'm fine now. Glad to not be there any more, sure, but looking back, it all just seems like bad luck.' I took a sip of my drink. Matt was looking at me, like he was waiting to see if I was going to say more. 'I suppose we learnt a few lessons about putting ourselves in the hands of someone we don't know,' I said. 'Maybe we were too trusting. There are a lot of oddballs out there.'

Matt nodded. 'A lot of dangerous people, too.'

I rested my chin on my palm and looked out of the window, thinking about this. 'I just can't work out *how* they could have done it.' I turned back to Matt. 'Not just how they got in, but the radio. I can't work out the mechanics of it. How could you connect the radio to the live wiring like that?'

'I suppose it would just be a simple case of removing the fuse. Because the fuse is an appliance's safety device. In the event of an overload, the fuse is the only thing that prevents—'

I laughed, cutting him off. 'I do know what a fuse is, Matt! But the radio wouldn't have worked at all without a fuse in the plug so that can't be it.'

He flushed. 'Well, yes, I suppose I don't mean removed entirely. I just meant moved from where it's supposed to be to somewhere where it will actually carry the current further. With more force.'

Matt wasn't making any sense but I could see I'd already embarrassed him by correcting him once, so I kept quiet. I did wonder, though, for the first time, if we'd been too quick to accept Matt's theory that the radio had been set up as a deliberate trap. He'd seemed so sure about it all that we'd had no reason not to take his word for it. Now, hearing him waffle on about fuses and wiring like this, I wondered if it was more likely that Anya's suggestion had been right – maybe it had just been an accident. A cheap appliance with dodgy wiring. Although I suppose that didn't explain how the radio had come to be in our kitchen overnight. Which, in a way, was the most alarming aspect of all.

I shook my head and sighed. 'I don't know. I guess it'll always be a mystery. I suppose I'm only still thinking about it because it used to be something that preoccupied me. Electrocution, I mean. It became a phobia, in a way. Or an anxiety, at least. You find yourself reading a lot about how electricity works when that's how your brother died. Probably wasn't good for me.'

Matt blinked, surprised at the flippant way I'd mentioned it. I thought about it all the time, so for me, the subject was always just below the surface. I realised though that that wasn't the case for others. That flinging my brother's death into the middle of a casual conversation could feel inappropriate. Upsetting.

'Sorry,' I said quietly.

'No,' Matt shook his head. 'It's okay. I was just surprised. I thought you didn't like to talk about what ha— About the accident.'

I looked up. 'Why? Why do you say that? Who said that?'

Matt's cheeks flushed. 'Anya mentioned something. Sorry.'

'What did she say?' It came out more sharply than I'd intended.

He shook his head, wide-eyed. 'Nothing. Nothing really. Just that. Just that you didn't talk about it. It totally makes sense, obviously. I assumed it was just too painful.'

'Oh. Yes. Yeah. It's . . . yeah.' I nodded and waited while my heartbeat slowly returned to normal.

8 June 2005

Lauren

'Okay,' Anya said. 'Right. Okay.'

We were sitting on the beach, both facing the sea. I'd asked Anya to meet me there and insisted we walk to the far end, where the wooded area was replaced by sand dunes, where we were unlikely to come across anyone we knew. Anya had offered to come to the house to see me, but I wanted to go somewhere we couldn't be over-heard.

I could tell Anya was concentrating very hard on what to say next. She had taken the news calmly. Or rather, she had pretended to. I was grateful for that.

'Okay,' Anya said again. 'So he . . . set the camera up in your room? On his own.'

'I don't know,' I said quietly. 'There *was* a camera. And then there were pictures. And Reuben had the pictures. That's all they actually know.'

173

Anya turned to look at me. 'Yeah. Okay. But putting two and two together . . . ?'

I closed my eyes – screwed them tight shut, trying to block out the outside. I opened them again. 'Well, yeah, obviously that's what *they* think. Because they didn't know him.'

Anya nodded. 'Okay. And what do you think?'

'They think maybe he was doing it for money. Selling them to people at school.'

'What do you think?' Anya said again.

To this, I didn't say anything at all. I looked out at the sea watching a kayaker struggling against the breakers. Normally Anya didn't tolerate longs gaps in conversations. Normally she would hurry things along with a follow-up question or a view of her own. Today, though, she said nothing. She sat and watched the man in the kayak and waited for me to think of my answer.

'I don't know,' I said eventually. 'I don't know exactly. But I don't think he did it. It could have been someone else. Lots of people have been in our house. I don't exactly keep my bedroom on lock-down.'

Anya nodded. 'So, the stills? Why did he have th—?'

'I don't know!' I shouted suddenly, making Anya jump. I picked up a pebble and threw it aimlessly towards the sea but it fell well short, smashing into another stone. 'Maybe he found them? I don't know. I don't think it was him, Anya.' I turned to look at her now. 'That's what I think. I think there's something else to explain it. Something that we'll never know.'

Anya nodded. 'Does anyone else know? About the pictures?'

I shook her head. 'Mum. The police. That's all. I don't want anyone else to know. Ever.'

'Yes. No. That's what I was going to say. I think that's a good idea.'

I looked at Anya again. 'You can't tell anyone. Never speak about it to anyone.'

'No. Of course.'

'Seriously, Anya. No jokes about it. No getting drunk and talking about it by accident. No telling someone as a secret that they swear to take to the grave. Not even in ten years' time. Not in fifty. Never, okay?'

'Of *course* not. Of course I'm not going to do that. Jesus, Lauren. I wouldn't.'

'Okay,' I said, quieter now. 'Good. That's good.'

Chapter 29

On the Friday that marked a week since Matt had offered to let me stay on, he sent me a message in the middle of the morning, asking if I wanted to meet for lunch. He said there was a little place near his work that was good, so at midday I sent off my morning's work, closed my laptop and headed out to find his office.

'It's sushi,' he said, as he led me down an unremarkable residential street. 'Is that all right? Sorry, I should've checked.'

'Oh, okay,' I said. 'Yeah, that's fine. Good.'

'You sound surprised?' He grinned. 'Did you think they only have Spanish food in Spain?'

I laughed. 'Oh god. Maybe I did think that subconsciously.'

The pavement was too narrow for us to walk side by side and, as Matt was the one who knew where we were going, he went in front.

'It's just on the corner there,' he said, pointing up ahead to where a small black sign with a red icon was sticking out of the wall. 'It should be—' He stopped suddenly, leading me to walk right into his back. 'Shit,' he muttered.

I followed his eyeline and saw a woman with white-blonde

hair and a loose blue sundress step out of the restaurant we were aiming for. She looked around her like she was trying to get her bearings, then crossed the road and walked quickly away from us.

Matt sighed and continued walking, his hands pushed into his pockets. 'Sorry,' he mumbled.

'Who was that?'

'No one,' he said.

But his demeanour had changed and in the restaurant he was distant and distracted. I asked him questions about the menu and he explained what things were, he asked me polite questions about my morning, but I could see something had upset him.

'Matt,' I said as the waiter cleared our plates. 'What's up? Who was that woman we saw? The blonde? Do you know her?'

He wrinkled his nose, then he nodded and said quietly, 'Yeah. Used to.'

'An ex?'

He nodded.

'A serious one?'

He smiled sadly. 'We were married.'

My eyes widened. 'Really? Married? When?'

'Got married . . .' His eyes flicked upwards as he did the calculation in his head. 'Six years and nine months ago. And divorced six years and two months ago.'

'Seven months. Right. Okay. So it was quite . . . brief, then?'

Matt laughed once, then sighed. 'And we only managed to actually live together for two months.'

'I see.' I was shocked, but I was trying to make it appear that I was taking all this in my stride, that we all have short failed marriages in our past. 'What happened?'

He closed his eyes for a moment. When he opened them

177

again, he said, 'I don't really want to talk about it, to be honest. The short version is that I was a stupid naïve romantic. A stupid naïve romantic who ended up with a broken heart.' He looked down, embarrassed.

I put my hand on his. 'Okay. I'm sorry. For the broken heart and for asking you about it. It's none of my business. And it's in the past. Over.'

He smiled. 'Over,' he agreed.

Chapter 30

I hadn't heard much from Anya since she and Sophie had returned home. I told myself she was busy catching up with the work she missed but it did sting. There would have been a time when my taking an unplanned extended working holiday would have filled Anya with a kind of curious glee and she would've been messaging me every hour to see what I was doing. I decided that when I got home I would go to see her, force her to talk to me, find out what was going on.

Sophie, on the other hand, had been much more forthcoming with the communication, sending me short messages most days complaining about the weather, asking me about work, chatting about what I was cooking that evening.

The day Matt had seen his ex-wife, Sophie and I were exchanging messages in the evening and I mentioned that Matt had taken me for lunch.

Sophie replied:

Oh really?? Do I sense romance on the cards?

This short, nine-word message completely reframed the insecurity I had sensed from Sophie the evening I announced I was going to stay on in Spain. I realised now that she'd thought that my decision might be the start of some romantic liaison between Matt and me. And there she was, newly single, setting out on her newly single life and she'd thought I'd be doing the same. We'd compared notes about what it was like to come out of a relationship, to find yourself on your own again, and she was obviously hoping for a few more months of this shared situation. But, as she'd seen it, I was moving on already, with a man I'd only known a few days, and in another country too. I could see that, if I was in her place, I too would feel disappointed.

I sent her a message to reassure her:

Me: Haha no! It's not like that. Haven't seen him that much anyway. Just having some time to myself.
Sophie: Oh, fair enough. My mistake. Probably for the best. Think of the ginger babies.
Me: I like ginger babies!

The next day, I couldn't make headway with my work until I received replies to some emails I'd sent out after breakfast, so I decided to reverse my routine; to begin with my walk around town and to come back to the flat to work later instead.

As I wandered through the pavements, trying my best to avoid turning down streets I had seen before, I realised my route had brought me to the back of Torre Sonrisas.

I'd never seen the place from this side before, the balcony side. I was standing in the space between the block itself and the high brick wall that, as we knew all too well, blocked any view the balconies may have had. As I looked up, I could see that the flat we'd stayed in, number 17, wasn't the only one where the owner had tried to perk up the outlook by brightening up the portion of the wall in front of their terrace. I could see the cityscape mural that had duped us in the photographs was in no way convincing from this angle, looking more like default desktop wallpaper on a new computer. Other apartments had tried different ideas – hand-painted rainforest scenes, underwater seascapes, bold floral designs. I guessed the owners of the flats didn't have any official permission to decorate that wall, but then I suppose no one was particularly likely to object.

As I looked upwards, I noticed a shirtless man, skinny and pale, leaning on the rail of the balcony. He was smoking a cigarette and tapping the ash over the side. I realised he was on the balcony of number 17. Was this him, I thought, the owner? The scam artist, the drug dealer? The source of all our troubles?

Without a face to put to the man who had taken our money and left us in a sub-standard flat at the mercy of his enemies, I'd built him up in my mind to be dark and dangerous. I'd imagined him to be physically imposing and smartly dressed. A ruthless mafia figure. But the man I was looking at now was short, scrawny and unshaven. He was sniffing as he smoked his cigarette and at one point, he took a handkerchief out of the pocket of his shorts and wiped his nose. Seeing him standing there, looking so ordinary and smoking a cigarette like he didn't have anything to worry about or anywhere important to be, I was furious with him. He was clearly a lazy waster who thought he'd hit on a great scheme to make a bit of easy money from some gullible tourists, with the added benefit of giving him the opportunity to make himself scarce while whichever petty criminal mates he'd wound up exacted their revenge on his property.

As I entered the front door of Torre Sonrisas and climbed

the stairs to the first floor, I was intent on getting answers. I wanted our money back, but I wanted an apology too. I wanted to show him that I was still there, the gullible tourist he thought he'd washed his hands of. I wanted to see him squirm.

It was only as I approached the door of number 17 that it occurred to me the man I'd seen on the balcony might not be the owner at all – that he might very well be the next unfortunate holiday maker, equally disappointed at where he found himself – so as I knocked on the door I was forced to dial down my anger to curiosity. I was just going to ask him some questions.

It took the man a long time to answer my knock, and when he did, his eyes were half closed, like he was very sleepy or very stoned. He made a grunting noise in greeting.

'Do you speak English?' I said, my voice bright and clear.

He made another grunting noise that didn't really answer my question one way or the other, but I decided to continue regardless.

'Is this your flat? Your apartment?'

'Yes,' he said. He folded his arms defensively.

'My name's Lauren. We – my friends and I – were staying here last week. We tried to contact you – about the break-in? The new keys?' My voice was still bright, but it was firm too. I was hoping to show that I wasn't prepared to be fobbed off.

He narrowed his eyes. 'You?' He angled his head towards me. 'You stayed here?'

'Yes. That's right.'

Then, without warning, he grabbed me by the arm, pulled me into the flat and slammed the door behind us.

Chapter 31

'Jesus, get off!' I pulled my arm free and backed myself towards the door, but he put his hand flat against it, holding it shut.

'You apologise! And you pay me!' He was pointing his index finger at me. It was a few centimetres from my face.

'What?' I stared at him. '*Pay* you?'

If he'd been a bigger man, I'm sure I would have been more scared, but he was so small, so skinny, he looked almost fragile. Like a sparrow. More than anything, I felt confused.

'You treat my home badly!' he said. His accent sounded German, or maybe eastern European. Not Spanish at any rate. He marched off across the lounge. 'Number one, this!' He stood in front of the wall of photos, the poor women killed over the years by lunatics and psychopaths. He gestured to it with both hands, his fingers splayed. 'You put up this . . . this pictures! Nails in the wall.' He removed one of the picture frames from the wall and waved his hand at the nail behind it. 'Holes!'

'I didn't put them up!'

He ignored me and crossed the lounge again, stopping in front of the bathroom door. He gestured at the fuse box on the way. 'And why you shut down power? Why you do this? I have food in freezer. Is now all bad! Why you do this?'

'We had to,' I said. 'Because of the radio.'

'What radio? There is no radio. I don't *like* radio.'

I crossed the lounge and headed for the kitchen. He didn't try to stop me. I stopped in front of the counter where the radio had been. 'It was here,' I said. 'The radio that was here. It was . . . faulty. It was dangerous.'

The man looked at me like I was mad. Or hallucinating perhaps. 'There is no radio,' he said slowly. 'What you mean? You make no sense.'

We were looking at each other now with matching expressions, faces screwed up, somewhere between disgust and confusion.

'Who are you?' He took the handkerchief out of his pocket and wiped his nose again. His voice was a little calmer. 'You are English? American?'

'English. We just came on holiday.' I made an effort to keep my tone non-confrontational. 'We booked it – this apartment – through the website. We found the keys, where you said, in the box on the wall, and we—'

'What website?' He shook his head. 'What "holiday"? You said you come for work. I only rent to workers. Single people, quiet. Three months minimum. Where's Gabriel?'

'I don't know who Gabriel is.'

He thrust his phone at me and I scrolled through a series of emails; from my scanned reading, I gathered that they were between him – it looked like his name was Alexander – and someone called Gabriel Cartos, arranging, quite informally it seemed, a three-month tenancy, ending in July.

'Gabriel said he had to go,' Alexander said. 'His work contract finished, and he leave Barcelona. So I come back.'

I took my own phone out. I found the message group where

Sophie had first posted the link to the flat. I clicked on it and turned the screen towards Alexander. 'See? We found it here. We booked it through this website. A holiday rentals site.'

Alexander frowned, then pushed the phone back towards me dismissively. 'There's nothing.'

When I looked at the screen it was blank apart from an upbeat error message – *Oh dear! We can't find that page.* The link was no longer active. The listing – the flat – had been removed from the site altogether.

I stared at it for a moment, trying to piece together what must have happened. This Gabriel Cartos person had rented the apartment from Alexander on a three-month tenancy, then had advertised it and sublet it to us, no doubt charging us – and other holidaymakers too, probably – considerably more than he was paying Alexander, meaning a tidy money-for-nothing profit for him. The added bonus features of our stay – the skull through the window, the night-time intruder, the booby-trapped radio – were still a mystery, perhaps par for the course for someone who makes his living out of short-term scams. But one thing was clear: whoever Gabriel Cartos was, Alexander was as angry with him as I was.

'Who is Gabriel Cartos?' I said. 'Where's he from, what does he look like? Have you contacted him?'

'I don't know!' Alexander shrugged and pushed out his bottom lip in an exaggerated expression of confusion. 'I leave a card in the window of my sister's shop. I say "Apartment for rent". He email me, say he want to take it, but no need to see the place. He pay in advance – cash in an envelope, under the door.' Alexander pointed at the floor and I looked down. 'I never see him! I never hear from him! Except yesterday, he email to say he gone. Then I come home. And these strange things – pictures, broken window . . . and a new key!' He stepped forward and picked up a single key

185

from the desk and held it up to show me. 'A new key in the secure box. Because new lock.' Alexander shook his head in bafflement.

Once it had become clear that Alexander knew no more about what had happened in the apartment than I did, I knew there was nothing to be gained by staying there. When I'd finally managed to convince him I'd had nothing to do with the damage to his flat and I had no idea who Gabriel Cartos was, I let myself out, leaving him muttering and trying to light a new cigarette on the balcony.

Outside the block, I leant against the wall and typed out a message to Sophie:

Met the owner of the flat. Turns out he rented it out to someone who subletted it to us. He's as annoyed as we are!

She replied quickly:

How weird. So, our tormentor is still at large. I was thinking – I really think you should probably come home now. It just seems safer that way.

Her concern was sweet, but I thought, overly cautious. A bit dramatic really. I decided I'd reply later and change the subject – tell her something silly or upbeat from my day. As I walked down the road away from the block, I was lost in my own thoughts. I wasn't especially shaken by what had just happened in the flat, but I was baffled. It had been a surreal few minutes. There were just so many strange people in the world, it seemed. Strange people living strange lives.

I was aware of a voice calling, 'Hey! Hey excuse me!' somewhere behind me, but I was so distracted that it wasn't until someone reached out and touched my elbow that I realised the voice had been aimed at me.

I jumped and spun around to see a woman in her sixties looking at me anxiously. She had hair the colour and texture of straw, and bright pink lips.

'Hey, love,' she said. 'Sorry. Didn't mean to give you a fright.' Her accent was Australian. 'Do you speak English?'

'I am English,' I said, more defensively than I'd intended.

'Oh. Yeah. Right you are. It's just . . .' She paused and looked around her. She lowered her voice. 'I just wanted to let you know – because you're a young girl and I've got daughters myself – that a couple of times I've seen a bloke acting a bit . . . you know. Off. Watching you, I reckon.'

'What do you mean? When?' I looked around me. 'Who?'

'I've been sat over there' – she pointed to a cluster of chairs outside a bar – 'all this arvo and I've seen him a couple of times. Fella in a hood, he was. In this weather!' She gestured to the clear blue sky. 'He was kind of skulking, you know? In doorways and that. I'm sure it was you he was looking at.'

I felt the skin on the back of my arms prickle. 'Where is he now? What did he look like?'

She shook her head. 'Couldn't see really, with the hood. Just a bloke. Seems to have gone now. I reckon he clocked that I was onto him. But you just watch yourself, all right, love? Keep that bag zipped up.' She nodded down at the canvas bag I had over my shoulder. It didn't have a zip but I tried to pull the top edges together to show her I was taking her seriously.

'Okay,' I looked around the street again. There was no one near us except a group of teenage girls wearing tiny skirts and carrying helium balloons shaped like ice creams making their way towards us. 'Thanks.'

'No worries, love. Careful how you go, yeah?' With a quick wave, she returned to her seat outside the café.

I looked around me again, and then over to the woman who was now engrossed in conversation on her phone. There were three empty beer bottles on the table in front of her. Was she just drunk? Could she have let her maternal instincts run away with her and lead her to misinterpret what she'd seen? I told myself that she could. That she had.

Nevertheless, I cut short my morning's amble and took the quick route back to the apartment. It was only when I was safely back inside that I let myself properly address the niggling thought I'd had in the back of my mind for several days now: *I know*, John had said, when I'd reminded him I was in Barcelona. *I know*. I know you're there and I still want to see you. Wasn't that what he'd meant?

My phone beeped and as I searched for it in my bag, I knew it was going to be him.

But it wasn't. It was Sophie:

Really, I do think you'd be better to come home.

Chapter 32

That evening, Matt insisted I have a night off cooking so he could make me his favourite paella dish. He pronounced it the Spanish way – 'Pai - ay - a' – but with an exaggerated accent to show he knew it was a little pretentious.

As we were eating, I told him how I'd found myself outside Torre Sonrisas earlier in the day and what had happened next.

'You saw the owner?' Matt lowered his fork and looked at me anxiously. 'What did you say? Are you okay?'

'Yeah,' I said. 'Yeah, I'm fine. It was just weird.'

I explained the initial confusion where we had both blamed the other for the state of the flat, before realising there was a third person – the subletter, Gabriel Cartos – who was behind it all. I left out the detail of the way Alexander had manhandled me into the flat. I had a feeling that Matt would get too attached to that, that he might come over indignant and gallant and want to teach Alexander a lesson, and really, it didn't seem to matter that much now. This was also the reason I decided not to mention my encounter with the Australian woman and the hooded figure she'd claimed to have seen. I had a feeling that my being in Matt's city, a guest in his apartment, had given him a sense of responsibility towards me that I didn't want to encourage, however well-meaning it might have been.

'Gabriel Cartos?' Matt frowned, searching his memory for the name. He shook his head when nothing came. 'So who's he?'

I shrugged. 'I don't know. The owner didn't know either. He said he lets his flat out to seasonal workers on a medium-term basis. He advertised the apartment in a shop window, and it was all arranged by email, so he never even met him.'

Matt made a face and went back to his paella. 'Who just lets some random person he's never met move into his flat?'

I shrugged. 'Don't know.' But then I thought for a moment and amended my answer. 'Well, I suppose everyone who has ever rented their flat out. So a lot of people, really.'

Matt laughed. 'Yeah. Fair point.'

I sighed and continued eating my dinner. 'Anyway,' I said. 'The upshot is, we're no nearer knowing who Gabriel Cartos is *or* if he was involved in anything dodgy *or* how we managed to get in the middle of it. I think probably that woman from the block was right. It was something to do with drugs. Turf wars. Us being there was just bad luck.' I looked out of the window. 'Just my luck,' I added quietly.

Matt put his hand on mine and gave it a supportive squeeze. Then he stood up and took a bottle from the worktop behind him. He refilled my glass. 'Meant to be a decent one, this.'

I took a sip and smiled at him. I didn't have the palate to have any idea whether the wine was particularly good or not, but it went down easily enough. I was in the mood to get drunk.

Conversation moved on from Alexander and Torre Sonrisas and we exchanged reminisces about our childhoods in Hoyle. We initially stayed away from the heavy stuff, remembering instead the huge toy warehouse on the outskirts of town that everyone had begged their parents to take them to every Saturday morning, the pavement chalk drawing competitions that had been held on the prom on the first weekend of the summer holidays, and how devastated we'd been when the ice rink had been knocked down to make way for a car park.

As the timeline of our trip down memory lane moved forward, though, entering our teenage years, we started talking about a camping trip that had been run jointly by the boys' and the girls' schools. It had been before I'd started at secondary school, but I knew Reuben had taken part.

Matt said, 'That was the first time I really hung out with Reuben actually.' He looked at me cautiously as if to check it was okay to mention him.

'Yeah?' I smiled to show that it was.

Matt looked relieved. 'Yeah.' He took a sip of his wine. 'Me and him weren't exactly into sports so we were both – independently – bunking off football and we bumped into each other trying to hide out in this little wooden hut they used to dry the boots. He looked at me, and for a moment I was, like, nervous maybe? Reuben always seemed so *cool*, with his long black coat, and the hair . . . and,' Matt laughed and shook his head, embarrassed. 'I don't know. I thought he'd tell me to get lost. Little ginger loser that I was. But he didn't, he just gave me this lazy grin and said, "Right shithole, this place, isn't it?" and he laughed and I laughed and then that was it. We were mates.'

I nodded and swallowed. I could feel I was starting to tear up. I'd never heard this story. I didn't really know what Reuben had got up to on that camp. I hadn't been interested in hearing about it when he got back. It hadn't seemed important then.

I think Matt sensed that the story had made an impression on me because he was quiet for a few moments. We poked what was left of our food with our forks and looked out of the window. The sun had gone down now. The sky was a vivid twilight blue and the lights were starting to come on to signal the start of the city's evening activity.

'I know,' he said breaking the silence. I turned to look at him. He began again, 'I know everyone does the "what if" thing and it's pointless and everything and you just have to accept what happened but . . . but that's my what if. The beach party. You know what we were talking about the other day? With Anya? What if I'd followed him, when he left the beach. What if I'd made him stay, just a bit longer, to calm down. What if I'd got it out of him, whatever was going on. I could see he was upset about something. Or annoyed or . . .'

'Agitated,' I said. 'That's what they'd said, in the inquest. He left the beach in an agitated state.'

Matt nodded. 'Agitated,' he repeated. 'If I'd gone I could've just got him home. But I just . . .' He trailed off, shaking his head. 'You know, I fell asleep?' He laughed once but the smile fell quickly. 'Right there on the beach. Woke up at 3 a.m. absolutely freezing.'

I nodded. I thought perhaps I should reassure Matt, tell him there was nothing he could have done, but how could I when I knew that what he said was right? If he *had* got Reuben to stay, or if he had gone after him, maybe it would have made a difference. Just the same as if I'd gone to the party or if I'd persuaded Reuben not to go or if any number of the infinite alternative versions of events that I had turned over in my mind over the last thirteen years had been the version that we'd lived.

But they weren't. And I couldn't say anything to make Matt

feel better about it in the same way I'd never been able to make myself feel better about it.

Instead, I stood up abruptly, making Matt start with the sudden movement. 'Let's go out on the terrace.' I picked up the bottle of wine from the table. 'You can tell me about the history of the buildings we can see or point out which constellation is which. Whatever it is boys like to do when they're showing off.'

He laughed as he got to his feet and followed me out of the kitchen and through the lounge to the glass doors. 'I haven't a bloody clue about stars, I'm afraid.'

We didn't talk at all in the end. We stood on the terrace, leaning on the railings and looking down at the city, at the people sitting outside the bars talking and drinking, the mopeds weaving around the web of narrow roads.

After a few moments, he put his arm around my shoulders and pulled me towards him. It wasn't suggestive or flirtatious. He sighed, and it was sad, in a way. Resigned. I felt like the gesture was saying, 'Here we are then' or 'Who would've thought we'd be standing here together, after all these years and everything that's happened.' And I thought, who *would*'ve thought it? And I was aware it was partly the wine, and partly the warm evening air and the flickering lights below us, but I was suddenly overwhelmed by the sense that I had found my way there for a reason.

This time a month earlier, as I'd carried my microwave lasagne through my damp hallway, tripping over the box of books I was still waiting for John to collect, I'd had no idea that in a few weeks I'd be standing on a beautiful roof terrace with a boy I hadn't seen in years. And that I'd be getting on with that boy better than I'd got on with anyone in a long time. Because, we did, I realised now. We got on so well. It was so easy and natural. With Matt, never once had I worried that I'd said the wrong thing or that he thought my questions stupid or my interests pointless. I hadn't had to make an effort to seem more fun or more interesting or more normal than I was.

And then it seemed so obvious, that of course this is what was meant to happen. I had to leave my hometown, to try out life in new places, to have some painful experiences with terrible people, before realising the answer to all my dreams was the funny-looking quiet kid I'd known all along.

'It's a tale as old as time,' I said.

Matt turned to look at me. 'You what?'

I laughed. 'Don't worry.'

And then I kissed him.

Chapter 33

'Woah okay, hello there!' Matt chuckled gently, but he quite deliberately – quite firmly – took a step away from me. 'I told you those wine glasses were bigger than you thought.'

I blushed and looked away. I forced myself to laugh like my throwing myself at him was a hilarious joke. 'I know! Honestly, three glasses of a mid-shelf white and I'm anyone's.'

'Hey!' he said, mock offended. 'Top shelf!'

He laughed too but when he stopped the silence was awkward. We could try to make a joke of it as much as we wanted, but we both knew what had happened. He turned and headed back in through the glass doors, muttering something about getting a glass of water, leaving me to contemplate my ridiculous behaviour alone.

The next morning, I woke early with a dry mouth, a pounding head and sense of what-was-I-thinking shame I hadn't had since university. My memory of the details of the night before was patchy, but one image I could bring to mind quite clearly was that of Matt's face – surprised, alarmed, disgusted even? – as he moved away from me. As he stepped back, out of my reach.

I sat on the edge of my bed and as I looked around at the room, I suddenly realised how stupid I'd been. I could see now that the feeling I'd had the night before, that sense that fate had somehow put me exactly where I belonged, was a ludicrous romantic fantasy brought on by too much sun and too much wine. I was an idiot. I didn't 'belong' here. This wasn't perfect and right and exactly what destiny had intended for me all along. I was a glorified squatter, a houseguest who had well overstayed her welcome. If indeed I ever had been welcome. Matt was polite and he was generous but I knew that given the situation he'd found himself in, he hadn't had much choice about it either. I had a flat and I had a job at home. I knew neither were much to shout about, but that didn't mean I could just latch on to some bloke I hardly knew from school and decide I lived with him now. And then to throw myself at him too! I closed my eyes, shuddering inside. Totally embarrassing, is what it was.

On my bedside table, my phone vibrated. I realised it had gone 10 a.m.; I should have been at my computer by now, replying to emails from work. I answered it, ready to give some excuse about a faulty internet connection.

'Hello?'

For a moment, I thought the line was dead, but then I realised there was someone there. They weren't speaking but there was a sound – a sniffing or a snuffling, like a small animal.

'Hello?' I said again.

'Lauren? It's Valerie Marshall.' Her voice was weak and shaky, like she was having trouble getting it out.

'Oh, hi. Hello. Sorry. Are you—?

'Lauren, John's dead. He's dead.'

Chapter 34

'What?'

But she didn't reply, and I didn't need her to say it again. Neither of us said anything and for thirty seconds or so, the only sound was Valerie's gentle sobbing.

'What's happened, Valerie?' I was trying to keep my voice gentle for her sake but I could hear a note of hysteria threatening to creep in. 'What's going on?'

There were a few more sobs, then a hiccup while she tried to gather herself. 'They found him, drowned. He went swimming in the sea. They think he was drunk. I told him – I told him! – *never* to go swimming after drinking. They're going to fly his body over. I told them I want it now! I want him back!'

'What do you mean? Fly his . . . fly him from where?'

'Barcelona!'

I felt a lurch in my stomach. Instinctively, I looked towards the door.

'I don't understand. Is he in Barcelona? Was that where he was, when you couldn't find him?'

'Yes!' Valerie wailed. 'He called me when he arrived.

He said it was a spur of the moment decision and he was sorry for worrying me, but that he had to see you. Didn't you see him?'

'No. No, I didn't. I had no idea he was even here.'

I heard her turn away from the phone then, to speak to someone in the room. 'She didn't even know he was there!' she wailed.

'Oh no,' said the person in the background. A woman. John's dad wasn't on the scene, hadn't been for years, but I knew there was an aunt, Valerie's sister, who was close by. I hoped this was her, that Valerie had someone there. 'Oh, Val,' the voice said.

'He just wanted to see you,' Valerie said into the phone. 'We said it wasn't a good idea, and that he should wait until you were home but he was hell-bent on it being a surprise. But he didn't even get to see you and now . . . and now . . .'

I heard the woman in the background speak again, first to Val – 'Oh Val, come on. Come here' – and into the phone, to me. 'Lauren? Lauren, we have to go now. Valerie will speak to you again soon, I'm sure. About arrangements and what have you.'

And the phone beeped twice and the line went dead.

I sat on my bed. As I looked at the phone in my hands I realised I was shaking. I pulled my sheet off my mattress and wrapped it around me, swaddling myself tightly. I wanted to call Valerie back, to get her to explain exactly what had happened, right from the moment John had left her house up until she'd got the news, however that had happened, but I didn't think she'd be capable of it even if I could bring myself to do it.

I suddenly felt very alone. I wanted to call someone, to be with someone. I wanted someone to come and take control and explain what had happened and what was going to happen next.

I scrolled through my recent contacts. For a moment my thumb hovered over Anya's name but in the end it was Matt I selected. The awkward encounter of the night before didn't seem to matter now. Matt was the one who was closest, and I knew he would be calm and capable and take charge. The call went to voicemail without ringing so I hung up and sent him a message asking him to ring me when he could.

Then I sent one to Sophie:

Can you call me when you're not with a student? Something's happened.

Within a few seconds my phone rang, the screen lit up with Sophie's name. I told her about Valerie's call.

'*What?* What do you mean? What was he even doing out there?'

'I don't know. She said he'd come to see me. And that he'd got drunk and gone swimming and, I don't know, I guess he got in trouble. They're flying his body back to England.'

As I said the words 'body' I suddenly let out a sob. 'I don't even know where he is now! He came to see me. I should have guessed he would try to do something like this. I should have messaged him. I should have answered his calls! He wouldn't even have been here if it hadn't been for me.'

'Hey,' Sophie said gently. 'Hey hey hey. It's going to be okay. It's going to be okay.'

'I didn't even reply to his last message,' I wailed. 'He told me he wanted to see me and I could have made an arrangement, I could have promised to meet him when I was home, and then he wouldn't have come. I could have spoken to him, to have heard him out. Then he might not have got so desperate. Then he might not have . . .' Suddenly I remembered something. 'Someone was watching me. Yesterday. A man. Watching me, or waiting for me, maybe? I thought it was him. I thought it might have been. So he could have been there! Couldn't he? Thinking about approaching me, but then he . . . he changed his mind and went to the beach and . . .'

'Lauren,' Sophie said. 'Come on. There's no point in this. He decided, all by himself, to come and see you when you were in the middle of a holiday, which isn't exactly something you could predict, is it? That isn't something most people would do. This is in no way your fault.'

I didn't reply. I just stared at the wall, feeling the tears on my cheeks.

'Listen, Lauren,' Sophie said. Her voice was low. There was traffic noise in the background. 'I still think, more than ever now, what I said before. I really feel you should come home. I can't really say why, but you being there is giving me a bad feeling. Everything that happened at Torre Sonrisas when we still don't know who was behind it, and now John. I don't want to worry you but I just have this strong sense that—'

'I am worried. I'm worried too, now. I was telling myself that things at the apartment were nothing to do with us, but now, I don't even know. Do you think whoever it was, was out to get John? And was trying to, I don't know, get to him through me?'

'I don't know.'

'Or – Oh my god Sophie – do you think it *was* John, all along? All of it? If he's been here the whole time, if it was him watching me, it could have been, couldn't it? Do you think he was trying to mess with my head, to get his revenge

200

for me leaving him? Maybe he didn't want to see me to try to get back together at all. Maybe he was furious with me. Maybe he was here to . . . to . . . should I go to the police and ask exactly what happened? Should I—?'

'Lauren,' Sophie voice was firm now. Cross, even. 'You need to come home. Collect your things, get a taxi to the airport and fly home.'

'Yeah,' I said. 'I had been thinking it was time anyway this morning, for other reasons, but yeah. It's time. I just want to be at home. I'll tell Matt what's happened. I'll tell him I need to go.'

'You don't need Matt's permission, Lauren,' Sophie said. 'Just leave him a note. I really don't think you should waste any time. If there's a police investigation into what happened to John, you don't want to find yourself in the middle of it. Those things can take weeks, and they'll insist you stay in the country until it's over.'

'But I can't help them. I didn't even know he was here. I don't have any idea what happened.'

'Yes, but they won't take that into account. They might not even believe you. They'll just know that John came to see you and now John is dead, and they will want to keep a very close eye on you until they're absolutely sure those two facts aren't related. You might find if you don't come now, you don't have any choice but to stay in Barcelona for the foreseeable future.'

I could feel my breathing becoming fast and shallow. I realised she was right. 'Okay. I'll come home. Today, if I can.'

As soon as the call ended, I began scouring the flat for my belongings. I packed my things quickly. I thought about searching online for a flight to make sure I had a ticket guaranteed before I set off, but it felt better to just get to the airport. If I was there, I would feel I was already halfway home. I wouldn't feel as if I was truly in Barcelona any more then, not once I was in the strange no-man's-land of the departures lounge. And that way, if there was a cancellation, a no show, on any flight to the UK, I could be the first to take up the spare place. Then when I was at home, I could find out exactly what was going on. I could find out when John left and where he'd been headed. I could find out if the decorated red and white skull was still in my kitchen.

With all my clothes packed, I just needed to gather my papers – my money, the printed details of the route to the airport, my passport – from the drawer next to my bed. I slid open the drawer and lifted everything out and into my ruck-sack, but I realised my passport wasn't there. I took the drawer out of the cabinet and looked in the space where it had been. I pulled the whole cabinet out from the wall and checked behind it. But it was gone. I searched the whole room, which didn't take long now I'd tidied all my things away. The pass-port had completely disappeared.

Matt had been almost comedically well-mannered about not going into my room while I'd been staying. If I was inside and he wanted to speak to me, he'd hover in the doorway. When he'd provided me with clean towels, he placed them in a pile outside the closed door, rather than, as I would have thought would be more natural, going in and dropping them on my bed.

The only person who had been in that room apart from me since Sophie had left had been Luisa, the cleaning lady. I remembered one afternoon when I'd come home to find her merrily hoovering inside the wardrobe. She hadn't seemed fazed when I'd appeared. She'd just carried on with her work, picking up my sleeping T-shirt from where I'd left it on the end of the bed, folding it into a neat square and placing it under my pillow. I'd been embarrassed to have been standing there while she tidied up after me, but she'd seemed quite unconcerned. I had a feeling that if she found something somewhere she didn't think it belonged, she would have no qualms about taking it and putting it somewhere more suitable – a filing cabinet or document drawer. Matt seemed the type to have something sensible like that. I just needed to know where it was.

When his phone directed me once again to his voicemail, I decided to head down to his office in person. I wasn't comfortable with the idea of leaving with just a scrawled note as a goodbye anyway, especially not given what had happened between us the night before. If I went to see him in person, I could ask him about the passport and at the same time explain everything that had happened and why I needed to get home.

I followed the route I'd taken the day I'd gone to meet him for lunch, crossing the main square then weaving my way through the narrower streets. It was as my progress was impeded by a group of American tourists and I was looking around for an alternative route that something caught my eye. It was a flash of fabric with a distinctive fox print. It took me a moment to register where I recognised it from, but I remembered it was the pattern on a skirt that Sophie had bought from a shop near Matt's flat on our last day together. As I looked up at the woman, my first thought was that the baseball cap she had protecting her eyes from the sun was incongruous with the flowing feminine skirt, but then as the woman moved her head to look to her left, something far more surprising struck me.

That wasn't just Sophie's skirt. That was Sophie.

Chapter 35

She was on the other side of the throng of Americans I was trying to pass, and by the time I'd pushed my way through their rucksacks and shopping bags, she was gone.

I stopped at the junction of four roads and looked around me. Could I be sure it had been Sophie? Or, as the skirt had been the same, had my mind jumped to conclusions, twisted some other woman's features into the shape of her face? How much had I really seen, underneath that cap?

I took out my phone and dialled Sophie's number. I knew it was quite likely she'd be with a student at this time, but all I wanted to hear was the normal ringtone. The ringtone that showed she was in the UK, and not the long monotone tone that sounded when a phone was abroad. But the phone went straight to voicemail, with no ringing tone at all. I sent her a message:

Random question but you're not back in Barcelona are you? My head's all over the place but I swear I just saw someone who looked exactly like you.

As I waited for a reply, I stayed in the area, going up and down side streets, hoping for a glimpse of the woman in the fox print skirt. Hoping that if I saw her again, if I could get a proper look at her, I would see that she wasn't Sophie at all.

Twenty minutes passed and there was no reply from Sophie, nor was there any sight of the skirt.

I typed a message to Anya:

Do you know where Sophie is at the moment? Have you seen much of her since you got back from Spain?

I knew she might be put out to get something so abrupt when we hadn't spoken for so long, that she might be annoyed that there weren't any questions about how she was doing or news of how my extended holiday was going, but I'd just have to smooth that over later.

Luckily, if Anya was annoyed, it didn't preclude her from replying. Her message was cool but it did at least answer my question.

She's in Edinburgh as far as I know. So no, haven't seen her at all. She decided to go and visit her cousin at the last minute, so I left her at the airport and she flew straight there from Barcelona. Why?

I read the message twice trying to make sense of it. My first thought was that if Sophie was in Edinburgh then she couldn't be here in Barcelona, but then all Anya had said was that she'd left her at the airport. Sophie might have said she was going to make this impromptu trip to Edinburgh, but it was unlikely Anya had actually seen the plane take off. All Anya really knew was that Sophie hadn't got on the plane to London with her, which meant it was entirely possible that she had stayed exactly where she was in Barcelona, and that the woman I'd just seen was indeed her. But I still had no explanation for what she was doing there. Or why she had lied about it.

Chapter 36

I suddenly felt vulnerable, standing in the middle of the busy street, without knowing who was able to see me or what they might want. Was Sophie still nearby? Could she see me looking for her?

I ducked into a small dark café, headed to the back and took a seat in the corner. I re-read Anya's message. Sophie hadn't gone home with her. There had definitely been no mention of a visit to Scotland while we'd been together. She had never talked about a cousin at all. If Sophie had decided to stay on in Barcelona at the last minute, that *could* make sense – after all, it was exactly what I'd done myself – but why would she tell Anya this story about Scotland? And why would she pretend to me that she'd gone home exactly as planned?

The only reason I could think that Sophie would want to stay in Barcelona without me knowing was if she wanted to avoid me. If she'd announced her intention to extend her break, then the natural assumption would be that we would continue to spend time together. So perhaps the reason for her lie was that she didn't want to do that, that she just didn't like me, even. But that really wasn't the impression I'd got. In fact, the feeling I'd got was quite the opposite.

I took myself back over the journey of our short friendship.

There had been that look, that double take, when we'd first met that had unsettled me. Her explanation, that she'd recognised me because of my connection to Reuben, made sense. It wasn't unusual for people I didn't remember from home to remember me – a tragic death in the family tends to raise your profile in a small town – but still, I couldn't deny that my first moments with Sophie had been strange.

Over the week we'd been together, Sophie had stuck closely to me. She would always choose my company over Anya's, and over Matt's. She seemed to gravitate towards me, wanting to be where I was, to know what I was doing. I remembered how keen she'd been to share a room with me, not just in the flat in Torre Sonrisas but in Matt's flat too, even when he'd suggested I should be the one to sleep on my own.

She hadn't wanted me to stay behind at all. The nearest I'd seen her to angry was when I refused to entertain her concerns that Matt didn't really want me to stay, when she'd wanted me to come home, with her, but I'd insisted on staying.

And then I remembered something else: her reaction when I'd been hit by the skull. She'd been so upset, so emotional. I sensed Anya felt it was an overreaction at the time, and really, it was. It seemed irrational, given that I really wasn't seriously injured.

I thought about the Australian woman who had warned me that I was being watched. She'd said the hooded figure was a man but how could she have been sure, if the hood was up? Sophie was five foot nine at least, maybe even five ten. Could she have been mistaken for a man, from a distance, in the shadows?

Sophie freely admitted she was finding her new life lonely.

Had she seen me as a solution to that? I remembered that joke – what I'd assumed was a joke – that she'd made on the first day of our holiday, about how as we were so unused to living on our own, we should just move in together. Was that what she was hoping for? Was she so anchorless, so lost and sad in her new life, that she'd allowed herself to form some kind of attachment to me?

I took three deep breaths. I'd just told myself a persuasive story, but I was aware I could be cherry-picking the evidence that suited my narrative. What I needed was to go through it with someone else to get another perspective.

I sent Anya another message.

Can you call me? Now? It's important.

Her name appeared on my screen almost immediately.

'What's up?' she said. 'Where are you?' She still sounded cool, but anxious too.

'Anya, John's dead. I found out this morning.' Saying it out loud again made me start to cry, exactly as it had when I'd relayed the news to Sophie. 'He's dead, Anya. I can't even believe it.'

There was a pause. 'What? Lauren, what do you . . . ? Are you joking?'

'No. No, of course not. His mum phoned me. He was here, in Barcelona. He drowned.'

'What? *What?* How? Were you with him? Where are you now?

'No. I'm in a café. That's the whole thing. He was apparently coming to see me, but didn't find me or changed his mind or something. Then he got drunk and somehow got in the water and . . . I can't believe it. I can't make my brain accept the information as true. Everything feels so strange, like it's part of a big disgusting joke to mess me up. And anyway, I'd just got the news, I was just on my way to see Matt to tell him and then I thought I saw Sophie. And that makes no sense either so—'

'Sophie?' Anya said. 'What, *Sophie* Sophie?'

I hiccupped. 'Yeah. I think so. I'm sure of it. But I don't get it. I only spoke to her a few hours ago and she didn't mention she was here. Why would she pretend? I feel like something's going on. What you said in your message, about her not flying back with you. What did she say, about this cousin?'

'She was strange as soon as we left the flat. I was waiting in the taxi for ages for her, so I had to go back to the flat to get her, and at the top of the stairs, I saw her talking to Matt. I couldn't hear what they were saying, but they both looked kind of grumpy, I thought. Which seemed weird seeing as it should have been more of a smiley bye-thanks-for-having-us type moment.

I asked her if everything was okay and she said it was fine, but she still seemed really preoccupied in the taxi, all the way to the airport. Then, as soon as we got there, she said she'd had this message from a cousin in Edinburgh saying her aunt was ill, and she had to go to see her. She said there was a flight she could jump on if she hurried and I barely had a chance to ask her anything about it before she scuttled off.'

'So do you think she could have stayed? That the thing about Edinburgh was a lie?'

Anya paused. 'Well, yeah, I suppose in theory it could have been. But why would she do that?'

I took a deep breath. 'Okay so I know how this might sound, but please just go with it for a moment.'

'I'm listening.'

'Do you think she might have stayed . . . for me?'

'In what way?'

I took Anya through the series of events, looks, comments, everything that Sophie had done since I'd known her that could be pieced together to paint a picture of a woman with a fixation. I was fully prepared for Anya to make a scathing comment, to laugh and suggest that the only person in this world obsessed with me was me. But she didn't. She said, 'Jesus. I think you could be right.'

'Really?'

'You know, I thought there was something a bit strange going on with her from early on, because – I didn't properly explain this because I didn't want to put you off her – but she really pushed to come away with us. She didn't directly ask, but the hints she was dropping were hard to avoid. I sort of dodged the comments at first, because it was meant to be your trip, to get over John, so I didn't think it was appropriate for me to invite my new friend along. But she kept angling, kept pushing. And I just thought she was lonely and you two seemed to get on okay when you met, so I thought, why not? Maybe it would be good for all of us.'

'I just thought you'd invited her without thinking it through and then you couldn't back out of it.'

'No,' Anya said. 'Not at all. I thought about it loads. I just didn't want you to think it was a big deal. And before we came away, she asked loads of questions about you. I thought she was just one of those types who's interested in other people, but when I think about it, it was a bit intense. You want to know the one topic she kept coming back to?'

'What?'

'John. She kept asking about my impressions of your rela- tionship, like if I thought you guys had been solid before the break-up or if he'd been bad news all along. And then it was like she'd realise she'd been grilling me a bit because she'd

211

sort of laugh it off, change the subject. But I definitely got the feeling she was keen for you not to be with him any more.'

'And now John's dead,' I said quietly.

'And now John's dead,' Anya repeated.

We were quiet. I could hear Anya breathing and the sound of her office in the background. 'Definitely just come home now, I think,' she said eventually. 'Just come home.'

'Yeah,' I said. 'I will. I am.'

'Good.'

'You know, I thought you were angry with me,' I said. 'The whole holiday. You were different. Distant.'

'Yeah,' Anya said quietly. 'I'm sorry.'

I didn't say anything. I wanted to give her space in case she wanted to add anything else.

'I just felt like I was losing you,' she said eventually. 'To her.'

'Why would you think that?'

'You two had your secret conversations right from the start. I realised that when we were picking the apartment and you called her and told her all that stuff about me always pressurising you into spending money.'

'What? She said *what*?'

'She said . . . I can't remember her exact words. But something about how you always thought I was flashing my cash around.'

'What? Anya, I never said that. Never!'

'Well, maybe she was paraphrasing.'

'There was nothing to paraphrase. I've never had a single conversation about money with Sophie. I didn't speak to her at all when we were choosing the flat. You wanted the expensive one, then you changed your mind. That was it. That was all I saw.'

There was a pause. 'Really? But you rang her and—'

'I didn't! It didn't happen, Anya. It just didn't.'

Another pause. 'Oh.'

'Is this why you've been weird with me?'

She sighed. 'I just thought . . . I thought that what it came down to was that you preferred her, and her cheerfulness and her optimism. That you liked that more than . . . my moods. My swearing. But I didn't think I could really say anything out loud. It was too hard to explain.'

'Okay. I get it. I think.'

'Where are you now?' Anya said.

'In a café. Hiding. I was getting ready to come home, but then I couldn't find my passport. I was going to ask Matt if he'd seen it but then I saw Sophie. And now I'm thinking . . . . does she have it? Could she have taken it before you two left Matt's place?'

Anya sighed. 'I have no idea why she'd do that. But who knows what she's thinking.'

30 July 2005

Sophie

Sophie scrubbed furiously at the glass on the oven door, her hands raw from the hot water and the chemicals. The little house she'd been renting for the last year in Hoyle hadn't been pristine when she'd moved in – far from it, actually – but she was compelled to leave it so before she went. She knew it was silly, she knew she was distracting herself from the real issues. She knew that anyone with even the most basic interest in psychoanalysis could tell you what that was all about: she was leaving a mess behind her. Lots of great big tangled mistakes that she couldn't fix, she couldn't tidy and put right, so to make herself feel better about it, here she was, channelling all her energy into cleaning up a house to please a landlord she'd never meet.

She'd written a formal letter to the head of Hoyle Boys' School explaining her decision. It was full of bland sentiments about being grateful for the opportunity but the time being right to move on. He was a pleasant enough man, but she'd sensed even in her interview that he'd been baffled by her. She probably wouldn't have been his first choice but he was under pressure from the Head of English who was keen to shake things up, to try to get some new – young – blood into the school. He'd probably be relieved to see her resign so soon. 'Ah well,' he'd tell the rest of the staff. 'I did think this wasn't really the place for that kind of teacher. Those kinds of methods. Good luck to her, I'm sure.'

She'd already arranged a new house. A little flat in a village fifteen miles outside of Sheffield. She knew the area vaguely from her university days, but really it was just about choosing anywhere that put distance between herself and the school, herself and Hoyle.

She hadn't applied for any new posts in the area's schools yet and she wasn't sure she would. She'd always thought she'd be a good teacher, and in some ways she was – she knew how to inspire, how to explain concepts clearly. But she felt uncomfortable taking on a position of authority, accepting that she was the one in charge. She didn't feel she had any right to be, that she had any more knowledge or understanding of the world than anyone else. And that had meant the boys hadn't always truly respected her role in the classroom. Some of them manifested this in disobedience, simply ignoring her, or making fun of her. She shuddered to imagine what the other members of staff would have made of it, if they'd seen what she let some of them get away with. Others seemed to like her – she was able to reach the boys who were left cold by traditional methods, by formality and structure – but she knew that very few of them considered her a 'proper' teacher.

She knew that at the heart of all her problems was her tendency to let her feelings lead the way. She'd drifted her way through that year, following her emotions, acting instinctively, when really what she should have done was taken a step back a good many months earlier and intellectualised things, thought everything through rationally and reined herself in. That, she was resolute, was what she would do from now on. She would be measured. She would assess every new relationship, every interaction, carefully and think through the likely progression of events and set the course herself.

She would never leave herself at the mercy of her heart – her passions – again.

Chapter 37

The waiter cleared my empty glass away so I ordered another drink to buy myself a little longer in the café. It felt better, for the time being, to stay there, tucked away in the corner, with a clear view of anyone who might come in and out until I knew exactly what the situation was. And exactly what I was going to do about it.

As the waiter set my refilled glass down in front of me, I realised there *was* something I could do – something that would help me solve a mystery that had been bothering me for weeks, although at the same time would raise a whole new set of questions.

I took my phone out of my pocket and opened Facebook. I typed 'Sean M' into the search bar and scrolled down the results to find the profile illustrated by the figure on the beach that I'd first seen when John had come to my flat to show me the message he'd received. I'd visited the profile before, of course, that night after John had left and several times in the day afterwards, but I'd never managed to find out anything at all about the man behind it, or why he'd claim we'd met.

I opened the profile again now, and was faced with the same limited information I'd seen before: the photo, the name, the work – 'self-employed' – but nothing more. I knew that the only way to unlock any more of the profile was to send a friend request to Sean M, and for him to accept it. But I'd been reluctant to do that and have him – whoever he was – realise he had my attention. Now, though, I had enough information to be able to try a new tactic.

I logged out of Facebook altogether and loaded a fresh log-in screen. I clicked on the 'Forgotten account?' link and was taken to a page that asked me to enter my email address or phone number to find my account. I opened my contact list, scrolled down to Sophie's number and copy-and-pasted it into the search bar. I hit the search button and waited. The results returned one matching account. I was deflated, although hardly surprised, that that account belonged to Sophie Rickson.

I paused for a moment, my thumb hovering over the screen as I thought about what to do next. I opened my inbox, found the email Sophie had sent me back in April with the details of our flights and pasted her email address into the search field. Once again I pressed the search button and waited to see which account – if any – had been set up via that address. A few moments later, I had the answer I had been looking for, but hadn't truly been expecting.

Unless somewhere along the line there had been some kind of unfathomable administrative confusion, Sophie was Sean M.

Chapter 38

I stood up. I had everything I needed. I was sure now that I wasn't letting my thoughts get ahead of themselves, that there wasn't some obvious innocent explanation that I was overlooking.

I still didn't know exactly what was going on but I did know two things for certain: that Sophie had taken active steps to keep John and me apart, and that John was dead. I also knew that she'd lied to both Anya and me repeatedly – about where she was and about things I'd said. I found it hard to accept that Sophie – gentle, cheerful, innocent Sophie – was someone so different to who I'd thought. I wanted to talk to her, to ask her directly what was going on and what she was trying to achieve, but I knew that I had to be careful.

My plan was this: to continue on my way to speak to Matt, to explain everything that had happened to him, then for us to approach Sophie together, somewhere public, where we could be fair and clear, firm and reasonable.

I made my way quickly to the GigCity office, keeping my head down, but taking frequent furtive glances around me in case I encountered Sophie again. I found Matt in the lobby of the building, signing an electronic handset held out by a parcel courier.

'Oh, hey Lauren!' He smiled when he saw me and approached the glass doors to meet me. 'What brings you here?'

'Sorry, I tried to call.'

His smile dropped as he registered my expression. 'I've been in a meeting. What's wrong?'

I looked around the lobby. The woman on reception was talking quickly to a man in overalls but there was no one else around. 'I don't know. It's hard to . . .' I took a breath and lowered my voice 'I feel like there's something going on. John's mum called me this morning. John's *dead*, Matt.'

His eyes widened. 'What? Your ex, John?'

I nodded. 'And Sophie's here.'

He frowned, confused now. 'Sophie? Where?' He looked over my shoulder to the street outside.

'I don't know, exactly. Just here in Barcelona. She never went home. She lied.'

'What? Why? How do you know?'

'I saw her.'

Matt looked carefully at my face for a moment, then he put his hand on my arm and spoke in a low voice. 'Go up to the third floor. Meeting Room 4 will be right in front of you as you get out the lift. Go and wait for me in there. I'll be two minutes while I cancel something.'

As I pressed the button for the third floor and watched the doors slide shut, I felt myself calm a little. I'd been starting to feel a kind of paranoia set in, an unsettling sense that everyone but me was part of some grand plan, a practical joke, the details of which I wasn't privy to, but I felt confident that in a few minutes Matt would point out some obvious explanation that my shock over John had led me to overlook.

As promised, a few minutes later, Matt came to join me in

the windowless air-conditioned meeting room he'd directed me to. There was a water cooler bubbling gently in the corner.

'Right,' he said, shutting the door behind him and taking a seat opposite me. 'I'm all yours. Tell me exactly what's happened.'

I recounted everything as accurately as I could; starting with the conversation with Valerie Marshall and working backwards, covering the last message John had sent me when I'd reminded him I was in Barcelona, the calls I hadn't answered and the visit to my flat where he'd shown me the strange message from 'Sean M'. This point brought me on to Sophie, how I'd discovered she'd been the one behind that message, the suspicions Anya had had about her from the start, and now, strangest of all, the sighting of her here in Barcelona, when she'd claimed to be elsewhere.

Matt blinked slowly. 'I don't understand,' he said. 'Why would she . . . ?'

'I've had this thought.' I said. 'A . . . theory. What if it's because of this . . . *thing* she has for me. This obsession, I suppose you'd call it. I don't think it's sexual, I didn't get that feeling from her. But just that she was looking for an answer to her loneliness and . . .' I trailed off.

Matt was still looking at me, his expression concerned but calm. He picked up a pen and clicked the button at the end a few times. Then he put it down and put his hands palms-down on the table. 'Okay, so, that – the message to John – I don't get that. You're right. I'm not sure what that was about. Maybe she genuinely thought he was bad for you? I don't know. But the rest of it, the reason she's lied, the reason she's still here, that she hasn't gone home . . . I think you're nearly right, about the obsession. But . . .' He narrowed his eyes, pulling a face that suggested he was uncomfortable somehow. 'I don't honestly think it's you she has the thing for. The obsession, or whatever we want to call it. Because I've suspected this for a while. Long before you got out here, actually.' He looked around the room then back at me. 'I think . . . what I think is more likely . . . is that it's more about me.'

Chapter 39

I blinked. 'What's about you? You mean, you think she's into *you*?'

He picked up the pen and started clicking it again. 'Yeah.' He sighed. 'Yeah, I think so. You see, there was this thing that happened, and we never really talked about it afterwards, but the first time I met Sophie – the first time when we met again that is, not when she was a teacher at my school – she sort of . . . made a move on me.'

I frowned, trying to work out where on the timeline of Sophie's life we were. 'Wasn't she married then? What about Caleb?'

Matt nodded. 'Yeah, she was. But I got the feeling she was unhappy. Or maybe just bored. She basically said a few things that made it clear she would like to be more than just friends. With me.'

'But nothing happened?'

Matt shook his head. 'No, I sort of laughed it off. At that point, I was still a bit weirded out by hanging out with her in a social way. You know, she was still just Miss Rickson from school. I mean, I got over that and we genuinely became friends, but . . . you know. Still wasn't interested in *kissing* Miss Rickson from school. Bit much.' He smiled awkwardly.

I tried to shuffle this new information into the picture of Sophie I'd spent the morning building up. 'But you think . . . what? She still hoped for something?'

Matt winced. 'Yeah. I think she did. Obviously I didn't see her in person much because of the distance but she would send weird messages about missing me in the middle of the night. And she was always trying to get an invite over here. At first I thought maybe she just wanted a free holiday, but then she did always talk about how nice it would be to stay in my flat particularly. How she wanted to go to specific restaurants *with me.*'

I remembered how keen Sophie had been when we'd been planning the holiday that we stay in Matt's flat.

'So why did you invite her – all of us – to stay with you? Surely it would've been better to keep your distance? If you were worried about giving her the wrong idea?'

'I guess I just didn't think it was that big a deal. I figured that even if she did have . . . feelings, or whatever, I could just ignore it. Play dumb. But as soon as you guys came to my place, I realised something wasn't quite right with her,' he went on. 'Just little things, but lots of them. For instance, remember when you were going to go out to look for a food shop just after you all arrived? I was going to come with you, give you a hand?'

I nodded. I remembered. 'She said she'd come. She sort of, jumped in with the suggestion, didn't she?' I sighed. 'She just wanted to stop us being alone together. Me and you?'

Matt nodded. 'I think so.'

'The day they left, Anya said she thought you and Sophie were arguing, while she was waiting in the taxi. What were you talking about?'

224

Matt closed his eyes briefly. 'Yeah. That was awkward. She was making a kind of last-minute speech. Telling me I didn't know what I was missing. And I got angry with her. I didn't mean to be cruel, but I was just so annoyed that she'd made everything so weird between us, when she could have just left it.'

I nodded slowly. 'Right. I see.' I felt calmer now things were starting to slot into place, now that I'd had the chance to talk things through rather than having all the disjointed, disquieting pieces of information floating around anchorless inside my own head.

Matt looked at his watch. 'Look, give me fifteen minutes to send a few emails and I can knock off here. Then we can go back to the flat and . . . and get our heads together. Seems like you've had a hell of a morning.' He looked at me carefully. 'I'm so sorry about John, Lauren.'

I nodded and looked down. 'I honestly can't believe it. I mean, he was . . . troubled, but . . .' I shook my head. I didn't know what I wanted to say.

Matt reached forward and squeezed my hand, then he stood up and turned for the door.

Suddenly I remembered why I'd been heading to Matt's office in the first place. 'I couldn't find my passport this morning. Do you know where it is? Do you think Luisa might have moved it?'

Matt pushed out his bottom lip. 'I don't see why she would, but it's possible I suppose. It must be in the flat somewhere, even if she did. She'll only have put it somewhere tidy. I'll help you look when we're back. Sit tight here for a minute.'

Ten minutes later, Matt returned, his leather record bag slung over his shoulder. 'Ready?'

As we made our way down the stairs to the lobby he said, 'I've just been on the phone to a friend of a friend. He works

225

for the police, just in the back office. I explained what we knew about John and he spoke to a few people and it looks like he went swimming in the sea, got out of his depth and . . .' Matt shrugged and looked down sadly. 'It was as simple and as horrible as that. It happens a lot, apparently. One a week, at least. Tricky undercurrents. Always catching people out. They were particularly strong on Monday apparently.'

I swallowed and nodded. 'Okay. Thanks for . . . finding out.'

Matt reached down and squeezed my hand. 'You didn't ask him to come over here. You didn't tell him to go in the sea. There was nothing you could have done.'

'I know.' I said quietly. 'I know.'

But as we made our way across the square to the apartment, something occurred to me. I stopped and looked at Matt. 'Monday? That was when he died? The day before yesterday?'

Matt took his sunglasses off and cleaned them on the bottom of his T-shirt before replacing them. 'Yeah. That's what my mate said. Why? Is that not what his mum thought?'

I shook my head and carried on walking. 'No. I don't know. She didn't say, specifically. I just thought it must have just happened. Today. Or yesterday, at least.'

Matt shrugged 'I guess it took some time to work out who he was. Who to contact.'

'Yeah.' I sighed. 'I guess.'

I still had my doubts about what the Australian woman had said to me the day before but one thing was clear: if there had been someone watching me from the shadows, there was no way it could have been John.

Chapter 40

When we got back to the flat, I made Matt check the cabinet where I'd been keeping my passport to make sure that I hadn't missed something obvious, and that it hadn't been sitting right in front of me the whole time, but it definitely wasn't there.

'I'd be very surprised if Luisa had moved it far,' he said, running his hand down the back of the unit. 'She normally puts things back where she finds them. But I'll ask her.'

He took out his phone but after a short conversation in Spanish that I couldn't follow, he reported that Luisa hadn't seen the passport, and hadn't looked in the drawer next to my bed at all. Together we scoured the rest of the flat, pulling the cushions off the sofas, taking drawers out of desks and peeling back rugs, but it was nowhere to be found.

Matt stood in the middle of the lounge, his hands in the back pockets of his shorts. 'Weird,' he said, shaking his head. 'But don't worry. If it really doesn't turn up, I can help you sort out a new one. The embassy basically prints them on demand these days with all the drunk stag parties losing everything they came out here with.'

'Really?' I said hopefully. It made me feel uneasy, knowing that going straight to the airport and getting on the first plane I could wasn't an option, for the time being at least. I knew I would feel a lot more secure once I had that passport back in my possession.

'Yeah, absolutely.' He paused. 'So, you still want to go, then? Because . . . sorry, I don't know how to put this without sounding harsh but . . . you going home now isn't going to do John, or his mum, any good. You can't do anything now. To change things.'

I thought for a moment, but then I nodded. 'I know. But I think I do need to go back. I think it's time for me to be at home.'

Matt nodded sadly. 'Okay. Of course. I get it. But let me cook something decent for you tonight at least? A goodbye meal?'

I smiled. 'That'd be nice. Thank you.'

That afternoon, I lay on my usual lounger on the corner of the terrace, the shadow of the building protecting me from the hot summer sun. Every so often Matt would ask if I wanted water or sunscreen or if I was okay and every time I would reassure him that I was fine, but my thoughts were bouncing frantically back and forth between Sophie and John. What had John been planning to do when he found me? What had he been thinking when he'd got in the water? Had he known he was taking a risk? Had he cared what had happened to him? Had Sophie seen John before he died? Where was she right now? Had she been watching me? And, if so, why? Was it about Matt?

I sat up suddenly, and Matt looked at me questioningly.

'All that stuff at the flat, at Torre Sonrisas – the skull, the break-in – do you think it was her? Sophie? Did she make it all happen, so we'd have to call you? So you'd have to let us stay with you?'

Matt looked at me for a moment and I thought he was going to reassure me that that was highly unlikely, but instead he just said, 'Yeah. I'd had that thought too. To be honest, right from when she first messaged me, told me about the break-in, I sort of thought . . . I thought how I wasn't surprised that she'd found an excuse to call me as soon as you all got out here. And now, with her still being here . . . I mean, I wasn't going to say anything to give you anything else to worry about but just now, I've been sitting here thinking, did she do it all? Did she make it happen so I had to rescue you all?'

I shook my head and stared blankly at the swimming pool. 'Jesus. *Jesus*. How much must you want something to do all that?'

Matt shrugged.

'Do you know what I feel most of all?' I turned to look at him. 'I'm just so sad. I really thought we'd shared a connection. That she got me. That we could be friends for life. I know that sounds silly – like something a kid would say – but . . .' I shook my head. 'It's hard to make new friends, as an adult, don't you find? And I thought maybe she would be one.'

Matt nodded and looked at me. 'Yeah. But . . . I don't know.' He sighed. 'I don't think she's all bad. She's just . . .' He looked out over the rooftops. ' . . . not well, I guess? Just not well.'

That evening, Matt cooked me the most extravagant Indian banquet I'd ever seen, preparing everything from scratch – grinding up spices in a huge marble pestle and mortar and folding the delicate samosa parcels one by one and laying them out on a board. I was in no mood for the festive, celebratory meal Matt seemed to be planning, it felt wrong to be carrying on as normal given the events of the day, but I knew cooking was just Matt's way of trying to look after me and I was grateful for that. He was adamant I shouldn't do anything to help, so I sat at the kitchen table and talked to him while he worked.

'What are you going to do about her?' I asked. 'About Sophie?'

He looked up, surprised. 'Do? In what way?'

'I mean, she's out there,' I gestured to the window. 'Thinking about you. Trying to . . . what is she trying to do?'

Matt carried a pan over to the sink. He shrugged. 'I don't know. I don't know that she's trying to *do* anything, really. I suppose she might come and try and see me at some point, but probably not while you're still here.'

I looked at him. 'Would it be better if I stayed, you mean?'

He chuckled. 'To protect me? I think I'll be all right.' He paused while he tasted a sauce and put the teaspoon down on the side. 'Not that it wouldn't be better if you stayed, obviously.'

I didn't say anything else and Matt busied himself making the final preparations of the meal. When he'd laid it all out, conversation for a while was dominated by where he'd sourced the ingredients and where he'd found the recipes. I asked the right questions and made appropriate noises of approval as Matt spoke, but my mind was elsewhere.

Where was John's body? What had they done with his things? He must have had some luggage with him, somewhere. He never went anywhere without his laptop. Would they send that back to Valerie too? What would she do with it? Would anyone ever read any of the stories he worked so hard on now or would the laptop just be stashed in a cupboard or a loft? When would his funeral be? Who would come? Should I speak? Should I write something about what he'd meant to me? What was that exactly? What could I possibly say?

When we'd finished eating, we went out to the terrace. Although I'd started the day feeling like I never wanted to look at alcohol again, especially not in Matt's presence after everything that had happened, I'd been glad when Matt had placed the wine bottle and the corkscrew on the table. Now, I was three glasses in and feeling sleepy but the tight feeling across my forehead that had been there since Valerie's phone call was starting to ease. As we stood side by side, leaning against the railings, it was easy to see how I'd misread the signs before.

As we gazed in silence down at the busy streets below, I just couldn't get my head around the fact that John was gone. Despite his faults, he'd been, until recently, the one person I spoke to every day. Without him existing, knowing he was no longer out there, I felt adrift. I wanted something – someone – to hold on to.

There was a long time when neither Matt nor I said anything at all. We just drank our wine and looked down at the city and listened to the sound of a steel band playing a calypso version of 'Sweet Caroline' in the square.

When the song finished, he turned to look at me. 'I did mean it. It would be better if you stayed.'

There was something intense about the way he was looking at me and I had a desire to break the tension.

I grinned. 'To protect you from Sophie?'

He just smiled and looked down. 'No,' he said quietly. 'Not really.'

And then he lifted his head up again, looked very carefully into my eyes, and leant down to kiss me.

20 January 2005

Matt

Matt had already been to Reuben's place twice that week.
On Monday, he'd gone over to borrow a music stand. He didn't
need it; he already had two but he fed Reuben some line
about the height adjuster being rusted and Reuben had
seemed happy to hand over his. It worked well as a strategy,
he'd realised, borrowing things, as it set up the opportunity
for a subsequent visit to return them. It had to be bulky items
he took, though, not things that could easily be passed back
and forth in school. It had to be the kind of thing you had no
choice but to collect in person from the house.

On Wednesday, he'd made an unplanned visit to see if
Reuben had a bike pump he could borrow. He'd told Reuben
it was unplanned, anyway – of course, his visits were always
planned. Reuben hadn't, but that didn't matter. While he'd
been there, Matt had taken the precaution of tucking his
library card down the side of the bookshelf in the hall on

his way out, thus setting up the perfect excuse for a house call today – Friday.

Matt hadn't seen Lauren on any of his previous visits that week. On the Monday she hadn't seemed to be home at all and on Wednesday her bedroom door had been firmly closed, leaving no opportunity for interaction. Today, though, he felt more hopeful. Matt knew that Lauren stayed late at school on a Friday to work on her art coursework, so if he timed his visit right, he would be there shortly after she got in, when she would be sitting in the lounge still in her school uniform watching the late afternoon quiz shows, twisting her hair around her fingers, her feet on the arm of the sofa.

'Oh, all right?' Reuben said when he opened the door.

Matt thought he detected a hint of irritation. He knew a third visit in one week was pushing it. He'd have to back off for the next couple of weeks if he didn't want to look strange.

'Yeah, I think I left my library card here the other day. You seen it?'

Reuben frowned. 'Your library card? No? Where?' He was still standing in the doorway, not showing any signs of inviting him in.

Matt shrugged. 'Not sure. Must have dropped it. Can I have a look for it?'

Reuben made a face and Matt thought he might tell him to get lost, but in the end he just held the door open and said, 'Okay. Whatever.' Then he turned and headed back up the stairs leaving Matt alone in the hall.

Matt got the sense that Reuben thought he was clingy, that Reuben thought Matt was keen for the two of them to be better friends than they were. This annoyed Matt as, really, he had very little interest in Reuben at all. The kid was kind of stuck up, Matt thought. Pretentious. If it hadn't been for

233

Lauren he would barely have bothered speaking to him at all outside orchestra practice.

Left alone in the hallway, Matt took a few books from the shelf and flicked through them, made a show of shaking them a few times as if searching for the misplaced card. He could hear the television from the lounge. The door was slightly ajar and through the gap he could see Lauren, exactly where he'd hoped she'd be; stretched out on the sofa in her school uniform.

He pushed the door open gently and stood behind her watching the television. The format of the show seemed to be that contestants had to give as many answers that fitted the category specified by the host before the on-screen timer ran out.

'Oasis singles that hit number one! Go go go!' the host shouted.

'Uh . . . "Don't Look Back in Anger"?' the woman on the television said, looking anxiously at the clock. ' "Wonderwall"!'

The host shook his head. 'Never made it to number one, I'm afraid. Twenty seconds left on the clock.'

'"She's Electric",' Matt said, making Lauren jump.

She looked at him and quickly set her face back to neutral. 'That was never a number one. Was it even a single?'

'Number one in Germany,' Matt said. 'And Indonesia.'

He was making it up. It almost certainly wasn't true. But that didn't matter. Lauren wouldn't know that.

Lauren went back to looking at the TV screen. 'Reuben's in his room.'

'Yeah. I saw him. Just came to pick something up.'

She didn't reply.

'You all right, anyway?' he ventured. He waited nervously for the answer. The inquiry was innocuous enough, but he rarely spoke directly to Lauren. He'd never asked her anything about herself before. It felt like a big step.

She looked at him, a slight furrow between her eyebrows. 'Yeah. Fine. You?'

He nodded and pushed his hands into his pockets. 'Yep. Yeah fine.'

She didn't show any signs of continuing the conversation and he didn't want to push things. He'd done enough. Tiny, careful steps were what was called for.

'See you later, then,' he said, his hand on the door handle.

'Yeah,' Lauren said flatly.

As Matt made his way down the road, his spirits lifted by his conversation with Lauren, he realised he'd left his library card where he'd hidden it on his previous visit, tucked between the recipe books on the fourth shelf down in the Henry hallway. Never mind, he told himself. Maybe that was just as well. Maybe if he was really lucky, Lauren might find it, might bring it to him, come and find him on the field or outside the school gates to return it and they could have a short conversation. He could look into her eyes as if seeing something no one had ever seen before, make her feel that he understood her in a way no one else ever had. He'd been practising that look, in the mirror in the bathroom. He was hoping he'd get to try it out on her soon.

But there was no rush. Lauren Henry was perfect for him. He knew that. He more than knew it, he felt it on an instinctual level. He just had to wait till she felt it too.

Chapter 41

The next morning, it took me a few moments to work out where I was. My first thought was that I had spent the night with John. As I came round, the truth came to me in small bursts – I hadn't slept next to John. I had slept next to someone else. I would never sleep next to John again. John would never sleep anywhere again. I felt a wave of nausea and swallowed hard. I rolled onto my back and stared up at the ceiling, forcing myself to take deep breaths.

Matt's bedroom had the same layout as his spare room, the one I'd been staying in, but everything was reversed, with the door on the left of the bed instead of the right. There were different belongings scattered on the bedside table too – a small foldable alarm clock, a metal pot with three pens in it. I was alone; Matt's side of the bed was empty.

I got up, retrieved the dress I'd been wearing the night before from the chair in the corner of the room and pulled it roughly over my head. I guessed Matt must have gone to work and I felt both silly and slightly indignant at the thought. It made me feel like a one-night stand, a cheap evening's entertainment that he didn't want to let interrupt his usual routine. But when I went out into the kitchen, he was standing by the kettle in his boxers. Despite the shared living arrangement, we'd been quite formal and respectful of each other's privacy up until now, so I was used to seeing him fully dressed by the time I got up.

He turned round to look at me, his hands pushed into his armpits. His red hair sticking up at all angles.

'Morning.' He grinned slightly sheepishly.

'Hello.' I found that I felt shy too.

'Just making some coffee,' he said. 'Then we can . . .' He looked around him and shrugged. 'We can do whatever you want. What would you like to do today?'

'Don't you have work?'

'I can pull a sickie. Can you?'

I smiled. 'I suppose. I need to sort out my passport, though.'

His smile faded but he nodded. 'Yes. Of course. I'll look up the details for the UK embassy after breakfast.'

We took our coffee out onto the terrace where the sun was already beating down though it wasn't yet nine.

'You still plan to head home, then?' Matt said. 'As soon as possible?'

I thought about this. 'I'd like to get my passport sorted out, definitely. So that I know I can go home if and when I need to. But . . . I suppose there's no immediate rush? Is there?'

He smiled. 'No rush at all from my point of view. Absolutely no rush at all.'

'What about Sophie, though?' I said.

'How do you mean?'

'I don't know exactly. I just feel like, if she's stayed out here to be close to you to you or whatever it is, then she's not going to be happy if she realises that we're . . . that there's something . . . that we're spending more time together.'

Matt shrugged. 'Then I guess she'll have to be not happy.'

237

I looked down. As well as feeling unsettled by Sophie's presence, the overwhelming feeling I had about it all was still pity. I wondered if Matt's version of how things were between them had been one hundred per cent accurate. I didn't doubt that it was the truth of how he saw the situation, but I wondered if somewhere along the line, he'd done or said something to give Sophie false hope. To make her feel there was some kind of potential there.

Matt reached out and took my hand. 'Maybe it will be a good thing if she realises I've got someone else. Maybe that will drive the message home. Wake her up a bit.'

'Yeah,' I said. 'Maybe. I guess.'

Matt went inside and came back out with a plate of sliced mangos. He set them down on the low table between our loungers and we talked about what we were going to do with our illicit day off work. We planned to spend the morning by the pool, then later on for Matt to take me to a rooftop bar he knew where the cocktails were good.

By eleven, though, we were back in bed.

Matt lay on his side, his left hand propping up his head and his right hand resting on my stomach. 'What's up?'

'Oh. Nothing. How do you mean?'

'You're . . . thoughtful. John?'

I sighed. 'I just can't believe it. Can't *believe* it. I didn't think I ever wanted to see him again. I was angry with him. But I didn't want . . . want *that*.'

'Yeah,' said Matt quietly. 'It will take some getting used to. It always seems surreal at first, when someone's gone. But it makes sense eventually. Sort of. In time.'

I nodded. I knew he was probably right in theory, but I couldn't truly imagine ever getting used to this new reality.

'You keep staring at me,' I grinned to lighten the mood. I knew I wouldn't be able to put John out of my mind that easily, but I wanted to give Matt the impression that I had. He didn't know John. I didn't want him to have to pretend to be sorrier about it all than he was. It was something I wanted to process slowly, on my own.

He smiled back. 'I know. I can't help it.'

'Plonker.'

It was nice, I remembered, having someone like you. Properly like you. John had been like that, for a while, before he realised how much I annoyed him. Before the complaints and criticisms had started creeping in.

I looked back at Matt's sleepy smile wondering what I felt in return. It wasn't my style to fall head over heels. All my relationships had been more slow burn – on my side anyway. I'd always been cautious. I read something about it once – that when you've lost someone when you're younger, you don't like people as quickly as other people do. You're more careful. You're protecting yourself from the hurt of loss by not getting too attached. I'd told Anya about the theory once, when we were at university and she was nagging me to reply to the messages of a boy who'd been asking to take me out. She'd sighed. 'Yeah, maybe there's something in that. *Or* maybe you're just fussy.'

'So what if I am!' I'd laughed. 'Not sure I want to go through my life being *un*fussy, do I? Taking anyone who comes along?'

She'd just shrugged and let it go, but since John I was wondering if she'd been right. If I waited for a full-force, smack-you-in-the-face, can't eat, can't sleep crush to come along, I might be waiting a long time. I realised I needed to be a bit more pragmatic about the whole thing. Matt was a nice man. We got on. He was kind and friendly and had lots of very useful skills. And most importantly, he liked me. I knew that this particular set of variables didn't come along together very often, and if I turned my back on them out of respect for John's memory, they might never come along again. That happened, didn't it? More often than you'd think. Some people just never found someone. And although I was afraid of what kind of person it made me, to have moved on with another man so soon after's John's death, I was more afraid of being alone.

Matt turned over onto his back and put his hands behind his head. 'Do you remember when we saw each other on the high street, in Hoyle that Christmas? Must have been 2011, 2012?'

'Yeah. You were so awkward! Looked like I was the last person you wanted to see!'

He turned his head to look at me. 'What? No way! Do you know how long I'd been hanging around hoping to bump into you? Couldn't believe it when you finally turned up, just walking along with all your rolls of wrapping paper. And then I managed to ask you for a drink and you turned me down flat! It was gutting!'

'Really? You actually wanted to go for a drink? I just thought you were making conversation!'

'I wanted to so badly!' He set his face into a mock pout. I laughed and kissed him and he pulled me on top of him.

There was a knock on the door to the flat. Matt groaned and pulled his arm up to look at his watch. 'Great timing.'

'Who is it?'

'Gavin, I think, the pool guy. He said he'd drop round to fix the filter this week. Can you let him in? He's mates with people from work and I don't want him knowing I'm bunking off.'

I climbed out of bed and pulled on my dress. 'Aren't you the boss? Don't you make the rules?'

Matt grinned. 'Sure. But I've got to lead by example,

haven't I? Don't want everyone to start phoning in sick so they can lie in bed all day with pretty ladies.'

I smiled in spite of myself.

'Just show him straight through to the terrace,' Matt said. 'He knows what he's doing.'

I checked my hair in the mirror in the hallway and smoothed down my dress, then crossed the kitchen, wondering if it might make Gavin smirk to find a dishevelled woman with bed hair roaming around Matt's flat.

But as I undid the latch and pulled open the door, standing in front of me, still wearing the fox print skirt, was Sophie.

Chapter 42

'Hey!' she beamed. 'Surprise!'

Before I had a chance to say anything at all, she pulled me into a hug. When she let me go, I stood upright, looking at her.

'Sophie.' I looked behind me but the door to Matt's bedroom was shut. So much had happened since I'd last seen her – last officially seen her that is, when she'd left for the airport with Anya – that I wasn't sure what to say, or even what tone to adopt.

Sophie had no idea that I'd seen her the day before or that I knew about her lies. She had no knowledge of the analysis and speculation that Matt and I had carried out as we compared notes and tried to get to the bottom of her bizarre behaviour. Now she was there, standing in front me, seemingly believing we were still the great friends we'd been when we'd last been together, I wasn't sure how to respond.

In the end, I just said, 'Why are you here?' I found I sounded surprised, and curious, but not confrontational. I added, 'Anya told me you were on your way to Scotland.'

She seemed taken aback for a moment that I knew that

detail, but recovered quickly. 'Oh yes! Well, that was the plan. But there was a mix-up with the flight I'd been aiming for and I couldn't make it. So I found a cute little hostel just on the edge of the city and I've just been spending some more time here while I wait for another opportunity to fly out.'

I looked at her. 'You haven't found a single other flight you could get home since then?'

She shook her head. 'No,' she said, wide-eyed. 'Not one with space.'

I frowned. 'So why go to a hostel? Why wouldn't you come back here?'

Her cheeks flushed. She paused. 'Well, I didn't want to intrude. Didn't want to be in the way but, listen, the reason I'm here is because I've met someone. A man. I don't know a huge amount about him but it's clear he's got a bit of money. And we've been talking and long story short, he's looking for original artwork. Obviously I told him I knew a very talented artist and he's pretty keen to meet you. He's not in town for long but he's around now, if you're free? I'll take you to meet him and we can—'

She reached out to take my hand but I pulled it away. 'Sophie! No. I'm not going anywhere right now. I'm busy.'

I heard Matt's bedroom door open and I looked round to see him emerge, dressed now, in shorts and a shirt.

'Sophie. Hello,' he called down the hallway, his voice polite and business-like. He came to stand behind me. 'How can we help you?' His arm wrapped around my shoulders protectively and I saw Sophie look at it, registering it, trying to work out what it meant.

She swallowed. 'Can I come in?'

'No,' Matt said simply. 'It's not a good time I'm afraid.'

She turned back to me. 'If you can just come for a minute, Lauren,' her voice had become high-pitched. Desperate. 'Or,

243

if you'd rather go on your own, I can tell you where to meet him. It really is a good opportun—'

'Sophie,' Matt said, his voice soft but firm. 'You need to leave, now, please.'

She looked at him. Her eyes were wet. I felt sorry for her but uncomfortable too. I couldn't work out why she was doing this to herself. Or to us.

'I have your passport!' She reached into her handbag and pulled it out. She held it up triumphantly like she'd just found it in there, quite unexpectedly.

'Why?' I said. 'Why did you take it?'

'I . . .' She began quickly but then stopped. She looked at Matt then back to me again. 'I must have picked it up by mistake.'

Matt reached out and took the passport from her. There was a brief moment where it looked like she wasn't going to release her grip on it. 'We've spoken about this before,' he said, 'and everything I've said still stands. You're aware of what the consequences will be if you continue.'

Sophie took one more look at each of our faces, then she nodded. Her expression hardened and she seemed more angry than upset now. She hitched her bag up her shoulder and turned and stepped into the lift. She kept her back to us as the doors closed, and then she descended out of sight.

Matt shut the door and leaned his back against it. 'Christ,' he said breathing out hard. 'She is . . .' He shook his head. 'She's getting worse.' He took my hand and pulled it up to his mouth and kissed it. 'Don't worry,' he said. 'I don't think she'll come back.'

I pulled my hand away. 'I'm just worried about her, really. I know she's lied about why she's stayed here – all that stuff about the flights made no sense at all – but I don't think everything I know about her can be wrong. Can it? I just don't think it's fair to write her off as a total lunatic. I think she's just . . .' I shrugged. 'Sad.'

Matt pulled me into a hug and kissed the top of my head. 'Maybe. I don't honestly know. Maybe.'

We went back out to the terrace. Matt got us beers from the fridge and a bowl of stuffed vine leaves. He began telling me long-winded stories about mishaps that had happened at work and I could tell he was trying to lift the mood, to crowd out any thoughts or concerns I might be having about Sophie with inane chatter, to make me feel her visit had been nothing but a minor inconvenience. I wasn't ready to let the subject go, though. Aside from my concerns about where Sophie was now, and what kind of emotional state she might be in, I had the growing sense that there were details of conversations that had gone on between Matt and her that I wasn't aware of, and that there was a dynamic between them that I didn't fully understand.

'What did you mean when you mentioned consequences?' I said.

My question cut off one of Matt's anecdotes mid-flow and he looked at me surprised. 'When?'

'You said to Sophie that she knew what the consequences would be if she continued.'

Matt hesitated. He pushed his lips together making them turn white. 'It's complicated.'

'Why?' I could feel my irritation rising. It was part of Matt's chivalrous nature, I was noticing, to reassure me that he was taking care of things, that I didn't need to bother myself with the details, but it was starting to grate. I didn't want to be treated like a delicate teacup that had to be protected from rough handling. 'What's complicated?'

He looked at me for a moment and I thought he was about to appease me again, but instead he closed his eyes tightly, screwed them shut like a kid in a game of hide and seek. Then he opened them again and nodded once decisively.

'Okay,' he said. 'Okay. I'll tell you the whole story. I was never going to be able to keep it from you forever.'

Chapter 43

'Wait here a second.' Matt got up, slid open the glass doors and disappeared inside the apartment. A few minutes later he was back, holding a large padded brown envelope.

I nodded towards it. 'What's that?'

He put the envelope down beside him on his lounger. 'I'll show you in a minute. But first . . . do you remember Sophie at all, from Hoyle? When she was a teacher at my school? At Reuben's school?'

I shook my head. 'No. Why would I? I didn't know most of the teachers at the boys' school. I was surprised she'd recognised me, really. But she'd known Reuben and she said she'd seen us together, and we did look alike so . . .' I shrugged. 'Why? What about it?'

'Well, you wouldn't know this as you didn't remember her, but she was only at our school for one year. She arrived in September 2004. By the new school year, September 2005, she'd gone. Left the school, left town entirely. Did you know that?'

'That she left? Yeah. Yeah, I think I did. I didn't know exactly when she left, but I knew she wasn't in Hoyle for long. She said it wasn't really her cup of tea. She was only in her early twenties, you can see why a backward little seaside town might not exactly be enough for her.'

Matt rubbed his eyes with his index fingers then placed his palms on his knees and looked at me carefully. 'This thing that she's doing. This obsessional stalking type thing. It's not the first time she's done it.'

'She's stalked you before?'

Matt shook his head quickly. 'No, no. Not me. No. But she's done it before. In 2005. In Hoyle. That's why she had to leave town suddenly.'

'Really? So she was sent away? By who? The school? Or the police or . . . ?

'Not sent, as such, I don't think. But more that she just realised she should move on, with everything that was going on.'

'What do you mean?' I had the sense that I was following Matt's story two steps behind. 'What was going on?'

'With Reuben,' he said quietly. 'After Reuben died. It was Reuben, Lauren. Reuben that she was . . .' He shook his head. 'I don't even know what she was doing, but it wasn't right.'

I laughed involuntarily. 'She was stalking Reuben? But he was only seventeen. And she was his teacher!'

Matt nodded. 'I know. I know. Exactly. That was the whole thing really. The whole problem.'

I didn't say anything for a moment. The idea was too absurd to process. Reuben had always had an interesting face. He had a kind of broody, artistic aura about him that a certain type of girl I'm sure would have gone for. But he looked young for his age. He barely had a hint of stubble on his chin. And looking back at photos of him now, I realised just how much of a *teenager* he had looked. His long dark hair, his hunched shoulders. The idea of a twenty-three-year-old woman, a teacher, finding him attractive – attractive enough to stalk – seemed almost funny.

'Are you sure? How do you even know? Reuben never mentioned Sophie, never mentioned a Miss Rickson at all.'

'I saw,' Matt said.

'When? Saw what?'

'May half-term. A few weeks before Reuben died. School was closed for the holidays but some of us were allowed access to use the practice rooms, to store our instruments and stuff. I walked into the music classroom one afternoon and they were in there. Miss Rickson – Sophie – and Reuben. He was sitting on the edge of the desk and she was standing right up close to him. Standing literally between his knees. She had a hand on his shoulder.'

I blinked, unable to picture this, even with the detailed description. 'And you're sure it was . . . you're sure you didn't just get the wrong end of the stick?'

Matt shook his head firmly. 'Nope. It was obvious. They sprung apart straightaway which told me everything I needed to know anyway, really. But then I asked Reuben. I got it out of him.'

'But, got what out of him? Are you now saying it was a mutual thing? A relationship?'

I hadn't known Reuben to so much as go to see a film with a girl so to hear that he had been in an entire relationship, with an adult – a teacher – without anyone knowing made me feel physically unsteady.

Matt scrunched up his nose. 'Well . . .' He sighed. 'Here's how I understood it: I think at the beginning, for a few weeks maybe, Reuben was flattered by her attentions. You haven't been a seventeen-year-old boy, but I have, and I can tell you that having a young, pretty teacher after you would be very good for the old ego. But I think when he'd had second thoughts, she kept it going. Wouldn't take no for answer. And she would have known that what she was doing was wrong. Illegal, in fact. He was under eighteen, and there are all sorts of rules and laws about teachers and students. She would have known the consequences if it was found out. Losing her job, never able to teach again. Signing some kind of sex register, I expect. So, after Reuben died, with his life and what he'd been doing over the last few months suddenly being looked at in detail for the inquest, I think she realised the best thing would be if she disappeared. If she avoided getting too involved in answering any questions.'

'But it never came up. In the inquest. No one ever found out. There was nothing mentioned about it.'

Matt shook his head. 'No. The only people who know about what she did that year are me and Sophie.'

'Why didn't you tell anyone? When Reuben died and all the questions were being asked. Didn't you think you should mention it?'

Matt looked down at the envelope. He picked it up and rested it on his lap. 'After Reuben died, everyone knew your mum was heartbroken. And that she was adamant that it hadn't been suicide. That he was a happy, *normal* boy. I knew that if it came out, about how Sophie had been, that it would have added some pretty hefty weight to the school of thought that said he was messed up, that he was confused and troubled. I knew that if it came out, it would make it more likely that the inquest verdict would come back as suicide. For one thing, I didn't think that was true. I don't think Reuben was actually that upset by Sophie's behaviour. As I said, I think he enjoyed it to a certain degree. I thought the best thing would be if no one knew anything about it. That if, on top of dealing with the grief of losing him, your mum – and you – discovered he had all these secrets, it would have been too much to cope with.

'So I took the precaution of taking the evidence. It wasn't hard to find, in his locker at school. I guess it was the most secure facility he had, but I'd watched him enter his combination into the lock enough times. And there it all was.' He put his hand on the envelope. 'All the physical evidence of what Sophie did is in here.'

I looked at it. 'But what is it? What's actually in there?'

'Oh, bits and pieces. Letters mostly. Notes. Some photos.' He held it out to me like he was offering me a plate of biscuits.

I took it but I didn't move to open the flap. I put it down in my lap. 'Do I want to see? He was my brother. Is it . . . ?'

'Oh it's nothing full-on. Well, not sexy anyway. A lot of it is just scribbled song lyrics and stuff like that.'

I opened the envelope and took out the first piece of paper my hand fell on – a few lines of handwritten text, green biro on a piece of lined notepaper. Something about the stars and infinity. It certainly looked like song lyrics. I looked at a few more of the notes. The only ones that made any sense to me were generic love sentiments – 'You are everything', 'I can't imagine a time when you're not the centre of my universe' – always signed with kisses. I'd never seen Sophie's handwriting to know if this was hers or not, and she'd never included her name.

Matt was watching carefully as I sifted through the papers. I looked up at him. 'Are you sure they're from Sophie? To Reuben? They could be from anyone. About anything.'

'Look at the photos.'

I reached into the envelope again and took out a small wodge of five Polaroid photographs. They'd clearly been taken by Reuben himself, his arm extended to get both of them in the shot. He was bare chested, lying on a bed I didn't recognise. Sophie – younger, but unmistakably her – had her

251

head on his shoulder. In some photos she was smiling dopily at the camera, in others her face was nuzzled into his neck. That was the moment where I was forced to admit that what Matt had told me was true. Here was photographic proof. It didn't matter that I couldn't imagine it. I didn't need to. Here was the image, right in front of me.

I slid the photos back in the envelope and put it back in my lap.

'I still don't understand, though. When you warned Sophie about consequences, what did you mean?'

Matt sighed. 'Oh, I don't know exactly. I suppose I was trying to remind her what I knew. That I had this. That if she carried on . . . making a nuisance of herself, that I could make things difficult for her.' He shrugged. 'I don't know. I'd probably never do anything about it. I was just trying to scare her off, I guess. It was the only thing I could think of to get her to back off.'

I nodded. 'Right. Okay.'

'I did feel weird about it. Since you've been over here. Since we've been . . . getting on. It was one thing, I know, keeping these secrets about your brother when I didn't think I was ever going to see you again, but it had started to feel . . . wrong. But then I didn't know what to do for the best. In a way, I thought it was better to say nothing. That what you didn't know couldn't hurt you.'

We were quiet for a moment. I looked down at the brown envelope.

'Are you all right?' Matt leant forward and put his hand on my cheek. He tried to pull me towards him, to lean his forehead against mine but I moved away.

'Yeah. Yeah I am. I just need some time to process everything. It's kind of a shock, to find out things about someone you thought you knew like this.'

Matt nodded. 'Sure. Sure. Of course. Do you want to talk about it? Have you got any questions?'

I shook my head. I leant back on the lounger, the envelope still in my lap. 'No. I just want to be quiet, for a bit, if that's okay. I just need some time to think.'

Matt nodded. 'Okay.' He crossed the terrace to a lounger in the corner that was still in the shade and sat down. 'Let me know if you do want to talk.'

Fifteen minutes later, I could tell by the gentle snores that he was asleep. I opened the glass doors and stepped onto the cool tiles of the flat. I collected my bag from the bed in my room and quietly let myself out of the apartment and took the lift to the ground floor. Only when I was out in the street did I take out my phone and send the message to Sophie:

Meet me by the supermarket. I'll be there in ten minutes.

Chapter 44

Sophie was standing on the corner as I approached, looking around her nervously. Her phone was in her hand and she kept looking down at the screen. I was almost right next to her by the time she noticed me.

'Lauren.' She closed her eyes very briefly. 'Thank God. Does Matt know you're here?'

I shook my head.

She reached out to touch my arm, but I pulled away from her. 'There's no man, I'm afraid,' she said quietly. 'No man to buy your art. I made that up. To get you to come.'

'Yes,' I said flatly. 'I did gather that. But I'm not staying long. I just wanted to ask you to explain what's going on. Why you're here. Why didn't you just leave, Sophie? With Anya? That story about the flights doesn't make any sense. Nor does the way you're hiding away in some hostel somewhere. Is it true? That you're in love with Matt? Is that why you wanted to come to Barcelona so badly with us? You needed an excuse to come to him without it looking like you'd come just *for* him?'

She looked around us at the people walking past and I

thought for a moment she might be about to turn and run away from me.

'Let's go somewhere,' she said. 'Somewhere we can sit down.'

I hesitated. I was reluctant to follow her anywhere when I still had no real idea what her intentions were or what was going on, but I also badly wanted to have a proper conversation with her. For her to explain herself.

I followed her as she led me away from the main shopping street and around the corner to a quieter side road with a café about halfway down, set back from the residential buildings that surrounded it. I took a seat outside, feeling it was at least safer to be in full view of the street rather than tucked away in a dark corner when she could pull any trick she felt like, concealed by the shadows.

'Can I get you a coffee? An orange juice?' Sophie picked up the laminated menu from the table and held it out to me. I saw her hand was shaking.

I took the sheet from her and placed it face down on the table. I shook my head. 'I don't want anything. Please, just explain what you're doing.'

She nodded. She opened and closed her mouth a few times.

'Why are you still in Barcelona?' I said again, in case she'd forgotten what the question was.

'To keep an eye on you.'

Instinctively I moved my hands away from her, off the table and into my lap.

'For you!' she said quickly. She reached out to touch me but I shifted my chair away, scraping it on the pavement. 'To make sure you were safe.'

I made a face. 'Safe? From what?'

'Matt.'

255

'What?' I shook my head, as if perhaps I hadn't quite heard her properly. 'Why would I . . . ? What?'

'Everything that happened at Torre Sonrisas – the break-in, the skull that hit you, even the pictures of the murder victims on the wall – it was all him. He arranged it all. He did it all, to unsettle us. Well, to unsettle you.'

The waiter approached our table but neither of us responded to his offer of drinks and in the end he sighed, muttered something cross in Spanish and retreated back inside.

'And why exactly would he do that?' I looked down the street, trying to remember the way we'd come. I'd been willing to give Sophie the benefit of the doubt and hear what she had to say but I was veering back to my original feeling that she was experiencing some kind of delusional episode and, by entertaining her ramblings, I was making things worse.

Sophie followed my gaze and obviously sensed she was close to losing me. 'Please.' She leant forward, forcing me to meet her eye. 'Just listen.'

I exhaled slowly. 'Okay. Go on.' I rested my hands on the edge of the table. 'Why would Matt orchestrate a campaign of terror? What has he got against me?'

I was tempted to point out that if he really had been harbouring some furious grudge against me since childhood, that he'd been waiting all these years to play a dark prank on me to get his vengeance for whatever it was I'd supposedly done, then the developments between us over recent days didn't make much sense. However, I didn't want to give her any additional information that she might try to weave into her wild theory.

'He hasn't got anything against you,' Sophie said. 'It's more about what he has *for* you. A . . . I don't know . . . crush. Although, that makes it sound quite innocent. An obsession, is closer to the truth.'

I didn't respond at all. I just continued to look at her, letting her know that she was going to need to present her case more fully, to provide some evidence, if she expected me to get involved in the conversation.

'I know it sounds mad, but that's because it *is* mad. But in essence, it was quite a straightforward scheme. Almost laughably so! He laid on a short series of alarming, seemingly inexplicable, events with the sole aim of encouraging us to leave that apartment and to move into his. He created a crisis simply to give himself an opportunity to step forward as our saviour.'

I remembered Sophie saying something to this effect the day we arrived in Matt's apartment, how she felt he had a penchant for playing the hero. I'd thought at the time it sounded a strangely cynical reading of the situation, but now it seemed like she'd let the idea fester and spiral.

'Right,' I said. 'And how did you work all this out? At what point did it suddenly occur to you that the most likely explanation for our holiday from hell was that the one person who was around to help us out was actually behind it all?'

'I didn't have to work it out,' she said calmly, without taking her eyes off mine. 'I knew it was him because he told me. He told me he was going to do it, and then he did it. And . . .' She looked down at the table. 'And I helped him.'

The waiter came to our table again and, realising he was likely to ask us to leave if we didn't order anything, I quickly requested two lemonades and he disappeared to fetch them.

'What?' My voice was impatient now. 'What are you talking about?'

'You probably remember it was my suggestion to come to Barcelona. Even though we all know it was quite inappropriate for me to have invited myself along to your holiday at all.'

257

Despite the strangeness of the conversation there was some deep-seated politeness within me that wanted to jump in to reassure her that it was all fine, that she was very welcome, that we were happy to have her along. But I remembered what Anya had told me.

'Anya said you were very keen to come with us.'

Sophie nodded. 'Yes. Yes, that's a fair assessment. I was quite embarrassed by the whole thing, I can assure you.'

I looked at her, my head on one side. 'So why did you . . . ?

She sat forward again, a new urgency to her demeanour. 'Because Matt told me to!' She was obviously torn between raising her voice for emphasis and keeping it quiet for privacy; the result was a low hiss. She forced herself to take a breath. 'Matt told me to bring you all to stay in his apartment originally, but when Anya didn't want to do that, he came up with his new plan: for me to bring you to an apartment that he'd rented. Remember how unsuitable the other two on my shortlist were?'

Suddenly something made sense. I shifted in my chair. 'Anya wanted the first one, didn't she? The expensive one. But that wasn't supposed to happen. And that's why you had to tell her I was worried about money.'

Sophie nodded once. 'Yes. Exactly. I had to think quickly to get things back on course. I *had* to get you to choose that one. Because that was the one Matt had taken on. And he'd decided that this was actually a much better way of doing things. Because, he believed, by terrorising you out of one place, you'd be grateful, and in awe of him, in a way you wouldn't if I'd just brought you to his place from the beginning.'

'So . . .' I took off my sunglasses and rubbed my eyes. 'So let me get this straight: Matt rings you up one day, says, "Hey Sophie, I've just remembered I'm obsessed with this girl I haven't seen for ten years. Can you pretend to be mates with her then bring her on a fake holiday so I can terrorise her into my flat?"'

She laughed once and closed her eyes for a moment. 'That's actually not too far from the truth.'

'What? And you just said yes, did you? Couldn't see any issues with this idea?'

She sighed and slumped back in her chair. 'Of course,' she said quietly. 'Of course I could. But you're just going to have to believe me when I say I had no choice. If I'd had any option then obviously I would have had nothing to do with Matthew Fabian at all.'

'What do you mean, "no choice"?'

She shook her head. 'You're just going to have to believe me,' she repeated.

I shook my head quickly and sat forward. 'What? No. You don't get to say that. To just shut down that question. You wanted to explain, so you have to explain. What kind of friendship is it you have with him anyway?'

Sophie laughed suddenly, like she found this question genuinely amusing. 'Friendship! We don't have a friendship. Matt is not my friend. He has never ever been that.'

'So why were you even in contact? If your only connection is that you taught at his school years ago . . . ?' For the first time since our conversation had begun I let the defensive edge to my voice slip. I was so hopelessly confused. I just wanted something to make sense.

'We weren't in contact. But he found me. He contacted me. To ask me for help, with this. And to remind me that if I didn't agree . . .' She took her eyes off me for a moment and gazed off down the narrow street. ' . . . he had the power to ruin my life.'

'Ruin your life? How?' I knew what was coming, but I wanted to hear it from her.

Sophie looked down. Her fingers were resting on the edge of the table, spread out like she was remembering how to play a piano tune. I thought she was going to ignore the question altogether but after a few moments of silence she said, 'I did something I shouldn't have. It was a long time ago and I believe it sounds worse on paper than it was in reality, but still. It was what it was. And Matt knows about it. So, as I see it, I have to do what he says or risk him revealing it to the world.'

I pictured the envelope with its handwritten notes. The photo of Sophie's head resting on Reuben's bare chest. 'You mean Reuben? The stalking? How you stalked Reuben?'

She jerked her head up, her eyes wide. 'Who said that? Did Reuben say that?'

'Reuben is dead.'

She flinched. 'I meant, did he say it when he was alive,' she said quietly.

I shook my head. 'Reuben never mentioned you. But then why would he? You were just a teacher. He was just a student.'

She looked down. 'I wasn't. He wasn't. He was everything.'

30 May 2005

Sophie

He had his hood up when Sophie opened the door, as he always did. She'd never asked him to do that, they'd never agreed the specifics of their rituals, but discretion ran through the heart of every interaction between them. She'd liked that at first. There had been something appealing – pure, in a way – about the world they had created just for the two of them. But she was growing tired of it. She was exhausted by keeping this enormous swell of feeling contained, buried deep within her, not able to let anyone know that there was someone who occupied every waking thought, much less who that someone was.

As usual, neither of them said anything until he was inside, the door safely closed behind them. Then he said, 'Hi' and kissed her gently on the cheek. He was always tentative at the beginning of their meetings, as if he was making sure she was still comfortable with him doing it, asking her permission for the whole relationship anew each time. This time, though, she jerked her head sideways, and took a step away from him. He stood in front of her, his arms by his sides. He looked hurt and confused, clearly taking the manoeuvre as a straightforward rejection. The reality was that nothing was straightforward at all.

'You've changed your mind,' he said. It wasn't a question.

She shook her head. 'I haven't. I . . .' She stopped. What she meant was that her feelings hadn't changed, but she realised that, in a way, he was right. She had changed her mind. Her belief that this could continue without consequence, that how right things felt when they were together was all that mattered, had changed.

'I'm a teacher, Reuben,' she said quietly. 'You're a student.'

He let out an exasperated sigh. 'Who cares! I'm eighteen in six months. If I'd gone to college rather than staying on at school this wouldn't matter. You're not even six years older than me. If we'd met anywhere else, no one would even look twice. If we'd met two years later—'

She reached forward and took his hand. 'I know *if* a lot of factors were adjusted then the whole situation would be different. But they're not. The facts are what they are.'

'Is this because of Matt? You're freaking out because of what he saw? I can talk to him if you like but honestly, we don't need to worry about him. He won't talk. He's got his own stuff to worry about.'

'Look. Look at this.' She took the sheet of paper she had printed that morning from her pocket. She hated that she'd had to do this, to come to the conversation armed with evidence like a barrister in a court room, but she knew he would try and talk her out of it and she doubted her own resolve.

She passed it to him and he read the headline aloud. 'Teacher jailed for sex with seventeen-year-old pupil.'

She saw that he was taken aback for a moment and she knew why. They'd read about other cases together, but they'd always been about younger students. Reuben had always argued there was a world of difference between a fifteen-year-old and a seventeen-year-old.

'But seventeen's legal?' he said.

Sophie shook her head. 'Read it. It's about the position of trust. I told you.'

Reuben crumpled the paper in his fist. 'Well, it's different. This is about a bloke. A pervy old bloke having a go on school girls. That wasn't a relationship. That wasn't . . .' He lowered his voice and tried to kiss her again. ' . . . this.'

Again, Sophie stepped away from him. 'It doesn't matter,' she said. 'No one cares about the details. No one cares who initiated it or how much we like each other. The law doesn't work like that. If this was ever public knowledge, I would be the teacher who groomed a student.'

'If anything, I groomed you!' he protested.

She carried on as if he hadn't spoken. 'I would probably go to prison. My life would be over. My career ruined.'

His face darkened. 'Your career. Sure.'

She found herself getting irritated then. He'd implied his feelings on this matter before, that her career was insignificant, and she should be happy to absorb its loss as collateral damage. Which was a perfectly reasonable belief to hold when you were not yet out of school and had a whole selection of careers, and lives, laid out before you to choose from.

'Yes. My career,' she said, her face hardening now. 'I know it might seem boring to you, but teaching is all I ever wanted to do. All I *can* do, more to the point.'

He exhaled deeply then stood up straight. 'Okay,' he said. 'I get it. It's a clear choice for you. Your job or me. And you pick the job.'

'It's not—'

'You pick a job in an ordinary school in a shitty place like Hoyle over what we have.' He shook his head. 'Like, seriously. I actually kind of wish you'd said this sooner. Really puts things into perspective.'

'Reuben.' Her voice was soft again now. She tried to take his hand but he snatched it away.

'It's fine. I need to get going. I need to . . .' His voice cracked and he turned his head away from her.

'Reuben, please. We can talk for a bit longer. We can—'

'See you around.'

He pulled up his hood, opened the front door and left.

It was the last conversation they'd ever have.

Chapter 45

Sophie was looking at me, watching me for a reaction.

'He was everything?' I repeated.

Sophie nodded. Then she laughed softly and shook her head. 'I know. It sounds . . . I don't know. It's the kind of thing we'd say to each other a lot. We were young.'

I think she expected me to smile at this reminiscence because when I didn't, she stopped laughing abruptly.

She swallowed. 'Although I did teach him, we only really got to know each other through the music department. We were both in the orchestra. Several teachers were. Although we rehearsed at the school, it didn't really feel like a part of school life, in the true sense. We were just two musicians. And you've got to remember, I was only twenty-three. There was a smaller age gap between Reuben and me than there is between the two of us, even.'

'It makes a difference, though, when one of you is seventeen. Don't you think?'

Sophie thought for a moment, then she shook her head. 'I don't think it does, really. Not always.'

'So how did it happen? One minute you're chatting about

Chopin in the school hall. Next thing, you're . . .' I pictured the photos again.

Sophie frowned slightly. 'It wasn't like that. It was very organic. We would talk while we were clearing away at the end of rehearsals. He knew where I lived because the cottage wasn't far from school; plenty of students had seen me turn up the path. He dropped round once, to borrow some sheet music I think. Then he came a second time, this time without a plausible excuse but I found that . . . I didn't mind. I was pleased, secretly. But still. I would never have acted on that feeling. Indeed, I resisted for a long time. I knew a line had been crossed but I thought we were still on essentially inno-cent territory. I was careful never to mention to anyone that he'd been to my home, but for several weeks our conversations were entirely platonic. Professional, almost.' She frowned again. She paused, then spoke more quietly. 'I do know I am not without blame in this bizarre situation but, although I wish I could change many things about my life, I can't truly regret getting close to Reuben. I will never meet anyone like him again.'

'Matt said you stalked him. That he'd lost interest and you wouldn't let it go.'

She fixed me with a hard stare. 'That's a lie. It's just not true.'

It was the very fact that she didn't offer any further explan-ation of this statement that made me believe her. 'So when Reuben died, you were still . . . ?

She shook her head. 'I'd ended things, a few days before.'

My eyes widened. 'Just a few days? How did he take it? Was he upset? Do you think that he was upset enough to—?'

Sophie put her hand on mine and this time I didn't shake it off. 'Lauren, no. I know the inquest considered the possibility of suicide and I know how anxious your mum was that that

266

shouldn't be the verdict and she was right to be. Reuben did not kill himself.'

'That's what I've always thought. But how can any of us ever be completely sure it was an accident? How are *you* so sure? Because I want to be.'

'Well, of course I can't be sure of anything.' Sophie paused. She narrowed her eyes and looked down the road again for a moment before turning back to me. 'But actually, I don't think it was an accident. It's possible, I suppose. But more and more lately I've been considering another explanation.'

'What do you mean? What explanation?'

'I think Matt killed him.'

Chapter 46

Sophie was looking at me, unblinking. I knew in a way, everything hung on this moment. Was I going to hear her out, or had she pushed me too far? Was I going to call her a lunatic, stand up and leave?

'You're going to have to talk me through this one,' I said. 'Because you're making a lot of big claims about Matt which I have to say in no way match up with what I've got to know about him over the last few weeks.'

She nodded. She couldn't deny this was a reasonable request. 'Okay, so.' She adjusted her position. 'Please bear in mind that in the six months before he died, Reuben and I were speaking every day. We had to be careful, obviously, about how and when, but usually he would come to my cottage after school, or late at night, after you and your mum were in bed. So I knew everything that was going on his life. He talked to me about school, about his music, about his family.'

'About me?'

Sophie smiled. 'Yes. Often. He even showed me your artwork once. Brought your sketch book round to show me.'

'Really? Did he?'

She nodded. 'He thought you had a real talent, but was worried that, on some level, you felt that the role of the family artist was filled. That people would think you were copying him if you tried to follow a creative career.'

I considered this. 'I suppose I did think that, in a way.'

'He was proud of you.'

She didn't say anything else for a moment. I felt a pain in my jaw, a heat in my eyes. I wanted so badly to speak to him just one more time. To ask him all the questions I'd built up over the last thirteen years.

'But he was worried about you too,' Sophie went on, her voice lower now.

'Why?'

'Because of Matt. Because he knew Matt was interested in you.'

'But so what if he was? It's so sexist, that overprotective brother thing. I told him that.'

Sophie nodded. 'I know you did. And he told me. And he knew there was some truth in it, which is why he wanted to be cautious this time. He wasn't going to say anything to you about Matt until he had something concrete to tell you, but he didn't trust him. And, shortly before things ended between us, not long before he died, he told me he was going to confront Matt. He wasn't clear on the specifics, but he said Matt had done something he wasn't going to stand for. So I don't know exactly what happened but I do know that whatever it was, it ended up with Reuben dead on that railway track.'

'Did you tell the police?'

She paused for a moment, then shook her head. 'I hoped if there was anything to be discovered about Matt's involvement in Reuben's death, it would come out as part of the inquest. But nothing seemed to transpire. And I didn't push them in Matt's direction because I was reluctant to be seen to be getting too involved in things. I didn't want them to look too closely at my relationship with Reuben. I knew I'd been playing a dangerous game while Reuben was alive, but if our relationship was unearthed once he was dead, it could only be worse. I would be blamed for his death. I was sure of it.'

'But just because Reuben was going to talk to him, to tell him to – what? To back off me? – how do you know that happened that night? That Matt . . . did whatever you think he did that left Reuben on the tracks?'

Sophie pushed her mouth to one side, like she wasn't sure how to answer that. 'I can't say specifically. I just think there's something about him. Something dark.'

I raised my eyebrows. 'Dark?'

'You know Matt was married once. Did you know that?'

I nodded. 'Yeah. He told me. We bumped into his ex-wife once, in the street.'

Sophie's eyes widened. 'Really? What did she say?'

'Oh, nothing. We didn't talk to her. She just walked in the other direction.'

Sophie nodded. 'I'm sure she did. Inga, her name is. I saw her myself a few days ago. I asked her to meet me. I wanted to see what her impressions were of him. If his behaviour with me, about you, was wildly out of character.'

'What did she say? Didn't she wonder why you were asking?'

Sophie nodded. 'She was reticent at first, but I positioned myself as a potential love interest. I said I'd been on a few dates with Matt but my instincts were telling me something was a little strange, and she seemed eager to warn me off. She gave me quite an interesting account of their relationship, I can tell you. She said for the first few months he'd been wonderful. Perfect. So perfect that they'd got married more quickly than she'd ever imagined. Even her friends didn't advise against it, she said. They were all charmed by him. But only a few weeks into the marriage the shift began. What had started off as Matt taking care of things became a kind of suffocating control. She was barely allowed out without him. He would do things behind her back – intercept job offers, tell friends to stay away. He tried to isolate her completely.' Sophie looked at me for a moment, waiting to see what I was going to do next. 'He had evidence,' she said eventually. 'Of me and Reuben. That was what meant I knew I had no choice.'

I nodded. 'The envelope.'

Her eyebrow twitched. 'You know about it?'

'I've seen it.'

Her mouth opened slightly. 'He showed you . . . ?'

I nodded but I didn't say anything. I didn't offer any opinions on its contents.

'I see. Well, in that case, you'll understand the power that envelope holds over me. Part of the reason for me staying here is that I just don't want to leave Barcelona until I have it. He'd told me that, once I'd done what he'd asked of me, he would give it back. That I'd be free. But when the time came for us to go home, he went back on his word. I fought him on this right until the last moment – I was on the door-step pleading, bargaining, demanding, with Anya in the taxi waiting – but he refused. And although I hoped he wouldn't, I always knew there was a chance he would do that. That he would break his promise. So while we were staying there, I took the precaution of getting a key cut. I've managed to sneak into the apartment a few times when you've both been out to search for it, but no doubt he stores it somewhere secure. I even thought he might keep it in his office, which is why I loitered around outside and tailgated my way in a few days ago, but there was no sign of it there either. But that's how I came across your passport. That's where he was

271

hiding it. It hadn't occurred to me he might steal it but as soon as I saw a passport lying there in his desk drawer, I realised that it was the most obvious thing for him to do if he wanted to stop you leaving. So I flicked to the back page, and sure enough, there was your name, your photo.'

I didn't say anything. I sat for a few moments, staring straight ahead, not moving.

'What are you going to do now?' Sophie said eventually.

'I'm going to speak to Anya.'

Sophie opened her mouth like she was about to question the decision but in the end, she just nodded once and said. 'Yes. Of course.'

I stood up, crossed the street and found a secluded doorway to make the call. It felt important not to have Sophie listening in, looking at me expectantly, trying to interpret every word, every facial expression.

When Anya answered, I ran through my questions, and after each one she gave me the information I had been expecting. She had questions of her own, of course, about what was happening and why I was bringing up this subject now, but I told her I would have to explain more fully when we could speak properly.

When the call was over, I returned to the table where Sophie was waiting for me, to tell her what Anya had said, and to let her have her chance to respond.

2 June 2005

Anya

Anya looked around the beach to see who she recognised. There were some girls from the year above who she knew from when she'd subbed a few times for the netball team last year, but she didn't feel much like talking to them. In fact, she realised she didn't feel like talking to anyone. The humiliation from her failed flirtation with Reuben stung, and now the sun was going down she was cold in her flimsy skirt and denim jacket. She just wanted to be at home, listening to music in her room, or painting her nails and watching something silly on TV. She didn't want to be here any more. She wished she'd never come.

She took one last look around the beach, mostly to ascertain if there was anyone who had noticed her, anyone who would be likely to mention her brief appearance on the beach to Lauren, but no one seemed to be paying her any attention at all.

She headed into the woods then made her way up the path to the main road. A quick look at the timetable on the bus stop told her it would be at least a twenty-minute wait for a bus to take her anywhere useful, so she decided to walk. She headed up the quiet residential road of big houses set back from the street and turned onto the high street. The only premises that were still open were the pub, the Spyglass, on the roundabout at the end of the road, and the late-night Co-op. She ducked into the shop to buy a sausage roll from their heated rack and it was as she came out with her greasy paper bag to continue on her way home that she noticed Matt on the opposite side of the road. He was walking quickly, with purpose, like he had somewhere to be. She paused for a moment and looked around, hoping, in spite of herself, that Reuben might be not too far behind. But Matt seemed to be alone and soon he turned the corner out of sight. Anya made her way home, dropping the sub-standard sausage roll in a neighbour's wheelie bin when she'd eaten barely a quarter, deeming it the final insult in a terrible day.

Chapter 47

When I let myself back into the flat, Matt was already in the hallway.

'Lauren!' he said coming towards me and pulling me into a hug. 'Where have you been? I thought something had happened. I woke up and you'd just disappeared! I thought—'

I wriggled free from his grasp. I reached into my canvas bag and pulled out a big bottle of beer and a packet of crisps. 'I just went to get some bits from the shop. You were out for the count, so I thought it'd give me something to do.'

He rubbed the back of his head and looked out at the terrace, towards the lounger where he'd been asleep. 'Yeah, sorry. I always drift off when I sunbathe.' He turned to look at me. 'I was just worried. With Sophie out there, I didn't know if she'd caught up with you somehow or . . .' He shook his head. 'I don't know.'

I looked at his earnest face. His cheeks were flushed and his hair was scruffy from sleep. I looked down for a moment, then I closed my eyes and sighed. 'Yeah. Okay. You're right. I'm sorry. It wasn't just about the beer. I went to see her. Sophie.'

His eyes widened. 'You went to see her? Why?'

'I just needed to.' I went over to the fridge and put the bottle inside. 'I needed to hear her side. Everything you said about Reuben is a big deal for me, you know? He was my brother and there were whole parts of his life I didn't know anything about. I just needed to see what she had to say about it.'

He swallowed and nodded. 'Okay. I get that. I just wish you'd let me come with you.'

'Yeah. I knew you'd want to. But I just felt it was something I had to do on my own.'

He nodded again. 'So what did she say?'

'About Reuben?' I took a glass from the shelf and went to the tap to fill it. 'Not much. She reckons she "loved" him.' I made a face to indicate I found the idea both absurd and distasteful and Matt mirrored it. 'But what she said about you was more interesting.'

'About me?' He placed his palm on the centre of his chest. He was standing in the entrance to the kitchen now.

I nodded and took a sip of my water. Then I went to stand in front of him, my body a few feet from his.

'She told me, Matt,' I said calmly. 'She told me everything you did at that flat. How you set it all up – the break-in, the photos – to get me to come here. To be here with you.'

Matt looked at me. His eyes were moving quickly from side to side like he was trying to read instructions from a script inside his head. His mouth was clamped shut.

'It was you,' I said, 'in the flat that night. I was sure I saw someone. It was you, wasn't it? Bringing that radio in.'

'She's lying,' Matt said. Then more loudly, 'She's making it up, Lauren! You must be able to see that? This is why I didn't want you to speak to her. She's—'

'Matt,' I kept my gaze steady and my voice calm. 'You might

be surprised what I made of the account Sophie has given me. You might be surprised to know how the conversation went between us. But, if you lie to me one more time, about anything, you will never find out. If you continue to treat me like an idiot, then I'm getting my bag and I'm leaving and you will never hear from me again.'

'I—'

'Do you understand? One more lie and we're done.'

He nodded slowly.

I breathed out. 'So, as I said: it was you, wasn't it? That I saw in the night. That was you, bringing that radio in. That . . . trap.'

Matt was still looking at me carefully like I was a wild animal that might pounce at any moment. 'Look, Lauren.' He moved towards me but I stepped back and he stopped. 'I promise I'll tell you everything but please, tell me what she said? You can't trust her. She has her own game going on. She's not the innocent angel she pretends to be.'

I ignored him. 'Why did you wait until night time to bring it in? Were you hoping that I'd see you? Or were you planning to hurt us?'

'No! No, of course not.' He looked down. 'I don't know. I was drunk. I was just walking past and I thought of you, asleep up there and . . .' He shrugged.

'But Matt, what the hell would you have done if I'd come right out of my room and found you out there? Or if Anya had? Just made a run for it?'

He shrugged. 'I would've thought of something. I suppose I would have told you . . . that I'd thought I'd seen someone coming up to the flat. So I'd come in after to check you were okay.'

I looked at him. 'Of course. You wouldn't have had any trouble coming up with a story. You're quite good at that kind of thing really, aren't you?'

He didn't reply. He was fiddling with the drawstring on his shorts, refusing to meet my eye like a chastised schoolboy.

I sat down at the table and rested my forehead on the heels of my hands. 'Jesus!' I said. 'Jesus *Christ*, Matt!'

I heard him take a step towards me. 'Look. Lauren. Please can we just sit down and talk and—'

'No.' I stood up. 'I'm going to my room for a bit. I need to be on my own. I will tell you when – *if* – I want to talk to you. I need to get my head round this.'

'Sure.' He nodded and backed away to let me pass. 'Sure.'

I thought Matt might leave the flat while I was in my room but as I lay on my bed going over the conversation with Sophie in my head, I could hear him moving around, putting things in cupboards, opening and closing the terrace doors. When an hour or so had passed, I opened my bedroom door and went to find him in the kitchen. He was standing at the sink, drying glasses. He turned to look at me as I went in.

'Hey,' he said gently.

'Okay,' I said. 'I'm ready to talk. I have questions.'

He nodded. 'Okay. Of course. Okay.'

Normally Matt decided where we positioned ourselves in the flat. He'd suggest we go out to the terrace or he'd pull out a chair for me if he wanted me to sit in the kitchen. I was used to him directing me, setting the tone of our evenings. But this time he didn't move. He stood quite still looking at me, waiting for instructions.

'It was my skull, wasn't it? That hit me. I *knew* it was the same one, even though the others were trying to convince me it was just a coincidence.'

Matt nodded. 'Yes. Yeah, it was. It took some persuading, to get Sophie to take it from your place. She was sure you'd notice it was missing. But I needed something to make it a bit personal. To make you feel it was about you, you know?'

I nodded. 'Yeah. I felt that.' I laughed suddenly. 'I definitely felt that.'

Matt seemed relieved by my laughter and tried a nervous smile of his own. 'It *was* all about you, Lauren. It's always been all about you.'

I breathed out hard and closed my eyes for a moment. 'I know,' I said quietly. 'I get it now. I do.'

Matt looked up, hopeful. 'Do you?'

I nodded. 'I've been going over it in my head. Over everything you did. And I had this thought. I thought, although it's really not okay and we're going to need to talk about this properly, over a long time, if I'm going to believe you really understand why, but . . . the truth is, no one has ever done anything like that for me before. No one has ever worked that hard to get me.'

Matt's face relaxed and he blinked slowly a few times, like he was coming round from a deep sleep. His mouth hung open slightly. He looked at me. 'Really?' His voice came out as a croak.

'Yeah. When she was explaining it all – everything you arranged – it was such a . . .' I searched around for the right word. ' . . . a *careful* plan. And so although I was furious when Sophie told me – and you know she's angry? I'm sure you know that – I do get it, in a way. I can see the logic.'

'And . . . are you angry now?' His voice was barely audible.

I paused. 'Yes. And no. I'm angry about how you did it – and I think you've got some work to do to convince me that you understand that it was wrong and how things are going to be between us from now on – but . . .' I took a deep breath. 'I am glad you did something. Something to make things happen for us. To bring us together. Because the idea of *us* is not one I would have thought of before we moved in here

– it had been so long since I'd seen you – but I think it is a good one. A good idea.'

He nodded and swallowed hard again. We looked at each other, not saying anything for a few seconds, him just searching my face with his eyes, then I let him kiss me.

'Let's go and sit down.' I nodded down the hallway to the lounge.

We sat together on his big white sofas, him in one corner, me in another, my legs tucked up underneath me.

We didn't say anything for the first few moments, then Matt began.

'To be honest, Carlos nearly ruined the whole thing anyway. It was nearly over before it started. When he told you how he thought the lock had been broken from the inside? I'd had to do it that way to stop the neighbours getting suspicious. I knew it would've looked bad, me crouching in the corridor, messing about with the lock from the outside. I thought someone would've called the police for sure. So I had to let myself in, do it from the privacy of inside.'

'Really?' I remembered the way Anya had turned on Carlos when he'd been the bearer of this alarming news, how he'd backed out of his theory when he'd realised it wasn't going to be a popular one. 'If anything that just made it weirder, I thought. That someone had a key. Far creepier than just a standard break-in.'

Matt thought about this. 'Yeah. Yeah, I guess you're right.'

I smiled suddenly, and Matt looked at me.

'What?' he said nervously. 'What's funny?'

'You know, I think Anya was ready to ditch the place as soon as she saw the view was just a big photo. You didn't exactly pick a palace for us, Matt.'

He looked down at his hands. 'Yeah, I know,' he said quietly. 'But that was kind of . . .'

'The whole point?' I finished.

He shrugged. 'Well, yeah. Sort of. I just wanted this place to seem extra nice. Extra special, when you got here. I just wanted you to feel so . . . relieved to be out. I just wanted you to *want* to be here. I can't claim credit for the wall mural, though. That was there when I got there.'

I smirked again, and again he looked at me questioningly, nervous about what I was going to say next.

'I cannot *believe* you electrocuted yourself.' I shook my head. 'Did you mean to do it to yourself? Or was that meant for me too?'

'Oh, no, it was always meant to be me!' He looked at me earnestly. 'Honestly, I would never have actually hurt you. I'm sorry you got hit by the skull, you were never meant to be in there. Sophie was meant to keep you out for longer, but she messed up the timings. I'd always planned to hurt myself, because then I thought . . . there'd be no way you'd guess it was me. If I'd been caught up in it too. I thought it would make you realise . . . I don't know. That I was on your side.'

I frowned but then shook my head, letting my face clear. 'Yeah. I suppose that makes sense. Sort of. It was mad, though. You do know that? To electrocute yourself on purpose. Totally mad.'

Matt nodded. 'I know.' He brought his knees up to his chest, hugged them close to him and rested his chin on top. 'Although . . . I mean, I only pretended. There was nothing wrong with the radio. I was just pretending it had thrown me to the floor. I wouldn't know how to electrocute someone even if I wanted to.'

I rolled my eyes. 'Oh okay, I take it back. Not mad at *all*, then.'

Matt's cheeks flushed and he hugged his knees tighter.

There were a few moments where neither of us said anything, then Matt shuffled up the sofa towards me. Tentatively he took my hand and I didn't try to stop him.

'Lauren, everything you've found out. Everything I did . . . I don't want it to distract from . . .' He stopped and started again. 'I mean the main point that I really want you to understand is that I really like you. *Really* like you. I love you, in fact. I didn't want to say it too soon but it's the truth. And it doesn't feel too soon to me because I've felt like that for so long. For so many years.'

I turned to look at him. 'I just had no idea,' I said. 'Why didn't you say something? Try something . . . more conventional? Maybe we could have . . .' I shrugged. 'If you'd just *asked*.'

'I did try. I messaged you after Reuben died, but you didn't even reply. And then when I saw you that Christmas on the high street. It'd taken me days to work up the courage to ask you for a drink and you just brushed me off.'

I shook my head. 'I know, I'm sorry. I told you: I didn't realise you were really asking.'

He smiled sadly. 'Even worse. Not only do you not want to come for a drink with me, you don't even entertain it as a serious option.' He looked at me. 'I've waited a long time,' he said quietly. 'A really long time. Remember when I used to call at your house, when Reuben was still alive? I was just hoping for a glimpse of you.'

I frowned in bemusement. 'I can barely even remember you being there. Did we speak, ever?'

He chuckled in a wistful sort of way. 'Hardly. Reuben wouldn't let me get anywhere near you. He decided I wasn't good enough and so erected a forcefield around you, practically. Even though you'd have thought he'd have his hands full with his own . . . love life.'

I twisted my face into an expression of disapproval.

'Sophie told me about everything between her and Reuben. More than I wanted to know, to be honest. Do you know, I think she thought I'd be on her side. That I might even think it was . . . nice, or something? Like her carrying on with a schoolboy was romantic?' I shook my head.

Matt nodded. 'It did work out well for me, though, in a way. That she had a secret. That day I saw the photo on Anya's Instagram – that one of you and Anya and Sophie together – I had a good feeling. I couldn't work out why, right away, but I just had this feeling that finding out that this woman I knew had a big secret was good friends with the woman I loved . . . I had a feeling I could work with that. Somehow.'

I laughed. 'I wouldn't say we were good friends. I think that photo was taken the first night we met.'

Matt shrugged. 'Oh. Well, it still worked, I suppose. Didn't it?'

I rested my head on his shoulder to let him know that it had. That he had done it. It had worked.

Chapter 48

'What are you thinking?' Matt asked some time later.

I hesitated. 'About John.'

'Yeah. Of course.' He nodded but I could tell my answer had disappointed him.

'But what I was thinking was . . . I don't know.' I shook my head. 'It sounds bad.'

'What?'

'That I'm glad, in a way. That he's dead.'

Matt's eyebrow twitched in surprise. 'Right. Okay.'

'I know it sounds bad,' I said again. 'But it feels . . . neater. A tidy end. Like it was meant to be.'

Matt frowned, trying to make sense of this. 'Yeah. I see. Sort of. I get that.'

'And you must be glad too, really?'

'Oh, I don't know.' Matt rubbed the back of his head. 'I wouldn't ever be happy a man was dead.'

'No but . . .' I grinned suddenly, which I could see caught Matt off guard. 'He was a bit of a tosser, though.'

Matt smiled back uncertainly. 'Yeah . . . he wasn't exactly my kind of bloke, to be honest.'

I looked at him, my head on one side 'But you never met him. Did you?'

Matt closed his eyes for a moment. He opened them again. 'Once.' He didn't say anything else. He was looking at me carefully.

'On the jetty,' I said.

Matt made a small sound, somewhere between a cough and a grunt.

'You killed him,' I said quietly.

Matt jerked his head up. 'No!' He shook his head quickly. 'I didn't! Of course I didn't. It was an accident. But . . . I was there. I *was* there.'

I took a deep breath and put my palms on the sofa either side of me to steady myself. Matt reached out to take my hand and I let him.

'God, Lauren, I'm not a murderer,' he said quickly. 'Please don't get the wrong end of the stick here. I didn't set out to get rid of him. He was the one looking for confrontation. He approached me down by the water, demanding to know what was going on between us, saying you and him weren't officially over. And . . .' He looked down, 'Well, I was showing off, I suppose. I was pleased and . . . and *proud* to have you living with me. So I probably rubbed his nose in it a bit, let him know that you were going to be staying here with me for the foreseeable future and that we had a real thing going on. And he took a swing at me, so I took one back. And he'd been drinking, and he was nearer the edge, so he fell in. Perhaps, with hindsight, I should have stuck around to call for help, but honestly, it could just as well have been me getting washed up on that beach. It was just a matter of chance that he was the one to fall in.'

I stared at the blank TV screen in front of us as I processed this account. 'Wow. Right. Okay.'

285

'I didn't mean for it to happen,' Matt said again. 'It wasn't planned. It wasn't even intended.'

'But how do you know no one saw? Aren't you worried?'

Matt swallowed. 'I'm not sure. But no one's come forward so far. And if anyone does . . . I'll be okay. I'll say I was somewhere else. It'll be my word against theirs.'

I looked at him doubtfully. 'If you're sure. If you're sure you can handle it.'

He grinned shyly. 'Course I can.' He reached for my hand again. 'I can handle anything . . . with you by my side.'

I groaned. 'Good god, Matt, where do you get these lines?'

He looked worried for a moment, but then I laughed and he smiled in relief and squeezed my hand.

We stayed in position on the sofas and spent the next hour or so going back through our teenage years, revisiting everything with the new lens of Matt's growing crush applied. Matt mentioned incidents that I could hardly remember, conversations we'd had that I had no recollection of but that he had apparently held on to as signs of our compatibility – 'And when we stopped at the drive-thru on the way back, they got our orders mixed up, but it didn't matter in the end because we'd both asked for extra mustard but no gherkin. Do you remember? Exactly the same!'

'One thing I've been thinking,' I said, stretching my legs out across the sofa, 'as I try to get my head round all this, is about the photos. They found pictures. On Reuben. After he died.' I watched Matt to gauge his reaction, but his face remained impassive. 'You know what they were pictures of, don't you?'

Matt nodded slowly. 'Yeah,' he said quietly. 'I have a pretty good idea, yeah.'

'The thing is,' I pushed on carefully, 'that I've always hated the idea of that hidden camera, of my own brother doing that, of him . . .' I shuddered. 'But – and I've never told anyone this – but secretly, I've always thought, if it had been anyone else who'd set it up in my room, who'd wanted that footage . . . Then . . . I don't know. In a way, I'd have been *flattered*. Does that sound ridiculous? I was just so used to Anya being the one that all the boys looked at that, in a way, it would've been nice to think that someone wanted *me*. Anyway, so now I'm hoping . . . I mean, you've promised to tell me the truth, haven't you? Because after everything you've said today, I'm wondering if . . . ?'

Matt groaned and covered his face with his hands. 'Oh god, I do know it was gross.' He looked at me. 'I know that now. But I was just a teenage boy and I . . .' He shrugged. 'I just thought . . . where's the harm? That what you didn't know couldn't hurt you.'

Matt liked that expression, I'd noticed.

2 June 2005

Reuben

Reuben took the long route from the beach – the route that took him past Sophie's cottage. He had no intention of going up to it, of trying to contact her in any way. Now school was over there was no reason they should see each other at all. She had made her decision and he wasn't going to beg or bully or harass her into changing her mind. He told himself that he was doing the dignified thing, that he was taking his rejection like a man and acting with honour, but there was part of him that knew this was a tactic. A strategy. Perhaps, he hoped, by withdrawing himself completely, she would realise the hole he left in her life. Realise she couldn't live without him, and that he was worth all the risks.

Anyway, right now, he had something else to take care of. The only reason he hadn't done it as soon as he found those rank photos and realised exactly what a fucked-up little shit Matt Fabian really was, was because he knew how angry, how humiliated, Lauren would be, and he'd thought for a while maybe it was better she didn't know. But now he was worried that Matt was going to get to her first, to make up some story about where the photos had come from, absolving himself completely.

The buses were crap at this time of night, so Reuben thought it would be faster to get the train one stop and walk the rest of the way. When he arrived on platform one, the digital display told him the next train would be twenty-four minutes. He sighed and sat down. It was still the quickest option.

Hoyle West was a tiny station, and although trains ran through it relatively frequently, they rarely stopped. Hardly anyone got on or off there so the platform was deserted. There were two floodlights – one at either end of the platform – but the east-side one was broken so half the station was entirely in darkness. Tall pines lined the metal mesh fences that surrounded the platforms, their long shadows moving slowly back and forth in the wind.

When Matt appeared through the gate to the platform, Reuben thought at first he was looking for him, but as Matt looked up at the LED sign then paced up and down impatiently for a few moments, Reuben realised that he was just there to catch the train as well. And he had a strong hunch that he was making the same journey that Reuben was: to find Lauren.

'Getting the train somewhere, Fabian?' Reuben called. He had his hands in the pockets of his jacket, partly to appear nonchalant and in control, but partly to keep his hand on the photos, to make sure he knew exactly where they were.

Matt spun around and scowled. 'Nothing gets past you, does it, Sherlock?'

Reuben continued looking at him for a few moments,

refusing to be the first one to turn away. Then he said, 'You're wasting your time. She would never have been interested in a ginger scrote like you anyway. Even before she found out what a pervy little toss-bucket you are.'

Matt ambled towards him, his hands in his own pockets. 'Yeah?' he said. 'Well why don't we let her make that decision? Why don't you let her think for herself, instead of flapping about her like the world's lankiest bodyguard?'

Reuben nodded. 'Okay. Fine. Let's do that. Let's see what decision she makes when I let her know about your little birdwatching hobby.' He patted the pocket containing the photos.

Matt's eyes darted downwards. He laughed, but he was less cocky now, Reuben could tell. 'You haven't got them.'

Reuben raised his eyebrows and pulled out a photo from the small pile. 'You reckon?' He didn't want to look at it again himself but he held it up long enough that Matt could be quite sure he wasn't bluffing.

Matt took his hands out of his pockets and stepped towards Reuben. 'You went in my locker? You thief.'

Reuben laughed. 'What are you going to do about it, call the police?' He shook his head. 'Christ, you're such a freak.'

Matt's faced darkened then, and in three long strides he was next to Reuben, pulling on his jacket, trying to get his hand in the pocket.

Reuben pulled himself free. 'Jesus! Fuck off, you psycho!'

But Matt was ready to go at him again. His eyes were flashing with fury. He looked possessed.

'You're a *psycho*,' Reuben said again and he jogged off towards the end of the platform. Matt waited for a moment but then began after him. Reuben wasn't the kind of boy who had ever had to prove himself physically before and he knew that if that was how this battle was going to be settled, he didn't stand a chance; Matt was half a foot taller than him and at least two stone heavier.

Reuben upped his pace to a sprint and ran down to the end of the platform, past the sign that said, 'No public access past this point' and down the slope to the grassy scrubland at the side of the track.

He immediately realised he'd trapped himself. With the high mesh fence to his left, his only option was to continue to run alongside the length of the track, and that would only save him until Matt caught up with him. Which he knew wouldn't take long.

Matt was standing at the top of the slope now. He laughed. 'You look like a scared little rabbit, Henry!' he called. 'A little frightened bunny with a really shit emo haircut.'

Then he jogged down the slope and onto the grass at the edge of the line and Reuben realised there was only one route open to him: across the tracks and onto the opposite platform.

All he had to do was remember to dodge whichever rail it was that carried enough electricity to cook a camel.

Chapter 49

'But Reuben found them? The photos?'

Matt nodded. His smile was gone. 'I knew I was taking a big risk, sneaking into your bedroom and then, yeah. Reuben found out. And he wanted you to know. But I knew – *knew* – that couldn't happen. I knew you would never speak to me, *look* at me, again. But Reuben was determined to tell you, even if it meant upsetting you. He was on his way to show you everything.'

I swallowed. 'I see.'

'But obviously I never meant for him to *die*.' Matt was looking at me anxiously. 'I was just trying to get him to hand over the pictures. It was just an argument. An argument that went wrong.'

'Like with John.'

Matt looked down. 'Similar, I guess.'

Neither of us said anything for a while. Then he said, 'Are you angry?'

I didn't answer his question. 'Mum was right then all along. It wasn't suicide.'

'It wasn't suicide,' Matt repeated.

I nodded but I didn't reply. We were sitting at opposite ends of the sofa again now, Matt watching me warily.

'What are you thinking now?' he said after a while.

'About Reuben,' I said.

Matt nodded. 'Yeah. Of course. Sorry.'

'He's always in the back of my mind anyway, but today's been a big day. The pain feels fresh again. Raw, you know?'

'Yeah,' Matt said quietly.

I picked up my phone and checked the time. It was nearly three. Nearly two hours had passed since I'd returned from my conversation with Sophie.

I turned to look at Matt. 'Can I see those letters again? In the envelope?'

He frowned. 'Why would you want to?'

I sighed. 'It was obviously an important part of his life in those last few months. Whatever happened between them. I just want the opportunity to get to know a bit more about that.'

Matt's frown deepened. He seemed confounded by the idea. 'Really?'

I nodded. 'Yeah. I think it would help me.'

Matt hesitated for a moment, but then he nodded. 'Sure,' he said. 'I understand.'

He went into his bedroom and came back out with the brown envelope. I took it from him and ran my hand over the smooth brown paper. Matt was watching me carefully.

I looked towards the terrace. 'I'm just going to go outside. Take some time to think about things.'

'Oh.' He looked surprised for a moment but quickly set his expression back into one of understanding. 'Of course. Sure. You go ahead. I've got some work to do anyway.' He picked up a small laptop from the sideboard at the back of the room and sat back down on the sofa with it. 'I'll be here,

293

if you want me.' He gave me a supportive smile and I slid open the glass doors.

The terrace was hot from the mid-afternoon sun, but there was a light breeze which made it more comfortable. I walked to the front of the tiled area and rested the bottom of the envelope on the bar of the metal rail. Below me, a tour guide was holding a plastic flag high in the air, a throng of dark-haired figures with backpacks drifted across the square after her.

I lifted the flap of the envelope and took out a letter. *See you at 10* was all it said. I wondered if Reuben had kept everything Sophie had sent him, every message, no matter how ordinary and perfunctory. I turned to look at Matt through the glass doors. He was concentrating on his laptop, typing fast. I slipped the paper back into the envelope. I didn't need to look through them. They weren't for me.

The realisation hit me with a sudden wave of dizziness: Reuben died for me. He hadn't intended to, I was sure, but he had confronted Matt because he wanted me to know the truth. He wanted to show me what Matt was like. I wondered what Reuben would be doing now, had he lived. Would he have made a career out of his music like he'd hoped? Would he be living in a lively, exciting city? New York? Paris? I wondered even, if he might still be with Sophie. Something that always struck me about Reuben was that when he did something, he committed whole-heartedly. I remember Mum saying once that she always thought he'd be the type of boy to marry the first person he loved.

I looked at my watch. Three fifteen. I took one quick look down the side of the building, but I couldn't make out the specific figures on the pavement below and I didn't want to spend too long trying. I turned around. Matt was no longer on the sofa, but I saw the bathroom door was shut. Now was as good a time as any.

I opened my hand and watched the envelope glide down towards the ground. But about halfway through its descent, it tipped and began to fall horizontally, with the flat of the paper facing downwards, the increased air resistance causing it to soar forwards, drifting off course from its vertical trajectory and moving out into the middle of the road. This meant instead of being able to collect it from the pavement, hidden by the trees that lined the edge of the street as we had planned, Sophie was forced to dart out into the middle of the road, to wave her apologies to drivers as she picked it up from the tarmac. At first, I was relieved to have been able to see for myself that the envelope had been collected safely, but then, as I looked to my right, I saw that Sophie's unscheduled appearance had had more serious consequences.

Matt had seen her too.

Chapter 50

I realised immediately that I should have slid the glass doors shut when I'd come out, so that if Matt did approach, the sound of them opening would have given me some warning. As it was, I'd left them open and, I suppose, on coming out of the bathroom Matt had seen me leaning over the railings and had gone to the nearest edge of the terrace to where he was – the far-right corner – and looked down himself, to see what was happening below.

His hands were still resting on the railing. He looked at me, then back down to the street. I did the same, but Sophie had now disappeared out of sight. He moved away from the edge of the terrace and took a few steps towards me.

'You were lying?' His voice was calm. 'Acting.'

I didn't have anywhere to move to. Behind me was the white stone wall of the edge of the terrace, to my left, the railing and the drop below, to my right, the pool. I took hold of the top of the metal rail in my left hand for support. Instinct told me that the best strategy was to keep the pretence going.

I blinked, feigning confusion. 'What? When?' I took another

quick look down below me. 'Did you see Sophie, just then? Was that her? It looked like her didn't it, but I thought I was just imagining it because she was on my mind. I think—'

Matt laughed. He shook his head and looked up at the sky, his hands on his hips. 'Lauren, you just *threw* the fucking envelope to her!'

I blinked again. 'What?' I laughed nervously. 'I didn't?'

'Lauren. Don't.' His voice was low now.

It was time to change tactic. I sighed. 'Yeah. Okay. I did. It's just, she'd got herself in such a state about it. What does it matter if she has it now, if it puts her mind at ease? You only had any use for it while you needed her to help you out and that's all done with now, isn't it? The plan's over. It worked. You got me.' I reached out and tried to take his hand, but he shook me off.

'Don't,' he said irritably. 'I could hardly believe it, that you still wanted me, after Sophie had ruined the whole thing. I don't know how many times I said to her, that whatever happens you can't find out that it was me. I knew it didn't sound good, if you have it all spelled out to you. I knew what it would sound like. I know it *sounds* mental. But it's like a magic show, isn't it? An illusion. Nothing ruins the magic like knowing all the ins and outs of how it's done. It was a show!' He held his arms out on either side of him. 'I was putting on a show! And then she royally fucked it up by . . . by giving you backstage access.'

I didn't say anything. I was acutely aware of how physically trapped I was in that corner. I took a step forward, being careful that I didn't move too far to the right and end up in the pool. 'Let's go back inside, shall we? It's so hot out here. It's giving me a headache.'

My movement seemed to alarm him. 'No!' he said, grabbing me by the arm and pushing me back into my corner.

'Matt,' I said. 'Stop being like this.'

He laughed for a moment. Then he stopped abruptly and put his face close to mine. 'You've treated me like I'm a fucking moron,' he said quietly. 'You and *her*.' He jerked his head towards the street below. 'But the problem for you is, I'm not a fucking moron, actually. Look at all this.' He gestured to the roof terrace, the apartment, the view below us. 'Do you think a moron could have it? No. Because I'm not saying I'm perfect but I'm not stupid. But maybe that's the problem. Because there's always been one thing that worried me about you, Lauren. The one thing that made me wonder how it would work out for us, in the long run. You want to know what that was?'

'What?' I'd tried to make my voice sound calm but the shake betrayed my nerves.

'You have a weakness for total losers. What *is* it about them? Do you like a project? A tortured soul to rescue? Maybe that's why you like those stray dogs you work with so much!' He laughed and threw his hands up in the air. 'Okay so, loser number one, Reuben Henry.' He touched the index finger of his left hand with the index finger of his right, as if counting out a list. 'A little bit of talent but a *big* bit of ego. Shame he didn't live to be an adult, really, because then you would've all seen how he didn't have the balls to actually make anything of himself. And loser number two,' he touched the next finger on his left hand now, 'John Marshall.' He laughed again and shook his head. 'Marshall T. John. What an absolute tragedy of a man. I know you don't even need me to explain the issues there. You knew all about them yourself really, didn't you? Although, didn't seem to stop you shagging him for god knows how many years.' He looked down at me in disappointment. 'Really, Lauren. What were you thinking?' He paused, looking out at the rooftops. 'You know, in the animal kingdom, it's perfectly acceptable for the stronger, more capable members of the species to kill off the weaker ones. The deadweights. It's essential, in fact. To keep things moving forward.'

I wasn't sure if he was still talking about Reuben and John, or if now he had moved on to me, if I was just another deadweight he thought the world would be better off without.

'Matt, I'm going inside.' I stepped forward now, ready to push past him, but the movement prompted a sudden explosion of anger.

'No you're fucking not!' He pushed me back into the corner, hitting my head on the stone wall behind me.

'Get off!' I lashed out at him, my arms flailing, trying to make contact with any part of him that would keep distance between us.

'Shut. The fuck. Up. You stupid. Little bitch.' He pressed his hands to my throat. I tried to call out, to scream, but the sound was trapped. Almost immediately I could see dark spots in my vision. I felt like my windpipe had entirely collapsed, like a hose with a kink in it. I swung my arms hopelessly. Matt's face was so close to mine I could see nothing else, the rest of the world was just a halo of light around the shape of his head.

But then the sensations began to abate. Matt's face was gone, the light was in my eyes and the pressure on my neck was released. I realised my feet were wet and I looked down to see Matt, splashing furiously in the pool to my right. And in front of me was Sophie. In one hand, she was holding the red and white skull. With the other, she reached out for me.

'Run!' she said urgently. 'We need to run.'

Chapter 51

I have Sophie to thank for a number of pieces of quick thinking that day.

Firstly, on looking up to the terrace as she collected the envelope and seeing Matt looking back down, knowing imme-diately that the realisation that he'd been tricked – made a fool of as he so hated – would trigger a flip in temper that could have grave consequences for me. She had then wasted no time in making for the entrance to the building, taking the lift up to the seventh floor and letting herself in using the key she'd had cut.

Secondly, as we made our escape from Matt, him thrashing his way angrily to the steps of the pool ready to exact his revenge on Sophie for hitting him with the skull, she hadn't made straight for the front door as my instincts had told me to. Instead, she'd stopped, closed the glass doors behind us and flipped the catch, temporarily locking Matt on the terrace and buying me the time to collect my bag and passport from my room before we left.

Even when we were clear of the apartment block, I remained in a frantic state, unable to think calmly and with the overwhelming impulse that we should head straight for the airport, get on the first plane to England, flagging one down on the runway if we had to. I just knew that we had to get out, get away.

But Sophie had led me down a quiet side road, put her hands on the top of my arms and told me Matt wasn't going to chase us into the streets wielding a revolver or a machete. That we were safe now. So we collected her things from the hostel she'd been staying at, then headed to the police station.

Sophie assured me that the alarm tactics she'd unleashed on me when I'd wanted to go to the police as soon as I'd found out about John's death – that is, her claims that they might try to keep me in the country indefinitely while they investigated – were manufactured by her in order to hasten my exit from Matt's apartment, and that she didn't genuinely believe there was a risk of them preventing our departure. At the police station, we found an officer who spoke English to take down our report of what Matt had told us had happened between him and John at the jetty and gave her, we hoped, enough information to allow them to investigate further. And investigate further they did, unearthing two separate eye witnesses who had, between them, seen enough of the fight that had knocked John into the water – and of Matt's repeated efforts to prevent John climbing back out – to convict Matthew Fabian of the manslaughter of John Marshall and earn him a sentence of five and a half years in Botafuegos prison.

As soon as the escape from Matt's apartment was complete, our report to the police made and a flight back to UK secured, my feeling towards Sophie had begun to shift. The sense of her as an ally – the two of us against Matt – started to wane. Back at home in my flat, the blinding sun of the roof terrace, Matt's enraged face close to mine, all seemed to have happened a long time ago. The scale of her deception, however compelling the reasons behind it, overwhelmed any feelings of solidarity I had and I made a conscious effort to distance myself from her.

I sensed she wanted to try to continue our friendship, although I guessed she knew there was a good chance I wouldn't be interested. Every so often she would send me tentative enquiries into my well-being and occasionally make vague suggestions that we might meet up, but I let these go largely unanswered. During the plane journey home from Spain that summer, questions on the details of Matt's scheme occurred to me and Sophie confirmed that her visit that Sunday afternoon, ostensibly to ease my loneliness, had been ordered by Matt with the express instruction that she should seize something of mine that would give his plan a personal touch. She also confirmed – not that I needed her to – that she had posed as Sean M in order to report my infidelity to John, with the aim that this would keep me how Matt wanted me: single.

I was still confused by this element, though. 'Why couldn't he have just sent this message himself?'

'He probably could. But throughout the whole plan he made it clear that, although he was calling the shots, I was to do what he wanted. I was his henchman, I suppose. By the time he saw you, I was to make sure you were unattached. How I went about that was my problem.'

On this point, Sophie was less apologetic than on other details. 'It was probably the one part of the plan where I could see a silver lining,' she told me as we queued to make our way through passport control at Gatwick. 'I knew you were wavering, that loneliness was making you consider asking John to come back, even though you knew all the obvious problems. So although I'd never have taken it upon myself to interfere like that if I hadn't had to, I suppose I consoled myself that giving him cause to keep his distance was no bad thing.'

It was during a conversation with Anya, in the end, that I realised I was ready to get back in touch with Sophie. It was over lunch, six months after our return from Spain, that she asked me how I was feeling about everything, now some time had passed.

'I've been trying to think about it rationally,' I told her. 'To carry out a straightforward risk–benefit analysis. And I've decided what she did is defensible.'

Anya pulled a face. 'You reckon?'

'I think so. The benefits of going along with what Matt was saying were obvious, right? Save her career, her reputation, her freedom. Save *every*thing. And what were the risks, really? The tangible, concrete risks? Maybe there weren't actually that many. Everything was designed to freak me out. Not to actually harm me. Me getting whacked on the head with my own ornament was an accident. She didn't intend that.'

Anya thought about this. 'Okay but what about the whole point of the scheme? To give you to Matt? To sacrifice you like a . . . a baby goat to an evil Satanist high priest?'

I sighed. 'All she did was arrange things so we stayed with him for a few days. I guess she was hoping I'd spot what a creep he was myself. She didn't know I was going to go all middle-aged gap year on you at the end and refuse to come home. She also didn't know what an awful judge of character I can be.'

Anya smiled. 'That's true.'

In the end, Anya conceded that I might be right, although she showed little enthusiasm for reigniting her own friendship with Sophie. I decided that regardless of what the outcome might be, I'd still like the opportunity to talk everything over with Sophie, now a few months had passed and I'd had time to come to terms with everything that had happened. Apart from anything else, she felt like a connection to Reuben. There weren't many people who had felt his loss like I had, and she was one of them.

We met just before Christmas in a dark pub near Victoria station. As I'd suggested to Anya, Sophie was keen to emphasise that she had analysed Matt's scheme carefully and had decided that at no time would I be in any genuine danger.

'I hoped that maybe we wouldn't even have to go there – to his place. Do you remember how I tried to talk you out of believing the skull was yours? I thought maybe if I could downplay everything, if I could convince you it was all just a bit of bad luck and nothing too much to worry about, we might be able to get through the week without moving in with Matt at all.'

'But then what about you? Would Matt have honoured his side of the deal?'

Sophie shook her head and shrugged. 'Who knows. But I hoped as long as I'd done everything he'd asked . . . got you to Barcelona at least . . . ' She paused. 'Anyway, when it was clear we were on the move, I still thought it would be okay. As I saw it, there would be four, maybe five, days when we'd be under his roof and I just vowed that I wouldn't take my eyes off you. That's why I insisted on sharing a room with you. I'd just never considered that you might decide to stay on, alone. That's when I realised things had got out of my control. Before that, I thought I could manage it. It would all be temporary. We'd go home, you'd be safe, and I'd have that envelope, so I would no longer be beholden to Matt. We could put the whole thing behind us.'

We left the meeting in Victoria on lukewarm terms but we were in touch over the next few months. What won me round in the end was remembering that fundamentally, I *liked* Sophie.

I suppose I'd thought our burgeoning friendship had been faked, just another part of the plan, but as she reassured me, when she'd begun, she didn't know me at all, and once she got to know me and realised she genuinely liked me, it was too late to stop. So we started to spend more time together, and then, in the May that marked nearly a year after Barcelona, we surprised everyone by ending the tenancies on our separate flats and moving in to a small, two-bed Victorian terrace in Greenwich. We'd both decided it would be nice to have more regular company, and I hoped that having a housemate would stave off the loneliness that I was susceptible to, and that I knew had led me – and risked leading me again – to make unwise decisions, to overlook my doubts about people, in the pursuit of companionship.

I went to the police in the UK with Matt's account of what had happened on the platform and investigations into what exactly happened to Reuben the night of his death have been reopened, but neither Sophie nor I are hopeful that Matt will be held accountable. As things stand, he's denying any knowledge of the conversation we had in his apartment shortly before he tried to strangle me. Even though Anya came forward to make it clear she'd seen Matt in town later that evening, and that he hadn't slept on the beach all night as he'd claimed back in 2005, the police have already told me it's unlikely that any of the new information will be sufficiently substantial and irrefutable for the inquest verdict to be revised, or for Matt to be charged.

Sophie is still in touch with Matt's ex-wife, Inga, and the word from the people they once both knew is that by the time Matt is released from prison, he will have lost both his business and his apartment. It transpired that, even before his trial, the company was in trouble, with clients becoming aware of the allegations concerning his treatment of Inga and withdrawing their business, keen to avoid their brands being associated with Matt's.

My own bad judgement is one of the aspects of what happened in Barcelona that I've found most difficult to come to terms with. I still find it hard to reconcile the person with whom I'd spent those peaceful weeks, the person with whom I'd seriously contemplated a romantic future, with the man who had pushed his face against mine, his bloodshot eyes staring wildly, and tried to crush my trachea in his fist. I felt a lot of shame at having been duped, at having being blinded by flattery and the feeling of being wanted, and it was only on the chance discovery of an article in an online technology magazine when I was searching for details of the trial that I realised I wasn't the only one to have been tricked by him – that his dual character had confounded many.

The Rise and Fall of Matthew Fabian

Matthew Fabian, founder of Barcelona-based event listing resource, GigCity, was featured on this site in 2015 as one of our Thirty Under Thirty to Watch, but three years later his business is in receivership and he finds himself serving jail time for manslaughter. Where did it all go so wrong for the young star who had seemed to be getting it all so right?

At eighteen, Fabian eschewed university in favour of travelling around Europe in a second-hand car, busking as part of a jazz duo to pay his way. It's a move that, on first reading, sounds like a definite case of choosing short-term fun over long-term success, but Matthew Fabian proved that it was possible to have both when he realised the Barcelona music scene was crying out for a 'one-stop shop' website of music event and gig listings. In two short years he took his idea from a one-page website thrown together on a laptop in his bedroom to a fully fledged business, employing over forty people and turning over two million euros a year in advertising revenue. Even his appearance was transformed, with those who had known him in his adolescence marvelling at how the awkward red-head they'd known from the quiet seaside town of Hoyle had become a confident public speaker, adept at charming his way to the best business deals.

But a closer look at Matthew Fabian's adult life reveals a darker tale. While employees and former employees agree he possessed many enviable skills – a flawless memory, a formidable determination – they also recall a man with a temper; a man fixated on control who couldn't accept that things might not always go his way.

Arjun Patel, who worked for Fabian as front-end developer in the early years of GigCity, recalls how on one occasion, the cancellation of a client account prompted Fabian to summon the entire workforce to the office so he could begin firing them indiscriminately. 'He made us all stand in a circle,' recalls Patel. 'He made all of us list everything we'd done for this particular client, every interaction we'd had, and based on what we said, he told us to go and stand either by the left wall, or the right wall of the office. At the end, he told everyone by the right wall they were fired. Everyone at the left, he took out for a huge meal, no expense spared. It was nuts. Totally bizarre.'

Along with the stories of unconventional leadership, there are many who pointed to his romantic life as further evidence that not everything about Matthew Fabian was as it first seemed. At just twenty-four years old, Fabian already had a failed marriage under his belt. We couldn't reach his ex-wife – Inga Nilsson, the model and acclaimed cellist – but a source close to her told us of a short, tumultuous relationship, dominated by Fabian's controlling house rules and dramatic mood swings, that eventually reached the bottom of its downward spiral with a court order that prevented him from making any contact with her.

Despite the numbers of people becoming aware of the more sinister side to Fabian's nature, he may have been able to preserve his reputation for years to come had it not been for the crime for which he finds himself imprisoned today – a violent altercation with an English tourist, John Marshall, 32. According to the prosecution's case, the row had at its heart a love rivalry, one Fabian was so determined not to lose that he decided he would rather leave a man to die.

Legal experts say that Fabian is likely to be released from prison in 2021, but it's clear that when he does return to society, it will be to a very different life to the one he left behind.

Sophie and I talk about Reuben often, and although it's painful not to be able to update the official record of what happened, it's reassuring that some of the unanswered questions about what happened in his final hour can be put to rest. It means a lot to me to know that Reuben wanted to live, and that he wanted to protect me.

I hadn't been sure how much to tell Mum about my time in Spain, feeling that she might be critical of the way I let myself be taken in by people I hardly knew – both Sophie and Matt. In the end, I decided not to share with her the details of Matt's scheme, largely as I knew it was unlikely to warm her to my new housemate. I did, however, let her know about Matt's account of what had happened between him and Reuben at the station the night Reuben died.

Mum looked at me, blinking slowly. 'He was just running away. He was trying to cross the track. It was an accident. He didn't want to die.' She paused between each sentence, delivering each one like it was a line of a poem.

I shook my head. 'No. And the photos weren't his either. They were nothing to do with him.'

'Oh,' she frowned. 'Of course. I never thought they were. Not from the moment that policewoman laid them out on the table. I knew there was far more to it than that.'

I felt ashamed then, that my faith in Reuben hadn't matched hers. I'd wanted it to. I'd told myself I knew there was some other explanation. But it was only once that explanation had been spelled out to me that I acknowledged the extent of my doubts.

Mum was quiet then, but she seemed contemplative rather than sad. I returned a week later, not wanting to leave it as long as I usually did between visits given the nature of our conversation at the last. When I arrived that Saturday afternoon I found her brighter than I'd seen her in years. She was wearing lipstick, I noticed, and as I took my usual seat at the kitchen table, she bustled around me trimming the stalks from a bunch of tulips and arranging them in a vase. The flowers had been a gift she told me, from Andrew, the friend of her colleague who had been so keen to get to know her, and whom she'd decided to start to see more of.

But it was upstairs where I found the most significant development. The door to Reuben's bedroom was open and I could see that the checked duvet cover and pillowcase had been stripped from the bed and the posters removed from the walls. It was still blue as he had painted it, but it had been cleaned and dusted. The windows were open and there was a water jug of daffodils on the chest of drawers.

It was when I returned from that visit that I found the letter in the hallway. My name and address had been written by hand in careful block capitals. As I was studying it to work out if I recognised it, I clocked the Algeciras postmark. With the sound of my heartbeat in my ears, I tore open the envelope.

Inside was a sheet of notepaper, folded in half together with another smaller square envelope. I unfolded the paper and read the three lines of text, written in the same neat capitals.

DESPITE WHAT YOU DID TO ME, I STILL MISS YOU.
   AT LEAST I HAVE PLENTY TO REMEMBER YOU BY.
   M xxx

The smaller envelope wasn't sealed, so I lifted the flap and pulled out the two pieces of smooth card. As I turned them over and set them side by side on the table in front of me, I was surprised by how calm I felt. I think part of me had been expecting it. The images were grainy – stills taken from video footage – and the lighting was dim, but it was clear what they showed. It was me in bed, in my bedroom in Matt's flat. In the room he'd made such a point of never entering.

*Now read on for an extract of Jessica Vallance's
first gripping thriller,*

TRUST
HER

Prologue

I've always found it easy to make friends.

I know how that sounds but I say it without a trace of conceit, I promise. There's plenty (seriously – plenty) I'm hopeless at. I just think for all our obsession these days with education and training and upskilling, for all the blogs and articles and shelves of books in Waterstones promising to help us better ourselves, the skills that really shape our lives are those things that come naturally. Those innate instincts that we're stuck with, whether we like them or not. And I do believe that even the most advantageous of personal attributes has its drawbacks. Even our strengths can get us into trouble from time to time.

For instance, I'm a people pleaser. I want people to know they can count on me. If I feel that I've let someone down, that there was more I could have done, the guilt nags at me like an itch I can't get to. I don't know why I'm like that but I always have been, even as a little girl. It's a bit pathetic, I know, to need other people's validation like that. It's had its uses though, over the years. I've had some good friends. I think people have appreciated me. I suppose I can hold my head up and say I've always done my best, even when things haven't worked out exactly as I hoped.

But I've no doubt whatsoever that my natural sense of duty, my amenability, was the reason I found myself trying to convince a taxi driver that a woman with blue lips and a Punch and Judy puppet on her hand was 'honestly, hardly even tipsy' whilst the woman in question undermined my case somewhat by waving the puppet in the air and shouting, 'That's the way to do it!' in a high-pitched squawk.

It isn't too much of a stretch then, to conclude that that same sense of duty was also the reason I didn't walk away from Luke. Not on that first night and not on any of the nights that came after. I kept coming back. I let him – I let all of them – get under my skin. I wanted to do the right thing, not just the easy thing. And more than that, I wanted people to *tell* me that I'd done the right thing. I wanted people to say, 'Charlotte's a good one, isn't she? Thank God for Charlotte.'

It's like I say – even our good qualities have their drawbacks.

Chapter 1

The evening had begun four hours earlier as I made my way through the twisting streets of Brighton's Lanes, the glow from the fairy lights looped between the buildings making the wet stones shine. Emily and Meredith, many of the women from work in fact, turned their noses up at the Lanes. They were 'overpriced', 'twee' and 'for tourist morons', they said. It was probably true, but I loved them. As I'd been in Brighton less than five months – I'd never even visited before I moved – I suppose I was still a tourist myself, in all the ways that counted.

The bar I'd chosen for our drinks that evening was called Laking's Dispensary and was styled around the theme of an old-fashioned apothecary. When I'd stumbled across it a few weeks earlier, I'd stared, mesmerised, through the windows at the dark wood interior, the shelves of brightly coloured mixers in glass bottles of assorted shapes and sizes backlit on the shelves behind the counter, the bar staff in Victorian waistcoats and bow ties, lab coats slung over the top.

Laking's Dispensary was different from most bars in that it didn't sell alcohol at all. Rather, customers were instructed to 'bring along a good-sized bottle of their favourite tipple' and then, for a fixed fee, the trained cocktail waiters would use the alcoholic base provided to create a whole evening's worth of exotic cocktails from the mixers, spices and syrups on their well-stocked shelves.

'You have to bring your own drink *and* pay for the privilege. Wonderful. Where do I sign up,' Emily had said in her usual weary deadpan when I'd suggested that one night we ought to give Laking's Dispensary a go. I knew, though, that she wouldn't miss a night out, whatever the format, so I'd stood my ground and sent her a text earlier in the week instructing her to meet me at seven-thirty on Saturday, to bring a bottle of decent gin and to see if Meredith was around too.

I'd arrived a little early and, as it was raining, decided to head straight in. The bar was small – perhaps just six or seven tables, each lit with a single tea light in a jar. Only two of them were already occupied: one with three men whose clothes, beards and tattoos were so similar I wondered if they'd agreed the uniform as a condition of the friendship; the other by a couple. He had his back to me, but something about them – the way she was staring down into her drink, using her straw to poke moodily at the ice, the way he was leaning back in his chair, looking around the room, out of the window, anywhere but at the woman – made me think that their evening wasn't going particularly well.

As I took my seat the barman approached the table. He was tall, with vivid ginger hair and round tortoiseshell glasses.

'Hey! So!' He clapped his hands together then held them like that, in a clasp. 'First time? Been before? On your own? Waiting for someone?' He reeled the questions off quick-fire, jerking his head from side to side as he delivered each one.

I smiled. 'First time, yes. Waiting for someone. Maybe two people.'

'OK! Great!' He clapped his hands together again. 'So, I'm Toby. I'll be your mixologist for the evening.'

I reached into my bag and took out the bottle of Glenfiddich twelve-year-old malt that I'd bought on the way. He picked it up and held it in his palm, nodding appreciatively at the label.

'Nice. I'll get you something while you're waiting. Any specific likes? Dislikes? Requests? Something you've always wanted to try?'

I shook my head. 'Surprise me.'

He nodded and grinned, and headed off to the bar with the bottle.

The man at the couple's table turned around briefly and as I caught a glimpse of his face, I felt I recognised him from somewhere. It took a moment, but I realised where it was: one of the dating apps I'd signed up to when I'd first moved to town.

I'd lost interest in them by this point – too many idiots only there to waste time – but I'd been quite keen for a few weeks and would log on to check for messages as soon as I got home from work each day. The same photos seemed to crop up on all of the different sites, so you got to know the faces of your local single population quite well. Still, it looked like this particular one had managed to find himself a date at last. Although from the look of things, perhaps he was wishing he hadn't.

A few minutes later the barman was back, carrying a tumbler garnished with a slice of orange and a cherry. 'Thought we'd get things off to a traditional start,' he said, setting it down in front of me. 'An Old Fashioned – just sugar, bitters and whisky.'

I thanked him and sipped at the drink, looking around the room. They had done an amazing job with the place, I had to admit. It was even better once you were actually inside.

Obviously I had very little idea about the historical accuracy of the decor. I had my suspicions that neither a mangle nor a set of Punch and Judy puppets would have had any particular purpose in your typical Victorian apothecary, but they gave the place the quirky, surreal impression I'm sure the owners were aiming for. With the rain now coming down hard against the window and the quiet, slightly off-key, saloon-style piano music tinkling gently in the background, I sat back in my chair and allowed myself a smile.

There had been many moments like this since I'd arrived in Brighton five months earlier. Moments where I'd looked around and thought, Yes. This is *exactly* what I had in mind.

Chapter 2

When I'd been working behind the admissions desk of Fourcross Medical Centre in Holten, a small market town in Devon, I'd daydreamed about scenes like this. I was twenty-seven, single. I didn't own a house. I had no children. I'd met people from up and down the country but had no particular ties to any one place. How then, I wondered, had I ended up in a town like Holten, where people went to settle down, to retire even?

I was no stranger to setting up life in new places, but up until that point there'd always been a trigger for my moving on that was beyond my control. The usual life developments – new jobs, the rental market, changes of circumstances. Things that made me feel that fate was leading me around by the nose, with little interest in what I really wanted. This time, though, the decision was all mine.

Once I was sure I wanted to move, it didn't take long for me to set my heart on Brighton and I began to scour the internet for jobs in the area. One of the first roles I'd applied for had been 'Digital Content Producer' at Good Stuff Ltd, a start-up that delivered boxes of organic produce to customers' doors once a week. It had been a long shot – I couldn't honestly have said what the job title even meant – but I'd figured I had nothing to lose by trying. A little friendliness went a long way, I'd always found, and, as it transpired, this was no exception.

Marcus was the name of the man who'd interviewed me and I made him laugh several times during the hour we spent together. Then, as we were finishing up, he closed his notebook, rested his hand on top and looked at me.

'I'll be honest with you, Charlotte. We've spoken to candidates with far more experience than you.'

I nodded, and smiled brightly. 'Of course. I totally understand,' I said, but I was furious with myself. If he'd wanted experience I could've given him experience, but I hadn't wanted to over-egg it. I'd thought the blank canvas, eager-to-learn shtick would make him feel flattered, important. But now I'd blown it.

'But,' he went on. I looked up hopefully. 'When we set up this business, it was about creating an ethos as much as turning a profit. We want people with the right attitude, the right mindset. God, we're all stuck in here forty hours a week, we want people who are fun!' He laughed, so I joined in supportively. 'The other stuff you can learn. I'm sure you'll pick it up. So as far as I'm concerned, the job's yours if you want it.'

Marcus was right, about the people being fun. Friends came quickly. I worked hard to get on with people, but the way things worked there made it easy. People were inclusive, welcoming. I liked everyone well enough, but it was Emily, Meredith and Alison who became my real friends. After a few weeks in Brighton, they were the people I saw not just for a shared sandwich in the park outside the office, or for a quick drink after work, but for dinner or an afternoon's shopping in town. They were the people I could ring if I was lonely on a

Sunday evening and wanted someone to watch television with. If I was passing any of their flats, I knew I could call in for a cup of a tea, and they wouldn't be worried that they were still in their pyjamas, dirty plates piled in the sink.

They were all great but Meredith had a little boy, so was often limited to social activities that were possible with a toddler in tow. Alison was a little older than the rest of us, and from what I could gather had spent the five years since her divorce working her way through a series of casual but insanely rich boyfriends, which meant that, come the weekend, she was often whisked away for a short break in Venice or to relax in a luxury spa retreat in a castle in the Highlands. Emily though, like me, was single, childless, completely free of responsibility and obligation. Emily was always up for fun.

It was strange then, I noticed, as I finished my Old Fashioned, that it was nearly eight and there was still no sign of her. I checked my phone for texts, fully expecting to see one of her hastily typed apologies – 'Fuck sorry, lost my fucking shoe. Found it now. On way' – her style of communication always giving the impression that she was flailing through life in a fog of swearing and chaos, which she was.

I scrolled through my contacts and hit call. She would probably be on her way, I figured, running through the rain, slipping all over the place in her heels, battling the wind to keep her umbrella under control. It would be easier to speak than for her to try to text.

She answered after three rings. 'Hello?'

'Hey!' I said. 'Are you coming?'

There was a pause.

'Sorry? Who's that?'

I laughed. 'It's me, Charlotte. Are you coming or what? This place is wicked, actually.'

'Oh, shit. Charlotte. No, sorry. I can't.'

I frowned. 'Oh, OK. Is everything all righ—? '

She cut me off. 'Sorry, really can't talk now.'

And then she was gone.

I looked down at my phone for a few seconds. The light on the screen went out.

Weird, I thought. But not unheard of.

Emily always tried to do too much. She kept a social diary that even an organisational wizard would've struggled to pull off, and Emily certainly wasn't that. She'd try to fit in a haircut at five, an early dinner with a friend at six, drinks with a guy from Tinder at half-seven and still be at her sister's in time to watch a film and would invariably manage less than half of it. So, although I was disappointed to be stood up, I wasn't surprised. I would get the full story later, I was sure.

I looked around the bar. The twenty-pound personal cocktail waiter charge applied whether I left now or stayed all evening, and twenty pounds seemed more than a little steep for one drink, especially as I'd had to provide the whisky myself. Besides, I liked the place. I'd wanted to try it for ages. I was a twenty-seven-year-old independent woman, I told myself. I was more than capable of spending an evening in my own company.

As I looked around the room I noticed that the table with the miserable couple was now just a table with a miserable woman. My friend from the dating app had obviously decided that he'd had enough for one evening. The drink that the waiter had just placed in front of the woman told me that she intended to proceed without him.

She caught me looking at her and lifted her glass in a toast. I returned the gesture. Then she got up, and made her way unsteadily over to my table.

'Mind if I join you?' she said, with a lopsided smile.

I opened my mouth ready to decline, to make an excuse

about somewhere else I had to be or someone else I had to be with, but I couldn't think of anything. And then, I thought, why not? Although it was true that I was an independent woman, capable of spending an evening in my own company, it would be more fun, wouldn't it, to have someone to talk to? Anyway, I wanted to know what her story was. It looked like something had gone down with her and the man. I was curious about what it was.

I smiled back. 'Yes. No. Absolutely. Please do.'